Praise For

ONCE UPON A TIME

Sam Blumenthal provides a taste of how God creates, restores, and redeems through stories that reach across a wide spectrum of life experiences. Read, learn, enjoy!

—Rose Marie Miller, Author of *From Fear to Freedom* and *Nothing Is Impossible with God.*

With the insight of a psychologist who has visited the deep realms of faith, Sam Blumenthal opens many windows to the soul in *Once Upon a Time*. Let his words penetrate your heart as you join him on the journey home.

—Robert Whitlow, best-selling author of *Chosen People*

Written with deep conviction, Sam's stories reveal the transformative work of Christ as the characters weave their way through life. His stories touch on personal and societal flaws with empathy and understanding. They are warmhearted and a delight to read.

—Chris Payne, senior pastor at New City Church

Once Upon A Time

May you find God's story
in your story.

Once Upon A Time

A collection of short stories for those
trying to find their way home

Samuel L. Blumenthal, Ph.D.

REDEMPTION
PRESS

Contents

Acknowledgments

There are many people who have made significant emotional and spiritual investments in my life, far too many to name here. All the teachers and mentors, the pastors and authors, the Christian brothers and sisters—you have each played a role in my spiritual journey and in the development of my mind and heart. Thank you all for your loving care, for your encouragement and enlightenment, and especially for coming alongside and sharing this precious journey with me.

More specifically I have to thank those whose patient instruction made it possible for you to hold this book in your hands. First and foremost, Jennifer Edwards, my private editor, who patiently and wisely guided me along until I could accept the truth that if I wanted to be a good writer I had to learn what *not* to say. Thank you as well to Redemption Press for being my partner in bringing this book to fruition. I especially want to thank Dori Harrell, managing editor, and Sara Cormany, project manager, for their countless hours of guidance. And finally, thank you to my daughter-in-law, Heather Blumenthal, for her beautiful cover design.

Most of all, may any benefit or blessing that comes from the words contained herein be attributed to our great Father, whose love is responsible for all that is truly good in my mind and heart and anything I might ever accomplish.

Author's Note

Once *Upon a Time* is a collection of short stories inspired by the greatest story of all. I believe all stories, including even your story and mine, are part of one greater story, the first story ever told.

Life is so busy, filled with so many details. It can be difficult to believe it all has meaning, that it is all somehow connected. But if we can slow down long enough to look closer, we may not be so confused and distracted by all the action and detail in the foreground but able to distinguish and discern the greater message and meaning in the background.

My hope is that these stories will give praise and honor to the greatest story of all and to its Author. That they will find you where you are, wherever you may be in your journey. Most of all, I pray they will help you along your way, from here to there, but eventually all the way home, back to the One to whom you belong.

𝔜𝔬𝔲𝔫𝔤 𝔏𝔬𝔳𝔢

I remember concerning you the devotion of your youth,
the love of your betrothals, your following after Me
in the wilderness, through a land not sown. . . .
What injustice did your fathers find in Me,
that they went far from Me and
walked after emptiness and became empty?
—Jeremiah 2:2, 5

Prone to wander, Lord, I feel it;
prone to leave the God I love.
—From the hymn "Come Thou Fount of Every Blessing"

O
nce upon a time, there was young love.

She was the girl with red hair, and he was the boy who lived across the street, one year older. One year seemed like a lot back then. She had lived there as long as she could remember, and his family had moved in when he was seven. She still remembered that day like it was yesterday. It was the first time she had ever paid attention to the activity of someone moving in—the people in constant motion, the things being unloaded and carried into the house.

Will they ever be done? she'd thought.

She didn't remember noticing him that first day. That came later. There was something about him she couldn't name. He would look at her a little longer than most people. Not rude, mind you, just longer.

And she didn't have words, either, for what she began to feel for him in her heart as the years went by. The first time she admitted to herself it was something substantial was the time she fell down riding her bike in the middle of the street. She was hurt, but her pride more. It wasn't the most graceful thing. It was like he came out of nowhere; she hadn't even noticed him before she fell.

And she would never forget that look in his eyes. It had almost dried up the tears in hers. It was a look she would come to treasure as much as anything in her life. His eyes spoke concern, but also calm, and . . . something else. She wasn't sure if her mother could have done a better job that day of consoling her and making sure she made it back home. It was a little odd to feel so much the child, so much in need, and to have that need so completely met by another child.

He didn't think as much as her, and would have never been able to say as much either, but seeing her for the first time struck him deeply. Even at seven years old, it caught him off guard. At first it was her hair, especially as it flowed in the wind when she rode her bike. He was watching her hair the day she fell in the street. That was why he was there so quickly. He felt drawn to her. *Drawn.* That was the word he would have used if he had known it.

It took some time to say much of anything to her besides "Hello" or "How're you doing?" He didn't really know what to say. He just knew he wanted to say something. Eventually, she made it easier for him, the way it seemed many women made it easier for men when they decided to let them in closer.

She would talk to him to draw him out, and after a while, it worked. By the next year, they were sitting next to each other on the bus, and when she was ten and he eleven, they were the first little couple their age on their street. There was something so natural about the two of them together that the other kids their age didn't tease them, as bad as they wanted to, as much as their jealousy and insecurity prompted them to do so.

As the two of them grew older, they developed different interests. He loved sports, especially baseball, and she loved horses. But they both preferred to have each other involved. He would never be quite right if she were not at one of his games, and she came to life if he was at the stable when she rode, although the two of them sometimes rode together. They had good friends, boys who were his friends, and girls who were hers. These friendships never required that much thought or effort because they had so many common interests.

It was different when the two of them were together, and this was something both recognized right off. They never quite knew what the other might think or say about something. When they were younger, it was hard not to be surprised by an answer you had never suspected in the least, and sometimes even harder to resist the temptation to laugh or tease when the answer seemed so silly. He, in particular, learned the hard way that this was not the wisest thing to do.

But since they could never predict how it might go, it was also impossible to get bored when they spent time together. They knew exactly how things would go when they got together with their friends of the same gender. It was safe and often fun, but after a while, could become quite dull. With their friends, they were different variations of the same theme. With the two of them, they were very different themes who, over time, wanted to become very much the same.

And it was really about their deeper connection. There wasn't a word for it, and if there ever could be a word, it would be a holy word. A word that might even have to go unspoken. Kind of like having to take off your shoes when you stand on holy ground. They had this connection from such an early age that they never quite realized the enormity of its blessing. It was the first taste of relationship either of them had outside of their parents. It took years for it to become as deep as it did, but it started early. By the time they were thirteen and fourteen, they had been together longer than some adults survive in marriage.

And some of you may have experienced something similar, how after a while your identity changes. You are you, and there is something about one person in body, mind, and spirit that is separate and always will be. Yet when you grow close to another person in a more intimate way, it is as if both of you make a choice to surrender your separate identity, your previous identity, to this new one—the new identity of the two of you together as one. "And they shall become one flesh" (Genesis 2:24). Is this in itself not a miracle?

The difference with them was the degree to which they made this surrender. Most of us hold back some part of ourselves. We know it. Sometimes we will even admit it to ourselves. Sometimes if we are contrite enough, we will even admit it to our lover. But more of the time, we believe we *should* hold back, that the other person doesn't completely understand us, that they will not be fair with us if we are fully forthcoming. Maybe we risked it before, and they stepped on this part of our souls. Maybe more than once. And maybe it can be us too, our own selfishness we are not ready to part with.

Things could have changed for them as their bodies matured, but they did not. I wouldn't even give them credit for how they were blessed in this way, although their parents did try to educate them about such things. It more seemed to be something from above, some greater grace that was just given to them. It wasn't that they didn't want to know these things one day, to feel them, to be even closer to each other than they had ever fathomed. But something deep inside made it clear this was for later, and it was not only okay to wait, but much, much better to do so. They had a peace about it, without ever having gone through the struggle. And so without this to muddy the waters, they continued to be blessed by all the things they continued to share.

Even though he was almost a full year older, they were in the same grade, as his parents had held him back in kindergarten. Their middle school years grew into high school, and in a way, life became simpler. While it can still be relatively easy to be childish in middle school, even though your mind has already grown in leaps and bounds, high school has a way of focusing you, a little like smelling salts. The beginning of the rest of your life is right around the corner, so you are compelled to think about it more, to make plans, to think about college and majors and careers. Neither of them felt pushed to make choices about any of this too soon, but one thing was clear. Whatever the future held, they would be together. They never talked about this. They didn't have to.

It's funny how life is so often about *things*. The things we have or the things we do or even the things we are, or think we are. The two of them could be prey to this as well, but they had always shared such joy in just being together, no matter where they were or what they were doing, and this went back so far for them . . . They knew in their hearts that *this* was what they lived for. They made every effort to spend as much time with each other as they could, but when life and school and other things got in the way, as soon as they could, they reached out to meet again. This was natural for them, as natural as breathing. And seeing each other again was especially sweet after a rough day or a big disappointment. At these times, it was as if they were saying, "You know, it wouldn't have gone that way if *you* had been there . . . if I had been talking to *you* and not *them*."

As it turned out, he had quite an arm. He had loved baseball as long as he could remember and enjoyed playing different positions, but the coaches had never wasted much time in putting him on the mound and keeping him there. When he was younger, sometimes he would be given relief from the mound, but only because he had been so unhittable that day that the other coach was embarrassed and the boys on the other team were crying.

As you get older, sports get more serious, and no lead can be big enough. By the time he was in high school, coaches and parents wondered just how good he might be. Because of all of them, he wondered as well. He wasn't sure he wanted to play baseball in college, or professionally, if he turned out to be that good, but others expected he would.

He could never tell what she thought about this, and this was not by accident. She truly wanted him to be happy, and she had no way of knowing herself what that might entail, so she was purposely noncommittal. To say it another way, she was waiting for him to make up his mind about how much baseball mattered to *him*, and then she knew they would deal with it together. For now, she was his best fan, in good times and bad. And that would never change.

Her battles were different. Even though girls are brought up different these days, being encouraged to think of careers and self-actualization and all that, and they less and less feel obligated to be the homemaker who stays home for the children and a husband, she never struggled with this. She actually looked forward to being a wife and a stay-at-home mom. A number of her girlfriends, however, told her she would miss out on many things life had to offer if she married soon and became a homemaker—so much so that after a while she stopped being so generous with her thoughts on the subject. But none of this deterred her. She felt confident many people nowadays really didn't know best about such things, that all things modern were not an improvement, and most things old fashioned had only become so once upon a time because they *made* such good sense, not because they lacked it.

As they grew older, more boys and girls became couples, but none of them had known each other as long or been as close. Neither of them spent as much time with their same-sex friends as most of their other friends, but when they did, it would happen from time to time that some conflict would come up. He would be playing baseball or just hanging out, and the time would arrive when he needed to go see her.

For him it never felt like a "must" to see her but was always something he wanted to do. His friends would tease him, you know, with some of the timeless male taunts, that he was "whipped" or "tied to her apron strings." The implication was always that there was some weakness in this, that he was giving something away, even giving *himself* away, his independence, in general, but for sure all the things he could be doing instead of being "with her"—as if there were no doubt that all those other things were better. You know, unless you have feelings for someone else like the two of them did for each other, you really can't understand. You have never known anything better than just being able to do what you want when you want, to have your independence. It is very hard not to think that in giving so much of yourself to another person, to the two of you as one, that you are making a mistake, and a bad one at that.

Similar things happened to her too, but girls are different. They are so wired to be relational, to be nurturers. Much of their conversation is about relationships to begin with, especially about their boyfriends. But none of the other girls spoke about her boyfriend like she spoke about him.

When she listened to her girlfriends talk about boys and the boys they were interested in, she never heard anything remotely similar to her own thoughts. So much of the time, they spoke of themselves, what they thought, or what they liked, or what they wanted, or even what they needed. Rarely did they ever speak of what the boy might think, much less what he might need. She was disappointed by this, but it was so common that she had come to accept it and not be judgmental.

Earlier on it did make her wonder if there was something wrong with her, and with him too. Why didn't anyone else think and feel the way they did? But it had always felt so right, she had never really doubted it. And as she grew older, she more and more felt pity for her girlfriends and for anyone else who just didn't understand. She didn't know why the two of them had always felt the way they did about each other, but she was glad for it, overwhelmingly glad, and wouldn't have traded it for anything in the world.

Neither of them looked forward to high school graduation. Most kids can't wait to get away from home. They have been waiting their whole lives to decide exactly when they'll go to bed and exactly what they'll eat and exactly when they'll study, if they do, and for how long. They are finally "free" and become intoxicated with this, although some are humble and honest enough to admit they're also a little scared. Everything has always been taken care of for them, and Mom and Dad will still only be a phone call away, but they can't be there in a moment to fix things for you. *You* will have to fix all the things that come up or go wrong in your day, on your own. And this is fertile ground for wondering on a deeper level if you are really up for the task.

The two of them, however, were not worried about these things. They had other worries. They knew the paradise they had lived with each other was going to become at least a little more complicated, if not get interrupted altogether. It would be ideal if they could both go to the same college, but even so, there could be many more limitations on how and when they could see each other than there had ever been at home. And if they didn't end up at the same school, what would that be like? For her it brought to mind images of herself as the lonely and anxious wife, stuck on a military base while her husband was serving overseas. Not a happy thought.

He, on the other hand, decided to give up baseball, at least playing for school and possibly later as a professional. His father was more than a little disappointed about this and tried to conceal it, but didn't do so well. Others were shocked and almost seemed to imply that he must be a little dimwitted, at least shortsighted. Did he not understand how big of a deal this would be if he really made it, with both money *and* fame? He tried to explain, but after a while gave up on this, realizing that many would never understand.

Something told him it wouldn't be a great a surprise if he ended up with a permanent shoulder condition or chronic pain. Many were willing to risk this for the glory, but he was not. Pitching is quite a severe and unnatural motion, a great strain for the body, especially for tens and even hundreds of thousands of times. But it wasn't just this that made the difference. It was also her.

All professional athletes miss a lot of time at home, but baseball? Baseball is the worst. There are 162 games in the regular season, played over a six-month period of time, and that doesn't even include the postseason. On average that is twenty-seven games a month, leaving only three or four days each month when there is no game. She had never said a word about this, about any of it. But he thought about it himself and realized just how much of the time he would be away if all went well. And it might go on like this for years.

As it turned out, it was not a hard choice, although it did make him sad for a time. He loved baseball; he had always loved it. Why couldn't it be something you could just do from time to time? Why did it ever have to become such a big deal? He knew he could play in college and then quit, but he didn't want his college choice to be driven by this. He also considered playing for whatever college he went to, if that worked out. But in the end he was a little exhausted by it all. It was time to let it go. Time to let it die so that even greater things could come to life.

Regarding college and if both of them would end up in the same place, he did his best to alleviate her concerns. He reminded her of their connection, that it had already survived some challenges as they had grown older, and they would survive even greater ones if they were determined to do so. She always felt better after he encouraged her in this way, but then she would also feel bad for having had doubts in the first place and would wonder why her thoughts had wandered when his did not.

The truth was that his thoughts and feelings could wander as well, but for some reason he recognized them sooner for the distortions they were and dismissed them. And this thought really helps in better understanding the deeper connection they had, the commitment they felt for each other. They both looked at it as truth. Not as *a* truth, but *the* truth—the truth about life and what it was supposed to be about. And anything else, any other scenarios about the two of them that didn't include, first and foremost, them as a couple, were *false*, distortions. They knew this deep in their hearts, but their feelings confirmed it. They did not have words for the love that they felt for each other, but the feeling itself was familiar. Very rich and deep and familiar.

As it turned out, she more and more thought she would love to be a vet, especially a large animal vet who takes care of horses. He wasn't as clear, but his father had been an electrician when he was a young man and then had the initiative to start selling electrical parts and became a wholesale distributor. The business had grown enough to have several locations in their city. He wasn't sure if he wanted to work with his father or in that business, but he could if he wanted. Getting a business degree would give him a lot of options. She decided to go to the state university that had a good veterinarian school, and he decided to go to another state university that was only thirty minutes away but had a better business school.

With some anxiety, they settled into their new living arrangements away from home but found a way to see each other at least every other day and talked on the phone when they could not. Neither had ever scanned the horizon for other romantic interests—they'd had each other almost as long as their memories. Such a thought had never even occurred to either of them. They were two very different people, but they shared an incredible self-confidence that was obvious and attractive to others. So without ever inviting it, without ever thinking of anyone else of the opposite sex as someone to flirt with or ever be involved with, others frequently would flirt with them. They both learned to politely but quickly extinguish this.

And *self-confidence* is really not the best word to describe either of them. There was actually very little self in them—that was exactly what was different about them and what made each of them so attractive. There was incredible freedom of spirit that allowed them to think very little of themselves at all, as if they had no self, or desire, or emptiness that needed to be filled. Their real need was for each other, but it was never a selfish need or one that worried, or fretted, or demanded. A great gift it was, the greatest gift of all.

I wish this story could go on and on, unbroken, forever and ever and ever. I am not the first one to wish that. Looking back, he never understood it. He just remembers waking up that dreary morning and feeling different somehow. It was one of those cloudy, rainy days that just goes on and on. It pours for a while and then stops, but then there is still so much moisture in the air, you can feel it as you walk. And then it pours for a while again and stops again, but it refuses to clear up.

She had always been the one who was more vulnerable to doubts—doubts about them and if their love would stand the test of time. For him, on this day, it wasn't like that. It wasn't that specific. He could never pinpoint a particular thought, or event, or occurrence, or anything else to make sense of it. There was a slight heaviness in his mind and heart he had never felt before, not unlike the feeling you first get when you might be coming down with a cold.

You have that first feeling of scratchiness in your throat, or that first tinge of aching in your head, or that first bit of congestion in your sinuses. *Is it just a little discomfort that will soon pass,* you wonder, *or is it the beginning of a real illness?* After more time goes by and it hasn't passed, you are still wondering, still hoping it is nothing significant, eventually even wondering if your focus on it has itself made it into something significant, when it really is not. And sometimes it passes and does not become a real illness. And sometimes it doesn't. He spent most of that day stuck in a similar state of mind: wondering what was wrong or if something was wrong, eventually concluding that something *must be wrong* because he could not stop wondering why he was wondering. Sometimes it just never gets clearer than that.

He decided to run some errands, hoping the distraction would help to clear his mind. It didn't. After returning home and putting some things away, he sat down in one of his more comfortable chairs to rest for a while. His eyelids felt very heavy, so he decided to close his eyes for a few moments.

And then it happened. He had his first thought of a life *without her.*

Once upon a time, there was another quite similar story. Some people believe this story is not just *a* story but the *first* story, upon which all other stories are based. This story is about the first man and the first woman and their romance with each other, but first and foremost, their romance with their Creator. This Creator for centuries spoke of His love for these creatures as a bridegroom speaks of his love for his bride—His passion but also His hurt. And centuries later He spoke of His love for these creatures as a father's love for his child—His passion but also His hurt.

Either way it is intimate. It is said that it was only for love that this Creator ever created. He wanted to love these creatures and for them to love Him back. He would create a whole world for them, an incredible world, but life was never meant to be about the world. The world would give them plenty to do and to care for, and there was good purpose in it. But His desire for a relationship with them was the only thing that was ever to give life meaning. They would have relationships with each other as well, and these relationships would be important and precious. But even in these they would only do well if they had learned how to love from the way He had first loved them.

As surprising as it may sound, the romance that the first man and woman had with their Creator did not last unspoiled for long. There was another character in that story, someone who interfered, a demon who had once been an angel. This demon has always been given credit for introducing the discord between the Creator and mankind, for disrupting their perfect peace. But to some degree I believe he has been given a bad rap. The whole thing should not fall on him. We are responsible as well. And I wonder if even he believed the lie he told that first woman and man. He seemed to have already been taken in by it.

And that lie was just this: That you can live a life of your own, independent of this Creator. That you can be your *own god* of sorts, in control of your own destiny. Why wouldn't you *want* to do this? Why would you ever leave this up to someone else, even Him? Why would you ever trust *Him* to know what is best for *you*?

I don't know if you noticed, but it was in this very moment, in this very first story, that the whole history of the world changed forever. It was in this very moment that self was born and its close companion self-love. Self didn't exist in the heart of man before that day, but ever since, one consistent and unalterable thread has been woven through every story that has ever come to pass: the saga and struggle of men being overwhelmed and overtaken by self and self-love, and from time to time men trying in vain to put it to death.

Maybe after all this time, everyone else was rubbing off on our young man. Maybe it was inevitable. Maybe the fact the two of them had survived as long as they had, thinking and feeling different than everyone else they knew, was in itself a great achievement, not anything that could have lasted. He began to feel things in his heart and soul that he had never felt before, things he did not have words for that did not include her.

The first thing he experienced was an ache of sorts, but worse. More like hunger pangs, but it ran deeper down inside him. He felt . . . empty, painfully empty. Those were the only words that came close to describing what he felt. And then he had thoughts of being filled, of being satisfied. But the pain returned and hurt so badly in his gut that he felt a little desperate. *What if it gets worse*, he wondered? *Will I be able to stand it?* And then he had thoughts of food and platters of food, of feasting even, but the sense of desperation, bordering on panic, remained.

After a while it decreased in intensity and then subsided, but he remained more than a little shaken.

And then he had sexual thoughts. Thoughts he had never had before, thoughts that were graphic and compelling but at the same time made him nauseous. He felt dirty. *How strange is that*, he thought? He tried to will these thoughts away, but they stubbornly refused. He began to have fantasies of being seen and desired by a woman and feeling this sensation build up inside him. He felt good and content, satisfied with himself somehow, but did not understand this. And then in a moment, it all passed. *Thank God*, he thought.

For a moment he felt better, but then he had visions of houses and buildings, and monuments and statues, and other things that men had built. Some looked better than others, something he had never remembered thinking before. Some were taller or bigger or more intricate. Some seemed more elegant or more valuable or more desirable. He felt this urge to create and build things for himself.

He considered different things he could create and evaluated them in his mind. *What would be most glorious?* he thought. "A skyscraper, a beautiful skyscraper," he said out loud. *How tall should it be*, he wondered, *how intricate? How tall could it be?* he thought. And then he saw other towers, many of them. He thought of statues and felt drawn to them. *What would a statue of me look like?* he thought. He felt uncomfortable in thinking this . . . but not enough.

After this he saw another vision of himself reposing on a couch made of the finest fabrics. He noticed the clothes he was wearing and was dumbstruck. He had never seen such fine and intricate cloth, and the workmanship—it must have taken someone a long time to make such things. A platter appeared out of nowhere from behind him, offered to him with a drink and some fruit and cheese. He turned and saw a man there, holding the platter.

He looked up to see who this was, wanting to greet and thank the man and expecting their eyes to meet, but the man's gaze was fixed downward and away in such a manner that would not allow this. And then he realized this was purposeful. This man did not want their eyes to meet. *Why would that be?* he wondered. This man seemed calm and content in providing this service, but yet there was something more. It was just a feeling, but it felt bad, diminished, even like a . . . death. How odd was that? And yet the feeling was unmistakable.

And then he began to feel uncomfortable in yet a different way. He felt fidgety, restless, and anxious. He had the feeling that something was at risk, that he was on the verge of possibly . . . *losing* something. He sensed that something was about to get away from him, and because of that, he felt this urgency to do something, to stand up and act. He could hear the ticking of seconds in his head, and then he had the thought that minutes and hours were getting away, falling away, being lost forever.

There is only so much time, he thought. *Why have I never thought this before?* He felt an enormous burden, the burden of all the possibilities of so many different things that could be experienced, achieved, possessed, but might not. They were right there, right in front of him. *What should I do?* he wondered. *What should I . . . choose?* He could almost taste these things in his mouth, but then they were snatched away. A feeling of irritation rose up in him, anger even, but it was more than that. *Indignant* would be the best word to describe what he was feeling, but it is not the word he would have used, for he did not know it.

And finally, he experienced other thoughts, strange thoughts, fantasies of himself in different situations. He could hear cheers in the background (there were people sitting in a baseball stadium) and the cracking of the bat against a ball that is well hit. It has that certain sound, loud and deep, which reverberates inside the park. The sound that makes you think it has a chance to make it over the fence. A bolt of excitement coursed through him. He pictured trophies, many trophies, in a case. And he heard the sounds of voices, many voices. He could not quite make them out, but he very much wanted to.

What are they saying, he wondered? Good things? Bad things? An incredible heaviness came upon him. Why did he care about what they said, about what they thought? Why should it matter? But he could not dismiss this, as hard as he tried. He felt weak, helpless, even captive. He forced himself to look at the trophies. They were trophies he had won playing baseball, and the thought of this felt especially good. An expansive feeling rose up inside of him, almost as if he were growing, becoming larger. And then even more strangely, the other people seemed to shrink, become smaller. He wondered if he was losing his mind.

And then just when he thought things could not get any worse, he had the worst thought of all. He realized that he had not thought of *her*, not once, all day. This had never happened before, not from the time they had become a couple when they were children. He couldn't believe it, and he wanted to go hide somewhere. He was so ashamed. How would he ever face her? What would he say?

Their relationship had been such that he had never been able to keep anything from her. Not one thing. Sometimes this could be a little embarrassing, but he would always be glad he talked to her, no matter how odd or weird or awkward it felt. There was a part of him that believed it would always be okay. They were so connected that telling her about this would almost be like telling her about something that had happened to him, something beyond his control. For that is really the way it had always felt to him, beyond his control, like he hadn't chosen it.

But on the other hand, he was deeply grieved because he knew this time was different. Although he didn't really understand, somehow, someway, it was different. Somehow he *had* chosen this. Some part of himself, down deep, had to have chosen it. He would have loved to blame it on something else, on someone else. Like that first man had blamed it on the woman, and that first woman in turn blamed it on the demon.

And then he had a thought that seemed to fall from the sky. A little thing, very little . . . but sometimes the littlest of things can slay the world. *I have a choice*, he thought, *but I only have it right now. I cannot put it off, or it will be too late.* He had the realization as clear as a bell ringing: *I can have my life as it was, or I can have it the way it was on this day . . . one or the other but not both. And truly I can have a life of love, shared with her, or I can have all the other things the world has to offer. One or the other . . . but not both. I cannot change the course of the world, but maybe, just maybe, my course can change. I want it to change. I want the strength to change it.*

And then . . . he woke up.

He had fallen asleep in the chair, and his head had just slumped over, awakening him. He sat there motionless for a moment, still groggy. What just happened? All of those things he had thought and felt, all those terrible things, did they not really happen in his mind while he was awake, like it had seemed? Did they *really* happen or not? Or had he dreamed all of it in the brief time, maybe even seconds, while he was asleep in the chair?

And then it was clear. It had all been a dream. Or maybe we should call it a gift. A vision of how things could be, of how they might be . . . but not of how they had to be.

"Thank you," he said out loud. "Thank you!" he shouted out. And he jumped right out of that chair and right into his car to go see her that very moment. For, you see, young love was still alive and well.

Unless You Turn

Truly, I say to you, unless you turn and
become like children, you will never
enter the kingdom of heaven.
Whoever humbles himself like this child
is the greatest in the kingdom of heaven.
Matthew 18:3–4 ESV

Let the children come to me, and do not hinder them,
for to such belongs the kingdom of God. Truly,
I say to you, whoever does not receive the
kingdom of God like a child shall not enter it.
Luke 18:16–17 ESV

Once upon a time, there was an old, strange man who lived far back in the woods.

No one knew if he had any family in those parts, or if he ever had. His small, worn-out house was so out of the way that no one would ever come upon it by chance. You did have to turn off the main road and around the first little curve of his driveway to come to the first DO NOT TRESPASS . . . NEVER sign, but that was all it took for most folks to get the idea.

It was as if he had thought about it long and hard. He had not put up a sign you could see from the road, for that might be an advertisement. You never know—some people are looking to cause trouble. He hoped you wouldn't even notice the small path on the ground that quickly disappeared into the woods. It was mostly covered with leaves and fallen branches, to the point you might wonder if it was a path or a driveway at all.

But just in case you decided, for whatever reason, to turn off the main road and start down it, as soon as you came around that first turn, you would be put on notice. And every one hundred feet or so past that, you would be reminded again, so much so that anyone in their right mind, or wrong, whoever made it all the way to his front porch, would not be that surprised when they were greeted by the two large barrels of his shotgun. He very much minded his business. Other people should very much mind theirs.

The man kept some chickens and pigs and even a dairy cow or two and had a garden, but most folks did in those days, especially out in the country. This allowed him to be fairly self-sufficient—he didn't need to come into town often. Some said he had cut down his own trees, milled them by hand, and built his little house and barn all by himself. And they were right about that. He had. That had been about forty years ago, give or take.

When he did come to town, it was either very early or very late, when fewer were milling around. And he had a way, almost magical it was, with his mule and cart of sauntering into town so slowly and quietly, so rhythmically, that almost no one noticed even when he passed right by. There are some people who tend toward isolation but seem to make a point of irritating others, almost picking a fight. They can't seem to make up their mind. He was not like that. Something greater in him had died long ago. He was more like a ghost passing by living souls, hard to see and living more of the time in some other place.

It is funny how things happen sometimes. Random things, or so it seems. Years can pass, even decades or more, and very little changes. And then, on one particular day, something occurs . . . forever changing the trajectory of life. Sometimes bigger things happen, like the bubonic plague in the fourteenth century, the dustbowl drought of the 1930s, or Hitler's invasion of Poland in September

1939, which left little doubt what he had in mind.

But sometimes much smaller things can change that trajectory as well, like someone losing a job, or being in a car accident, or maybe, just maybe, a little boy who is lost in the woods. A mildly retarded boy who loved to explore and knew enough to stay within the landmarks he had been taught, but on this day he fell ill from something he had eaten, and in his clouded and confused state of mind, just kept walking straight on. Until he came to the old man's driveway just about dusk. He happened to turn to the right instead of to the left, which would have led him to the main road. After a few more steps, he came to one of the no-trespassing signs.

He knew the words "DO" and "NOT" but not this larger word "TRESPASS." He tried to pronounce it out loud, as he had been taught by his father, saying "tra . . . ppp . . . sss," but had no idea what it meant. "NEVER" was not a word he knew either. But it didn't matter. His heart would have never understood this sign, or believed it, even if he had been able to read it.

By the time he made it to the house ten minutes later, he was walking slowly.

The old man heard him approaching—barely a squirrel moved on his property without him noticing. It was good the boy was small, but his gait had become so labored and irregular the old man knew right away something was wrong.

It had been years since he had said more than two words to anyone, or wanted to. He had picked up his shotgun as soon as he heard footsteps in the distance and walked outside, but after seeing the boy, laid it down on the porch before the boy had time to see it. The two met in the driveway about twenty paces from the house, and just as they did, the boy collapsed in his arms. It was good that the situation was just this clear. Left with any choice at all, the man would not have chosen as he did. He carried the boy into the house, laid him down on his bed, and ministered to him.

The boy was not completely unconscious, but then nodded off to sleep. The man knew someone would be missing this boy very much and was tempted to try to rouse him right then to learn where home was so they could be on their way. But instead he let the boy sleep, and as he did, dusk moved on to dark.

The boy was not quite five feet tall, and from his overall appearance, the man thought he might be eight or nine years old. You wouldn't think that home could be that far off, but back in those days, especially out in the country, distances were much greater, telephones were new and not in every home, and word passed a lot slower. The man did not have a telephone, nor did he care to have one. He knew the family names of those whose lands were closest to him, plus a few other names, but almost never had contact with any of these people, did not know who had children or their ages, and so had no clue himself who the boy might be.

The man had served in the first Great War when he was young and had learned basic first aid. The boy's temperature and pulse seemed normal—hopefully his illness was something minor. As soon as he was feeling a little better, they could start on their way, and he could have him home before it became too late.

After an hour or so, the boy stirred, opened his eyes for a moment, and then closed them again.

The man tried to wake him so they could talk. "Young man," he said. The boy didn't respond. "Young man," he said again a little louder, taking hold of his arm and moving it a bit. The boy opened his eyes more fully. "Maybe you should sit up," the man said. "I need to talk to you, to find out where your home is so we can get you back to your family."

The boy's eyes were still unfocused, but he slowly sat up, allowing the man to place a pillow behind him so he could lie back more comfortably against the headboard.

"And so, young man," he started again, "can you tell me your name?"

"My name is John," the boy said.

"Where are you from? Did you walk here all the way from your home?"

"Yes," John replied hesitantly. "At my home we have a house and a barn and cows and pigs and big fields of corn."

"I see," the man said, "but *where* do you live? Where is your home?"

"Where?" John asked. "My house is right next to the yard, and the barn is right down the hill."

"But how would we get there from here?" the man asked.

John looked at him with a blank expression. Why did he not seem to understand? It was a simple question. The boy had walked all the way to the man's house from somewhere close by. He was old enough to be familiar with basic directions, to know landmarks, to know how to get from here to there in their little community. It was a very small town; there were only a few roads.

The man took another tack. "Tell me a little about your family. What is your father's name? What does he do?"

"My father's name is Pa. Pa is a farmer. He loves to work the land. Yes, he loves to work the land. He always tells me that."

"But what is your last name, your family's last name?"

"Last name?" John asked, again not seeming to understand.

And with that response, the man knew something greater was wrong, like his mind was not right. Like it never had been. Maybe he was mentally deficient. John looked like he was eight or nine, but his responses were more like that of a three- or four-year-old. The man didn't want to wait until morning, but even if it turned out that John knew some landmarks after they started out, he might not recognize them in the dark. His parents might be frantic, but it seemed better to wait and set off in the morning. The closest neighbors would be their first stops, but if these did not prove to be fruitful, they could continue from there. There were also several individuals in town who might know the boy and his family. If all else failed, the county sheriff lived two days away by horse-driven cart. Hopefully, it would not lead to that.

John did not want anything to eat, but he drank plenty of water and seemed to feel better. He looked around the room and noticed the large head of a bear mounted up high on the wall. "Is that . . . a bear?" he asked sheepishly.

"It was a bear, once upon a time. Almost killed me, it did. I would have never wanted to shoot it otherwise. Incredible creatures, they are. He came upon me while I was camping in the woods, right here as I was building this house. He went through my food pack, but he lunged at me once . . . wasn't sure what he was going to do. It still bothers me, thinking of it. He might not have harmed me. But I didn't know that. If I had waited just another moment, this might be *his* house you were sitting in, and you would be talking to *him* instead of to me, and you might be looking at *my* head up on that wall."

John's eyes grew wide, and you could almost hear the wheels in his head turning, but this was not something he could make sense of. The man realized his blunder right away and smiled, adding, "I'm sorry. I was just kidding. That was just a *joke*." John looked a little puzzled for another moment, but then smiled and seemed to get the idea.

Our bodies and minds are incredible things. They are capable of so much and learn things so well, that before long they perform many functions by habit. It had been so long since the man had smiled but also meant it. It had been a long while since he could actually feel the corners of his mouth stretch beyond the place to which they had become accustomed. The sensation surprised him but then disturbed him. He didn't want anything to stir him, to cause him to think of the past. And then he came back to this world and realized he had just been sitting there, staring off into space.

John was looking at him.

"Oh . . . I'm sorry," the man said. "I was just thinking of something. I didn't mean to ignore you." John may not have understood his meaning, but he understood the man's heart and responded with a smile—a genuine and forgiving smile. This triggered something even more in the man, but this time he was more able to conceal it.

"Are you sure you couldn't eat something? Maybe some soup?" the man asked.

"*Chicken* soup?" John asked as he perked up. "Do you have any of *that*?"

"I do," the man said. "I made some just this morning. I like it too."

John sat at the table and had some soup with bread. The man joined him and had some as well, but more to encourage John to eat. The man wanted to engage him in some conversation but wasn't so sure the best way to do this. And then he realized that if John was more like four in his mind, the man could just pretend he was talking to a child that age.

"Do you help your mom and dad on the farm? Do you have any chores?"

"My mom died when I was born," John said matter of factly.

The man felt terrible. "I'm so sorry," he said softly.

"Oh, it's okay," John said. "Pa said that God just couldn't go without her any longer. He had a much better place for her in heaven with Him. Pa said that we will both see her one day and . . . make up for lost time? Yes, that's what he says. But we will have to wait awhile. He says he misses her, misses her a lot. He wishes she could have been my mom. He says she would have been a great mom . . . the best."

"And I am sure she would have been," the man said. He figured there might have been complications during the birth, maybe the same complications that caused John's limitations. "Do you have any brothers or sisters?"

"I have two brothers, Matthew and Peter. Matthew is seventeen and Peter is nineteen. They are much bigger than me. Pa says that mom loved the Bible; that is why she named all of us after Jesus's best friends."

The man smiled again, but this time didn't notice. "Do your brothers help your pa with the farm?"

"They do," John said, "they do a lot. I help too. Pa said that one day I will be able to help a whole lot more, when I get bigger—bigger and stronger."

The man was relieved that at least John's father had been given some good hands with the farm. The three of them might just be able to manage a family farm if it wasn't too large.

As they were eating, John looked around the room, the main room of the house. They sat at a table in a rear corner. Only one chair was at the table, which the man had given to him. The man had retrieved a stool from the bedroom to sit on. A large woodstove occupied the middle portion of the back wall. There was a smaller woodstove for cooking and also a sink and cabinets in the opposite corner of the back of the room. In the middle were two larger chairs covered with cloth and a wooden chest in between, which also served as a coffee table.

"That chest looks just like the one my pa has," John said. "He keeps some of his favorite things in it. I have to ask his permission to go in it."

The man was suddenly transported back in time to a moment a couple of hours earlier, just before he had first heard John's footsteps outside. He had been sitting in one of those chairs in the middle of the room, his shotgun on the chest next to him. He had just felt a great burden lift off his shoulders, a great relief, the greatest he had felt in years. Many times over in the past he had approached this place in his mind, but he'd never gone further. This time he was resolute, and for a moment he felt free, or so he thought. He was just getting ready to pick up the shotgun and turn it on himself when . . . he heard the boy's footsteps outside.

"Sir?" John said, jolting him back to the present moment.

"I'm sorry . . . again," the man said. "I don't mean to be rude. I was just thinking of something else. How's the soup?"

"It's good," John said, "but not as good as my pa's"—noted without the slightest tone of criticism or judgment. The man could not help but smile at John's utter honesty and transparency, at his complete innocence. And then the exact timing of the day's events struck him.

Every ounce of his will had finally decided to pull that trigger. It was as good as done. He had never felt this feeling before; it was completely novel. It was just this that had convinced him this time would be different, that he could really do it. If the boy had approached the house just a minute later, maybe even just seconds later, the two of them would not be having this conversation. The boy, well, would likely still be lost and might be in very dire straits. He might have stumbled into the house and would have found quite a mess, something he would have never forgotten. And himself, well, he wasn't completely sure where he would have been. But at least he wouldn't have been in this place anymore. At least he didn't think so.

The man thought a little more about the boy. What it must be like to be intellectually challenged, if other kids made fun of him, about all the things in life he might miss as he grew older, if he would ever be able to live on his own, to marry, to have a normal life. He felt somewhat sad about this but then realized just how happy the boy acted. He didn't seem to have a care in the world, but maybe he wasn't old enough to even realize something was wrong with him. All children know how to live in the moment, to see the joy in little things, to just . . . be a child.

The man recalled how his life had started out. He had been blessed in so many ways. He'd grown up in a family that was financially secure, with both a loving mother and father, supportive brothers and sisters—heck, he even went to college and married his college sweetheart. But the man's thoughts came to an abrupt stop at this point. He had drifted off, and back. Again.

"Would you like any more soup?" the man asked.

"No. No thanks, I mean," John replied. "I feel better now. I sure didn't feel good when I was walking in the woods. I almost threw up once."

"I'm thinking, John . . . that it would be better for you to spend the night here. It's already so late, and it will be much easier for us to find our way to your home in the daylight. I have a cot you can sleep on. We'll eat a little breakfast first thing in the morning and then start out. I have a mule and a little cart we can ride in. How does that sound? Would that be okay?"

"It would," John replied. "I've never spent the night anywhere but at my house. It will be fun! You're a very nice man."

The man was taken aback at first by this comment, so much so he almost physically moved. But in a moment he forced a little smile so John could see this. And he was glad as well that John felt this way. He hadn't felt very nice in a very long time, or wanted to. It was a little encouraging to hear this and to realize that maybe, just maybe, there was still something down deep inside of him that was good, that had come to the surface, that had actually touched John. He would have bet otherwise.

The man started to glance around the room, a room that was as familiar to him as the back of his hand. But it all looked a little different now, almost as if he were looking at something new. This seemed odd to him at first, but then he realized he hadn't planned on still being in this room at this point in time, on still being alive.

It is a surreal feeling if you have ever felt anything like it. Any type of near-life-and-death experience can cause it. Anything that just occurred that could have had a much different result, like a near-miss in an automobile accident, or a serious health scare, or a gun discharging by accident, or anything else that might have been fatal, like a trip on the edge of a cliff that could have resulted in a fatal fall. It was as if he was living on borrowed time. "Existential" was the word he would have used if he had known it. That's a big word for country people, but what it really means is that you start having "why" thoughts instead of "what" thoughts. *Why* do we do what we do? *Why* does life turn out the way it does? *Why* are we even "here," for crying out loud?

Usually when you start asking "why" questions, it doesn't take too long for it to go pretty deep. The man wondered what this little boy might think if he realized the depth of the impact he'd had on this old, strange man by walking up to his house on this day. John would never be able to understand why an adult would ever want to take his life, what could be so bad. But what if he could? He probably viewed himself like most little kids, as very small and very insignificant. If only he knew.

After they had both finished the soup, John seemed to feel much better and became more talkative. "Are you a farmer like my pa?"

"No," the man replied, "I used to be a carpenter. Do you know what that is?"

"No," John replied.

"A carpenter is a man who works with wood, who builds things out of wood, like this house, for example. Built it all myself, every board of it."

John's eyes grew wide again as he looked all around, and up and down, and then all around again. He seemed to understand, but it was a little too much for him to take in, building something so big from scratch.

"I don't work anymore. Haven't in a long time."

John continued to look at him.

"A man doesn't have to work his whole life. Usually when you get old, as old as I am, you don't work anymore. Many times you can't. Your body gets too worn out."

John had never thought of this before—he hadn't spent any real time around anyone old. His grandparents did not live close by. He felt very sad, almost as if he was going to cry.

"Oh, it's all right," the man said. "Everybody has to get old one day. Can't live forever."

"You can't?" John asked. "Pa said he and me and my brothers will live forever; that's when we are going to see Ma again."

"Well, I didn't mean that," the man replied. "I just meant we can't live forever in these bodies. They get old. They wear out."

John looked up and down at the man's body and then at his own. His wheels turned again, even faster this time. Then he looked up and smiled at the old man.

It touched the man deeply. He didn't know why—it just did. A tear almost came to his eye. It had been many years since he had felt anything like this. It was as if he was coming back to something he had lost long ago and was only now remembering.

The man had laid his shotgun on a little table by the front door when they had first come into the house. He noticed it lying there, and he stood up to hang it in its rack on the wall.

"My pa has a shotgun too," John said. "He told me he would teach me how to shoot it one day when I grow up . . . but *never* to touch it. I wouldn't want to. It sure is loud when he shoots it."

"Your pa is very smart. You don't need to ever touch it—it could hurt you."

"Why do people have shotguns?"

The man was surprised by this but then realized again just how young John really was. "Well, that's a pretty good question, John. Let me see, how should I answer that? For starters, a gun can be used to shoot game, like deer and animals that we can use for food. It can also be used for protection, like when I had to use it to shoot that bear right there." He pointed. "And then, well, it can be used for protection from people too."

"People?" John asked.

"Yes." He thought how he might explain this to John, or if he should, but then began to try. "Sometimes people can be mean. Do you ever get angry or mad about anything?"

"Angry?"

"Yes, like upset, when someone does something to you?"

"Does something to me?" John didn't seem to have any idea what the man was asking. Was it possible, in his little world, with a loving father and two older brothers who had likely always felt a little guilty they had been born normal when John had not, that he had never been picked on or treated harshly . . . by anyone? They had to have lost their patience with him, you would think. But relative to what most people experience, maybe John couldn't understand what he was trying to say.

"Well, think of it this way," the man said. "There are people in this world who are not very nice. Sometimes people even go to war against each other."

"War?"

"A war is when one group of people fight against another group of people, and they use guns—even bigger guns."

"Why would they do that?"

And with this question, the man realized that he wasn't making progress but losing it. And then it occurred to him that maybe, just maybe, this conversation wasn't going the way it was because John, bless his little heart, was so limited and so *unable* to understand things that anyone else of any age or any degree of intelligence would grasp immediately—but that the rest of the world had *lost* their way many, many ages ago and had never found it again. And maybe, just maybe . . . John was the only one who was still sane.

It was war that had changed the man's life. Changed it from a bright and sunny day to a stormy one with no end. His mind drifted off again, and he wondered why he had chosen to use the example of war with John, why he had lost his focus, his self-discipline. He became angry at himself. He had promised himself in the past he would never again give it this much credit, even mention its name out loud.

War had taken everything from him. And then years upon years of reflection on it, with the hope that would help, that one day he would finally move through it all, turned out to be a waste of time, even worse. His heartbreak never healed; it would never leave him be. For him, thinking about the past just gave it the opportunity to assault him all over again. He had never been able to make any sense out of it, and so he decided he would do his best to not let it intrude into his thoughts any longer. He would at least have the last victory by shutting it out of his mind, even if it was a small one. And he had won this little war for many years, until just a few moments ago.

John yawned long and wide, and this interrupted the man's thoughts. "Well, John. What do you think about going to bed? If we go to bed now, we can get an earlier start. I know your pa has to be worried about you."

"Okay," John replied, and rose.

The man set up the cot in the main room. He did have indoor plumbing, and both of them visited the bathroom before bed.

"Good night, John. Hope you sleep well. I'll be right in my bedroom through here. I'll leave my door open in case you need anything. Just come right in, okay?"

"Okay," John said, "good night."

The man crawled into bed, and as he laid his head on his pillow, he again could not help but think how different the day had turned out than he had planned. He'd intended on ending his life right after lunch. He wanted to have one more pork sandwich, or he would have done it in the morning. Kind of silly, huh? He had particularly grown fond of the particular pig this pork came from. He never knew quite what it was, why he always wanted to give her a little extra food, something a little better. And he'd felt more grief than normal when the time had come to slaughter her. He had even given her a name, something he had never allowed himself to do with all the other animals that had been destined to have much shorter lifespans. Mabel. He had called her Mabel.

As he thought again about the day's events, he wondered if Mabel and John had somehow conspired with each other. Mabel's part would be to supernaturally call out to the man through her flesh, confusing him, wooing him for one last taste, causing him to wait just a little longer—until John could find his way down the driveway, all the way to the house. He smiled at this. He could not remember the last time he had actually made up a joke to tell himself.

And then after lunch, he'd decided to linger. It was like he wanted to take one more trip around the block, so he did. He had never expected anyone to disturb him—it had been the better part of a year since anyone had driven down his driveway unannounced. He revisited many of his memories that afternoon, many of his good ones. Maybe even a part of him was hoping that with a little more time, he might change his mind. But most of him knew better. The pain far, far outweighed any good memories. And it had become unbearable, unbearable with no end in sight.

But now as he thought about tomorrow morning, starting off with John on their search, he felt a small sense of anticipation, even a little peace, although he wouldn't have called it this. Someone once said that the greatest feeling is not joy. It is relief. The events of the day and the time he had spent with John had proven this theory correct, again. After a few more minutes, the man nodded off. And he never would have expected it, but he slept more peacefully than he had in years.

The man awoke to something tugging on his arm, and as he opened his eyes, he was startled by the sudden appearance of John's face only several inches from his own.

John had never seen anyone's face as old as the man's. He was in pretty good shape for seventy-seven, but his skin was much more wrinkled and decorated with spots here and there than anyone John had ever seen. "Wake up, wake up!" John said joyfully. "What are we having for breakfast?"

The man sat up and tried to collect himself. "Well, John. How did you sleep last night?"

"I slept great."

"Well, let me see. Let's go outside to the chicken coop. There should be some fresh eggs. And I have some bacon I could cook."

"Can I help?" John almost yelled.

"Of course you can, John," the man replied.

John could hardly contain himself as the man rose and dressed.

The man couldn't help but be struck by the extent of John's joy over breakfast. At first he was irritated, a feeling that had become his closest companion. He had been irritated at everything and everyone for a long time. But as quickly as his irritable thoughts began, they were interrupted. *It is wonder*, the man thought as he looked at John. Wonder. Sheer wonder over the littlest thing, the littlest joy in life.

And then he was struck again, this time by a great contrast. On the one hand, John's innocent and childish joy that would not be contained, and on the other, the man's own great emptiness, a great void, the utter loss of his own joy, many years earlier. For years the man had had no patience for the pleasures and happiness of other men. He had convinced himself that they were just fools. One day life would crush them, too, and wipe their smiles right off their faces. But this morning was different. The overflowing of John's cup had convicted him. He had been drawn in, not provoked or pushed away. He wouldn't have been able to put it into words right then, but something inside him stirred for the first time in a very long time.

At first he noticed he was getting his clothes on faster than normal, to the point he'd almost lost his balance and fallen on his face as he slipped on his overalls. And as they walked out the back door, he noticed his step had quickened as well. And what was this feeling in his chest? Could it be a little excitement? Excitement over going to the chicken coop to retrieve a few fresh eggs? Over something he had done over ten thousand times in his life, the great majority of which he had been daydreaming about something else? But not on this morning.

"Don't you have a name?" John asked the man as they were walking out the back door.

The man couldn't believe he had not properly introduced himself to John after all of this time.

"My name is Lucas," the man replied. "People used to call me Luke. There was a man named Luke who knew Jesus too."

"Really?" John replied.

"Really. My mother and yours must have thought the same way when it came to naming their children," he said with a smile.

The two of them found four eggs on that morning, and with some bacon and bread and milk to drink, had quite a breakfast. But they had more fun in getting it all together and cooking it on the stove. John had become a good helper in the kitchen at home—this was an area in which he could really contribute.

As they were finishing breakfast, the man wished it could go on a little longer. Soon John would be home, and their time together would be over.

As they started out from the house, the man told John that he knew his father would be worried sick to try to prepare him, but then explained this was only because he loved him so much. The first house they came to was not John's house, but they knew where he belonged—just a little farther down the road and around the bend. Pretty much everyone in that part of the county knew each other. You had to know other folks in those days; you never knew when you might need someone's help. Lucas had chosen different though.

As they trekked farther down the road, John recognized where he was. "Right here." John pointed. "This is our road. Our house is just over that hill." As the house came in sight, the noise of the cart on the road caused John's father to come out onto the porch.

What a night he must have had, Lucas thought. Maybe they should have set out last night, but it hadn't seemed like a good idea at the time.

John's father, whose name was also John, and Matthew and Peter were so happy to see John that they all couldn't stop yelling for five or ten minutes. John's father was a little suspicious at first of this old, strange man who had lived so close for so many years but who he did not know at all. But he only felt enormous appreciation for all he had done after he heard the whole story.

They invited Lucas to stay for lunch, and he actually accepted the invitation. He was a little uncomfortable at first—he hadn't been around people like this for forty-odd years. And John made him promise to come visit often before he left.

On the way home, Lucas wondered again if he should have tried to find John's house the previous night. And then he realized that only because he had not, a greater miracle had been able to occur. He could not help but smile at the irony of it all. He had been thinking he had been doing everything he could to care for this lost and sick boy, to help him to find his way home because he was just that—lost and helpless. And maybe he was.

But it had been he himself who had been truly lost without any hope of being found. Lost, very soon to be dead. And it had been a little boy, a mildly retarded boy at that, who had been the real hero and rescuer on this day. Can I get an "Amen"?

Maybe Lucas would give life a second chance. Maybe little John and his family could use a "grandpa" who lived a little closer. You never know.

Losing Oneself

The biggest danger, that of losing oneself, can pass off in the world as quietly as if it were nothing; every other loss, an arm, a leg, five dollars, a wife, is bound to be noticed.
—Søren Kierkegaard

For the time is coming when people will not endure sound teaching, but having itching ears they will accumulate for themselves teachers to suit their own passions, and will turn away from listening to the truth and wander off into myths.
2 Timothy 4:3–4 ESV

Once upon a time, there was a little village.

It sat in the loveliest foothills you could ever imagine, with majestic trees, flowering meadows, and vibrant rivers and streams. The village was in the Kingdom of Everlasting and ruled by King Glorius IV. He was a strong and courageous king, but no less gentle and kind in his dealings with all his subjects.

In years past there had been many wars, but Glorius I had always been victorious. He'd battled time and again with enemies who never seemed to tire of their desire to expand their boundaries. Glorius I finally made peace by giving these enemies three choices: "Lay down your arms and peacefully come to live with us. Move to some faraway place so we will never see your face again. Or die right where you stand, this day—you, your wives, and your children."

It seems these foreign intruders needed everything to be made that clear. But after it was, each made his choice and either lived with it or died with it. You see, their rulers did not have the integrity of Glorius I. They had always used their subjects for their greedy territorial desires. But something in the hearts of these foreigners very much responded to Glorius being so straightforward with them, and most of them changed their allegiance that day.

The Kingdom of Everlasting was blessed with so many resources. The land was fertile and would grow almost anything the people planted. The climate was temperate, usually warm, and summers and winters were never extreme. There were many trees, and no one had to travel to find the wood for fires and stoves or to build a house or barn. There was always plenty of rainfall, but not too much and never a drought. The rivers and streams were full of fish, many crops flourished in their fields, and large herds of cattle and flocks of sheep grazed on their lands.

Life was good, as some people say these days, but the people knew in their hearts this was not because of them or anything they had ever done, nor was it by chance. They had been given two great gifts: such a rich land and such a benevolent ruling family.

There was a young boy named Halam in the village, whose great-great-grandfather had been one of those foreigners long ago who'd decided to lay down his arms and join the Kingdom of Everlasting and who'd hoped that maybe, just maybe, Glorius I might be a more benevolent ruler than his own. His family had flourished ever since, and he had died just ten years earlier. On his deathbed he had made a point of making no reference to the family's history prior to their immigration. And he'd asked that going forward, no one ever mention it again. It would be an old and well-forgotten memory. From this point on, their family would always be known as members of the Everlasting clan, nothing more, nothing less.

Halam was a rambunctious boy who lived life to the full. If you ever wanted to find him, you should look outdoors. The landscape was so beautiful and so varied it was impossible to ever become bored with it. Halam did have school, although it was not called that. The word "school" comes from the idea of setting apart hours of the day to learn important things and for lectures to be given, which will assist you with the rest of your life. Learning in the Kingdom of Everlasting did include some lectures, but that would not be the best way to describe it. And learning was not just for children but for everyone.

As a matter of fact, there was not a single word for this activity, as if it were some discrete thing that one did at certain times and not at others. The people's education, if we can borrow another related but still inadequate word, was integrated with the rest of their lives. It was part of it and woven through it. They did have two words for their greater beliefs—"The Way."

First and foremost, The Way was an acknowledgment, and especially a gratitude, that all good things had been given to them through nature but by the hand and desire of the Great King, who had ruled since the beginning of time. The Way bound them to be loyal subjects to their respective king, who in the last century had come to this honor through birth. The king was set apart to rule with both courage and humility. He dedicated every ounce of his being to the good of the kingdom as a whole and to each and every one of his subjects, in particular, to his death, if that was ever required. And the good of each of every one of his subjects would only come to pass if they learned The Way and practiced it all their days.

The Way had been written down by their ancestors so long ago that no one actually knew the date or year, but these manuscripts had been preserved, unchanged, for countless centuries. It taught those in the kingdom how to live their lives. It did this not so much by instructing them *what* to do but by *how* to do it. The most important thing was their attitude of heart, and if their heart was set on the welfare of others before themselves, all would joyfully go about their business each and every day, and all would peacefully rest their heads on their pillows each and every night.

Everyone mattered in the kingdom, from those with the most basic occupations all the way to the king himself. It was quite a thing to have a king who sat in the place of greatest honor and for whom any one of his subjects would gladly sacrifice their lives in battle. But an even greater thing was that any one of those same subjects would extend themselves to the same length for anyone else in the kingdom, no matter the need, no matter the circumstance.

Everyone played a different part, but every one important, every one essential. Life itself in the kingdom was a celebration, but the people also very much loved to have special celebrations and had many of them.

One day Halam and some friends were swimming in a stream that ran by a great forest on the edge of the kingdom. After a while the children climbed out of the water for a rest and lay on the soft grass. One of the boys lay on his back, looking up into the sky. It was one of those days when the sky is so blue and so clear and the clouds so white and so scattered across the whole sky that it is hard, once you notice, to stop looking.

"Look," the boy said, "that cloud there looks like an elephant. Do you see?" and he pointed to help the other children find it. "And a rabbit," said another child, "right there." This went on for a while, as it often does. Children love to play this game, and some adults too. The game always goes better if it is one of those days when there is a steady breeze high up in the atmosphere that keeps the clouds moving across the sky at a fairly good rate but not so brisk that the clouds break apart. That way anyone trying to find a cloud has plenty of time to find it and join in the fun and commentary, and everyone has a different palate of choices to pick from every ten or fifteen minutes.

If you looked off a little to one side, you could catch the tops of some of the trees of the great forest. The trees were so tall that their branches seemed to blend in with the sky. One of the children made mention of this, but no one said anything further. But then she continued, "I once heard my father say that the trees at the center of that forest are so thick that no light can penetrate. It is completely dark."

An eerie silence followed. For one thing, the forest lay outside of the kingdom, and so no one had ever ventured there or felt the right do so. But the greater truth was that very rarely did anyone speak of it. None of the children could remember being told *not* to speak of the forest, but the sheer fact that most of them could not remember even one time anyone had ever done so left a void in their memories, so abrupt and obvious, that it now stood out.

But there was something more about this forest, something different, something foreboding, that caused them to *not* want to speak of it, maybe not even think of it. Maybe their parents had always felt the same way . . . with the possible exception of this one girl's father.

No one spoke for a time, but then one of the boys said something further. It was as if the first girl's comments had stirred up some confidence in the rest of them. Or something. "I wonder if that forest is really that different from all the other forests in *our* kingdom?" he said. "No one really knows, after all, do they? No one from our kingdom has ever been there, have they?" The boy asked all of this very much on purpose. If someone knew of something more, if anyone had ever heard of anyone going there and what they had seen, he wanted to know. No one spoke because no one had an answer, but no one really wanted to consider it either. His question had penetrated much too far too quickly.

It was one thing to think a little further about the forest, to poke at the idea of it. It was another thing entirely to start talking about what it might be like if you went there.

And this was enough for one of the other boys to offer an out for all of them, a retreat. "Well, I'm glad that it *doesn't* lie within our kingdom," he said. "For it is not anything we ever need to worry about." The boy might as well have said he believed they had already broken an important rule by mentioning it to begin with and it would be best if no one said one word more. And no one did.

Some of them did continue to think of it though, whatever the conversation had provoked in them. Halam was not immune and was particularly struck by just how odd it was he had never once even thought of the forest but now could not stop.

One of the other girls had lain back down and did her best to start the cloud game back up again. "There is a woman there, with long flowing hair. And it looks like she is holding something. Is it a baby? The woman's head is tilted down. Is she not looking at it?"

"Yes, I see," said one of the boys. "It really does look like that."

Sometimes the good in the world finds a way to console us at the very time we need it the most. And a couple of the other children mentioned seeing one thing or the other, and the game continued for a while longer, as if they were trying to rinse the conversation about the forest out of their minds. It usually takes a few good dips in the water and several times wringing it out to get the rag clean again.

It was nearly time for dinner, and one of the children mentioned this. They all sat up and gathered themselves for the walk back to the village. Halam sat up at the same time, not so much because he wanted to but because he felt he should. He kept looking at the forest, however. One by one the children stepped back down into the stream and waded across at its shallowest point. They then climbed back up the opposite bank and headed home.

All except Halam. He had so quietly stayed put that none of the other children had bothered to glance back, and no one noticed he was not with the group. All the children were so used to everyone doing as they should and as they were told that no one had ever developed the habit of checking on others who were stubborn or strayed. No one ever had.

Even after the children had disappeared in the distance, Halam sat right where he was for a while, looking at the forest. It was still a good way off, at least several hundred feet. But after a while he edged closer. The trees were so tall that before long he walked into the shadow they cast from the afternoon sun. Something in him shuddered as soon as he did.

For the most part, he couldn't believe he was doing this. He had *never* done anything like this. He had this terrible feeling, a mixture of fear and restlessness and foreboding, but there had to be something more or he would have been on his way home with the others.

Two men can be on the opposite sides of a door that swings both ways, both trying to push their way into the other's room, and the door may stay right within its frame and not move for some time—a stalemate. But if it ever moves one way or the other, the man pushing in that direction has to be pushing harder.

Halam did not know or understand what was compelling him toward the forest, but since he was walking to it, it had to be stronger than all his reluctance. There was something about the mystery of the forest, about the unknown, that was drawing him.

And Halam didn't notice, but as he had drawn closer to the forest's edge, there were little mosquitos flying about. They flourished in the moisture of the forest itself, but some of them flew out beyond it into the adjacent field. One of these mosquitos lighted on his forearm, and as mosquitos are compelled to do, sank the needles of its mouth into Halam's skin. Halam felt the little itching from this and swatted at his arm.

After a few more steps, he entered into the forest, and after a few more moments, he disappeared into its darkness.

Halam's parents were very alarmed when he was not home for dinner. He had never been late for dinner, nor any of his siblings. The other children felt terrible when they noticed he was not with them. They were just entering the village, when one of the boys spoke out to Halam, wanting to confirm their plans for the next day. The boy turned around as he spoke, expecting to see Halam behind him, and when he didn't, they all realized for the first time he was not with them.

Since the last time anyone could remember seeing him was when they were sitting on the grass, they didn't know if he had ever begun the journey back. Or he might have been separated from them along the way. And that is really the way they were thinking about this—something must have happened to him, something against his will. None of them could fathom anything else, nor their parents. It didn't lie within their minds and hearts. There wasn't a circumstance that any of them could conceive of that would have included Halam somehow *choosing* not to return home at the appointed time.

Halam's parents went to the elders of the village, and a meeting was called for immediately. It was about an hour's walk to the stream where the children had spent the afternoon. At the meeting it was decided that whoever was available to go would meet at the village gate in twenty minutes. There was only one road that went in the direction of the stream, but there were many side paths that had to be explored. After the search party started out, one or two individuals volunteered to check out each side path or clearing or any other tangent as they went, while the larger group continued down the main road, until they finally made their way to the stream. They first saw the stream as they came over a hill, and there, just behind, the great forest.

It never entered Halam's father's mind until the forest came into view that it might play a part in this. His name was Yalam. He immediately dismissed the thought, however, and quickened his gait toward the stream, envisioning Halam lying there on its banks, fast asleep. Halam had just grown tired after an afternoon of fun and had fallen asleep lying there. Otherwise he would have already started on his way home, and they would have met him along the way. Yes, that had to be what had happened.

But when Yalam made it all the way up to the edge of the bank of the stream and looked down into it, and across to the other side, and each way up and down its edge . . . Halam was nowhere to be seen.

After some time had passed, all the adults who had explored side paths caught up with everyone else at the stream. It was decided that everyone would fan out a little broader from that point in all directions, since that was the last place Halam had been seen. Maybe he had fallen ill or was hurt. He could be quite close by but unable to call out or move. Those on the far side of the stream could only go so far because of the forest, but they covered all the meadow up to the forest's edge.

It was a difficult and depressing day. No one could remember anything like this happening before. As the sun started to set, there was nothing more to do but start back to the village and hope they would find Halam along the way or that somehow he would already be home.

Neither of those things happened, however. And the night was cruel to Halam's parents as they tried to sleep and did not have the faintest idea of where to even begin in trying to understand what could have happened to their son and where he might be.

Several days passed, and the people in the village hoped that Halam would return on his own or be found by one of the additional search parties that went out, but neither occurred. Finally the village elders met again. The discussion was varied and erratic. No one had any good ideas about what might have happened or what to do.

And then one of the men said, "You know, I hate to even mention this, but I am. We seem to have exhausted every other possibility we can think of. There is no reason to think there have been any new intruders from foreign lands who might have taken Halam back to their country. We have not heard of anything like this from any of the neighboring villages or from the king. It has been decades since any large animal who lives in these lands went rogue and harmed a human. That stream where the children were that afternoon is right there near that great forest. Does anyone think that somehow the forest can have anything to do with this?" And it might not surprise you, but this man was the father of the girl who had first mentioned the forest the day the children were at the stream.

There was a deafening silence for what seemed like an eternity, but then the chief elder spoke. "I have been thinking the same thing but hoped beyond hope that Halam would be found first. He has not. I believe we at least need to consider the forest. Maybe we should also talk again to the children, but this time mention the forest, just to make sure we are not missing something."

All the council agreed. So each set of parents who had a child who had been at the stream the day Halam went missing were instructed to talk with their child again. They were to probe as much as possible but specifically ask about the forest. And all the parents did so. The little girl who had first mentioned the forest that day held out for a while but then finally broke down and confessed to bringing it up in conversation. And the boy who had subsequently pressed the children to talk about the forest even more broke down and confessed as well. And he added, "You know, it wasn't too much longer after our conversation about the forest that it was time to leave for home. That was the last time any of us can remember seeing Halam."

Only the elders knew there had been rumors in past centuries that mysterious creatures lived in the forest, or at least had once upon a time. Creatures that looked like people and may have been human in the past, but something had happened to them to change them. Or maybe they had just decided to revert back to a more primitive existence, forgoing permanent shelters and farming the land. This was all anyone had ever heard about this, and most believed that even these were just fairy tales. And there had been rumors that several individuals from the village had gone into the forest in years past, but nothing more was known. As the stories went, they were never heard from again.

Most of all, the people could not even fathom why anyone would ever *want* to venture into the forest—it was outside of their kingdom, after all. Everyone in the kingdom had always known that everything in the kingdom was theirs, to have and to use and to nurture, but nothing more. This was the way life was and always had been. And it had always been enough, so much so that no one had ever thought it should be any different.

The elders resumed their conversation as soon as all the parents had spoken to their children and reported back. "I do think it is likely the forest has something to do with this since it is something the children were talking about just before they left for home," the chief elder said. "More than one child mentioned seeing Halam on the grass just as they were getting up to leave. No one said they remembered seeing him after they had begun to walk back to the village. I still do not understand this, but if Halam does not arrive home by tonight, in the morning a small party should go search for him one more time, into the forest if need be. Are there any volunteers?"

The chief elder asked this question as if any volunteer would do, but it was a rhetorical question, a way to be polite. All the men had similar ideas about who should go in such an instance that followed from The Way. Yalam should go. How would any father who loved his son beyond all comprehension not go to look for him once he is lost, or leave this job to someone else? And a couple of other single men should go, who had no wife or children they were responsible for. Someone who had never married would be a good candidate, or someone younger who had not yet married. Yalam said nothing but stepped forward. And within a few moments more, two men spoke up, one matching the former description and one the latter. The older man's name was Ray, and the younger's was Nachash.

The next morning came, but no Halam. The three men set out with supplies to last for some time, not really sure how long they would be gone or what they might need. They did each take a sword, all of which had been hanging on their walls and collecting dust for nearly a hundred years now and had belonged to great-grandfathers who had fought for Glorius I. They also took plenty of dried food, several changes of clothes, and some other odds and ends. The rest of the elders gathered together to pray over them and send them off. The chief elder raised his hands as he said, "May the Great King guide and protect you as you go and as you return. May you always fear Him, for your good always, that He might preserve you alive, as you are this day." And the men set off toward the great forest.

Little was said between the men on their way. There is an ancient story of another journey that involved a father and son, two companions, and the specter of life or death for the son. Very few words were exchanged on that journey as well. It is difficult to break such a silence with just any words. Yalam was no more in the presence of the Great King on this day than any other, but because of the circumstances, he was much more conscious of being in His presence, of *wanting* to be, of wanting His protection and blessing.

There was so much in Yalam's life he was grateful for, but especially his family. He had wanted a son for many years, and then he was finally blessed with one. With every step he took on this journey, he realized more and more just how great a sacrifice he would make to have his son back healthy and whole. He would even give his own life.

As the men grew closer to the great forest, Yalam remembered that ancient story himself, and it washed over him. For the first time, he understood the depth of that ancient father's grief. *Love is so beautiful,* he thought. And a father's love in particular. But such a burden too. And he was almost overwhelmed by the aching of his heart. *How does the Great King do it?* he wondered.

The journey to the stream went just as all the previous ones, bearing no fruit. When the men got to the stream, they again explored it up and down, but they all knew they were just putting off the inevitable. After a short while, Yalam simply looked at both of the men and said, "It is time." They understood. They came abreast of each other with Yalam in the middle and started toward the great forest. He was not sure if he should, but just before they entered, he drew his sword. The other men did the same. And all of Yalam's senses came alive as they had never been before.

The men walked slowly into the forest. None of them had ever been in battle, but each one found himself crouching down in battle position as he went, ready to spring forward or back if need be, and widening his view of sight as much as possible. After they had walked a hundred feet or so into the forest, the beating of their hearts slowed. Nothing so far had looked any different than any of the other forests they were familiar with in their kingdom. Thank goodness.

A mosquito lighted on one of Nachash's arms and bit him. He felt it instantly and brushed his arm with his other hand. "Darn mosquitos!" he blurted out.

The others had noticed them flying around but had not been bitten. After a few more moments of continuing on their way into the forest, Yalam and Ray noticed that Nachash had not kept up. They stopped and turned around to find that he was twenty feet or so behind them, not even looking in their direction but standing in place, looking up into the trees.

"Nachash. What are you doing?" Yalam called out.

Nachash did not respond but kept looking up. Yalam and Ray walked back to where he was, and as they approached him, he was still gazing up.

"These trees are so tall," he said. "They seem to go up forever."

"Nachash!" Yalam exclaimed.

This time Nachash turned around to face him and had the oddest look on his face. "What did you call me? Do I know you?" he asked, as if it were the most natural question in the world.

Yalam and Ray were taken back, not only by his words but by the look of lost and innocent wonder on his face.

Teasing and playing jokes was not something the people in the kingdom indulged themselves in. Not that they didn't tease from time to time or enjoyed having fun. But they were all aware that jokes can easily be taken the wrong way, and taking this chance was never as important as maintaining the best will possible with fellow members of the kingdom. And if there could ever be a time to tease and play around, this was not it. Nachash was not pretending, and they knew it. It was as if he had never seen either of them. They were both dumbstruck and did not know what to say.

After another moment or so, Nachash turned away again to look back up into the trees. "I wonder how old they are? How long it took for them to grow so tall?"

Yalam collected himself for a few moments, considered the situation they now found themselves in, and began again. "And so, my friend, how long have *you* been in this forest? The two of us just entered some minutes ago."

"Well, that is a very good question . . . *friend*, if I may call you that. Now that you ask, I am really not sure how long I have been here. All of my life, I guess. I cannot remember anything more right at this moment. Is this forest not all there is, in this . . . *world*, if you would call it that?"

And if Yalam and Ray were not already at a loss for words, they were now. What on earth had happened to Nachash? And then it occurred to Ray—all of this happened just moments after the mosquito had bitten Nachash. "Quick," he blurted out, "cover your arms and neck with some other clothing! It's the mosquitos . . . the mosquitos!"

Yalam and Ray hurried and covered their skin as best they could, even pulling a wrap over the top of their heads. Only their faces were bare. And then it occurred to Yalam, if all of this had happened to Nachash because he was bitten, maybe the same thing had happened to Halam. If the mosquito bites affected everyone the same way, this would explain why Halam had not returned home. For the first time in many days, Yalam felt hope. Maybe Halam was still in the forest, lost and wandering around. Yalam decided to see if he could learn any more about this illness from talking to Nachash.

"Uh, sir, excuse me. I am not sure how I should address you. What is your name?"

"Are you talking to me?" Nachash replied.

"Yes, I am," Yalam said.

"What is that word you used . . . *name*, did you say?" Nachash inquired. "I have to say that I don't know if I have ever heard that word before. What does it mean?"

"A name is the word others use to refer to you—it is what you are called. It is *who* you are," Yalam explained.

"Who you are, do you say? My, that is a strange idea. I am not sure if I have ever thought of that before. Who I am? Ummm. I am not even sure where I should start to try to figure that out. How do you know *who* you are?" Nachash stared at them again with the same innocent and childlike expression.

"Well, our parents gave us our names when we were born," Ray said.

"Your *parents*?" Nachash asked. "What are parents? Are they *people*?"

And with this last exchange, Yalam and Ray realized the utter depth of the problem before them.

Ray leaned over to Yalam and whispered, "Do you think he knows anything, remembers anything at all about his life prior to being bitten?"

"I am not sure," Yalam responded. By this time Nachash was already looking back up into the trees, not paying them any mind.

"It sure does not seem like he does," Yalam continued. "It seems like he has complete amnesia, but oddly enough, he does not seem to *know* that he does. Have you noticed it's only our questions that have caused him to question anything at all? Otherwise, he seems quite content, and I am not so sure if we left him here that he wouldn't just continue to look up into the trees, admiring them, and not have a care in the world!"

"Yes," Ray said, "I very much get the same feeling. What kind of illness or madness could this be?"

"I don't know," Yalam said. "But think of it. If you had amnesia, but you at least *knew* you had amnesia, that something must have happened to you because you could remember all sorts of other things about life in general and how it works, but for some reason you had just lost hold of your own personal history, your identity, your family, and so forth, that piece of the whole. You would at least have some idea about how to begin to search for answers and would very much want to. You would be very lost and disoriented, but you would know this, know that something was terribly wrong, and you wouldn't be able to rest until you either learned who you were or had at least exhausted every possible avenue for doing so. Your sense that there had to be a larger story, and especially that you had to have a place in it, somehow you had just forgotten, would ground you and drive you to search until you found the truth of who you were.

But Nachash's problem seems much different than this, much worse. He has amnesia, but he does not even realize that anything out of the ordinary has happened to him, that there was a previous time and he had a previous life, but somehow he lost all knowledge of it. Without that realization, how would he know what to do but to just come up with the best understanding of things he can from what he sees in front of him at this very moment?"

"He wouldn't," Ray replied. "He wouldn't even know anything about the Great King." And as soon as these words left Ray's lips, they both stood motionless, staring into each other's eyes, dumbstruck.

"My lands, you are right," Yalam said.

They both continued to stand there in silence for what seemed an eternity. Nothing like this had ever occurred to either one of them or to anyone in their kingdom. How could there be life without the Great King? That would be like trying to live without food to eat or, even more, without air to breath. Neither said anything further, but the thoughts in both their minds led to their natural conclusion, supplied by Yalam: "Is that even possible? Could someone actually live without the Great King, without knowledge of Him, out of relationship with Him? What would such a life be like? What *could* it be like?"

After a few more moments, both gladly left those thoughts

where they were for the time being and came back to their present predicament, feeling more compassion and desire to help Nachash welling up within them than they had ever felt for anyone in their lives.

No one knew how large the great forest was, but they imagined that it could be quite deep, maybe going on as it did for countless miles. Halam could be anywhere. How would they search all of it, and how would they not lose their way or retrace the steps they had already taken and not know it? For whatever reason, they hadn't even thought of this until now. The two talked about this quandary and decided on several things.

They could use the sun for direction as long as they could see it, but they sensed the farther they went into the forest, it might be blocked from view. They would go back to the place where they'd entered and make an X with their hatchet on one of the trees, on the direct opposite side from the way they had entered. And they would continue to mark a tree every time they took another hundred paces into the forest and would do the same one hundred paces to either side, marking all of them the same, on the opposite side from the way they had first come. This way the marks should be easy to see on the way back but also indicate the exact direction from which they had come, the way home. They might get a little off course, but hopefully not too much. In this way they continued forward but also branched out to some degree. They might not be able to cover all of the forest in any reasonable length of time, but they were going to try. Good that they had brought a few basic tools and other odds and ends just in case.

Now, what would they do with Nachash? Maybe he would come with them if they somehow gained his confidence. As it turned out, this was not difficult—he was as easy to lead as a puppy and as willing. They had to watch Nachash closely, however, as he would be distracted by the least of things and wander off. Everything seemed new and inviting to him . . . because it was. He continued to look up more than anything else, however. He could not stop gazing up into the trees and commenting on them: how huge they were, how old they must be. After a time, he chatted about them as if they had human qualities, wondering what they thought and felt and if they ever spoke.

"Nachash is really losing it," Ray said. "Have you been listening to him?"

"I am trying not to," Yalam replied. "I'm trying to keep my mind on what we're doing here."

In several hours they had made good progress. They could still see the sun to some degree coming through the tops of trees, but less and less, for the forest was getting thicker. They had started off early that morning from the village, so it was still only midday. They decided to go as far as they could as long as there was any light and then to make camp. There had not been any mosquitos deeper in the forest, but that did not allow them to forget about them. It would only take one bite and they would lose themselves—maybe forever.

As they made camp that night, their hearts were more hopeful. It had helped to be busy all day with the task of moving into the forest and carefully marking the trees in just the right way. And they had come a good way, many miles it seemed. Yalam had been fairly successful in convincing himself that of all the things that could have happened to Halam, this was the most likely. If everyone who was bitten by the mosquitos had the same degree of amnesia as Nachash, and were also as fascinated with the trees, you would think they would just stay in the forest. With no prior memories to prompt them to go elsewhere, they might just stay there forever.

The next day, they were making considerable headway, and Yalam heard something just beyond them. "Did you hear that?" he said. "It sounded like someone walking and stepping on some small branches."

"I did hear it," Ray responded.

Yalam rushed forward as quietly as possible, while Ray stayed put with Nachash. There were no additional noises to draw Yalam in a more precise direction, but he kept moving forward. In the distance he thought he saw something move, but his eyes were just playing tricks on him. But then he saw something else a good way off. He couldn't make it out so far away, but it was different in shape and color than the rest of the forest. As he moved closer, he saw that it was the back of someone's head, possibly a man, who was kneeling on the ground in front of one particular tree. It might have been the largest tree Yalam had seen since he entered the forest.

As he approached, he tried to be as quiet as he could, but it was impossible not to make some noise walking on the forest floor. The silhouette looked more like a boy, but he did not turn around. Yalam continued all the way to one side of him and saw that it was Halam. His heart almost burst out of his chest, and tears flowed from eyes. Only when he touched Halam's shoulder with his hand did Halam finally turn his head and look at him. As Yalam feared, Halam's expression indicated that he did not recognize his father.

Yalam made every effort to keep his fear over Halam's plight from breaking out all over his face and to be as calm as he could. With a deathly serious but weak voice, Halam asked, "Are you here to worship the great tree as well?"

Yalam and Ray were eventually able to convince Halam to join them with Nachash around a fire. As Ray prepared something to eat, they noticed how famished Halam looked. The previous night Nachash had not wanted anything to eat, but they didn't make much of that, with everything else. Now they wondered more about this, and they tried to convince Halam and Nachash to eat, but neither would.

The oddest thing was that they did not seem to recognize the food as food or to respond to it in any favorable way. Not when seeing Ray take it out of his pack, not when watching him put the dried meats, fruits, and nuts on some small plates, and especially not when watching the two of them eat. They both did drink water, however—Halam especially.

Both Yalam and Ray held the food up to their mouths, took a bite and chewed, and then held out the food to Halam and Nachash, inviting them to do the same, like you might do with a small child or even a tamed ape. But this still resulted in no response. Halam and Nachash looked at both of them as if they were crazy, then looked away again, usually up into the trees. There were many berries in the forest that Halam could have eaten over the last several days if he were in his right mind. Evidently, he had not been.

They decided to camp for the night where they were, as Yalam and Ray were emotionally exhausted. For the rest of that afternoon and night, Yalam and Ray observed that Halam and Nachash would talk a little to each of them but not at all to each other. From their facial expressions they seemed suspicious of each other, maybe even afraid. In the morning, when Yalam opened his eyes, Halam was in front of this great tree again, on his knees, head down, seemingly in deep thought. When Nachash awoke and saw Halam at the tree, he walked over and knelt himself beside Halam, purposely imitating everything Halam was doing. The novitiate seemed to be learning from the sage.

"It's so odd, is it not?" Ray whispered to Yalam. "It is almost as if once their minds are erased, they need to find something to replace it with, something greater than themselves, something beyond themselves."

"Maybe," Yalam responded. "I've not been thinking too clearly myself. I am so worried that I may never have my son back again, not as he was."

"I understand, my precious friend," Ray replied. "Maybe the elders will have some idea of what to do to heal them, to bring them back."

"I certainly hope so," Yalam said. "Let's get everything together so we can start back to the village."

The journey back through the forest went well—their system of marking the trees worked to perfection. They did come across something disturbing, however, that they had missed the first time through—the skeleton of what seemed to be a grown man, mostly covered by many winters of fallen leaves and twigs on the forest floor.

"This madness, whatever it is, may end in death sooner than later because they simply will not eat," Yalam said.

"I was thinking the same thing. They have nothing to sustain them," Ray replied. "Let's not waste any time on the way home."

And they did not. Their two patients continued to be obedient but quiet subjects. From time to time, they would stop to gaze up at the trees again, but a simple tug and smile would do the trick to get them moving again.

But as they ventured within sight of the meadow just beyond the forest's edge, Halam and Nachash came to an abrupt stop. The edge of the forest was filled with more light and looked different, more colorful and detailed. Yalam and Ray gave them each another nudge, but this time neither budged. Their faces were full of alarm, terror even. Yalam and Ray had done well the last two days remaining relatively calm, in spite of their constant fear that at any time they might be bitten by a mosquito and immediately transformed into some type of mindless ghost. Coming within sight of the meadow only quickened their desire to finally be out of the forest. Their sense of urgency caused them to raise their voices and to push and pull Halam and Nachash more forcefully, but the two resisted even more.

They each lay down on the ground and countered by pushing Yalam's and Ray's hands off them. They even began to strike out.

"I am afraid one of us will have to go for help," Yalam said. "I am thinking it will take several men to carry each of them out of the forest, as much as they are resisting. You go. I will stay here with them and see if they will stay put. If we are not right here when you return with the others, come just a little further—hopefully you will find us. I might need to move a little further in to calm them. And let us both pray in the meantime that the Great King will prevent any further tragedy."

They bowed their heads and asked for the Great King's protection and blessing for this last challenge.

It seemed like an eternity for Yalam, but in less than two hours, Ray returned with eight additional men. The two had stayed right where they were on the ground, but had both turned themselves around so they could look *into* the forest, not out of it. The other men had heard most of the story from Ray but were still amazed when they observed Halam and Nachash for themselves. All were carefully bundled up to protect themselves from the mosquitos.

At first the men stood together as Yalam and Ray spoke of the events of the last two days. But then they spread out in front of Halam and Nachash. Yalam decided to try one more time to reason with the two men before dragging them out of the forest. It had become obvious that just dragging them out was not a final solution. What would stop them from wanting to run back in? Would they have to bind them so they would not? Would they have to remain bound? None of this was satisfactory.

Yalam looked at them firmly. "Listen, both of you"—he motioned back and forth with his arm—"there are ten of us here now. We can carry both of you out of the forest if we want." He pointed out into the meadow. "We want to take you *home*. I don't think you remember, but both of you have lived with all of us for all of your lives. Your village is our village. Something happened to you—we think when you were bitten by mosquitos in this forest. It caused you to lose your memory of everything in your life before that moment. You both had a good life with all of us. You can again. Am I making any sense?"

It would be difficult to fathom what might have been going through the minds of these two as they listened to these words— what they understood and what they did not. What, if anything, remained in their minds and hearts from all their previous years in their blessed village and what this madness or curse or delusion was filling their minds with instead.

And maybe it was more the tone and compassion in Yalam's voice than his actual words, but something seemed to get through. This was, in fact, in keeping with everything they believed with The Way. Form was always more important than color. Process over content. Heart over mind. Motive above all else.

As Yalam continued to speak, the alarm in both of Halam's and Nachash's faces lessened. The muscles in their bodies relaxed, and in a few moments more they seemed more childlike again. Yalam reached out his hand to Halam to help him up, and Ray did the same to Nachash, and they both responded in kind.

Yalam gave them a moment to stand comfortably and then leaned in the direction of the meadow. "Okay, now," he started.

"We're all going to walk out into the meadow. It's going to be all right. All of us came from out in the meadow. We all look all right, don't we?" And Yalam stepped that way slowly. All the men took another moment before they did the same, being patient, very much wanting to communicate to Halam and Nachash that they wanted this to be their choice.

Nachash looked intentionally at Halam, and Halam back at him the same, as if they were saying to each other, "I am willing if you are." Halam took a step to follow Yalam, and Nachash began as well.

Something deep in Halam's heart was stirred. Many years ago, when he was just a toddler, it was Yalam who held his hand when he took the very first steps of his life. He felt a sense of peace he did not understand.

One step led to another, and the two confused men walked steadily from that point on all the way into the meadow. They did almost come to a stop before stepping onto the grass, but then went ahead and stepped forward, like a small child who has never walked on grass before and first sees but then also feels just how different it is on the soles of their feet.

All the way to the village, none of the other men spoke to the two for fear they might interrupt their good fortune. No one knew it at the time, but once Halam and Nachash had come out of the forest and the light of the sun shone on them, they began to regain their senses. By the time they reached the village, they were still disoriented but recognized some of the landmarks, and then their own homes, and finally their family and friends.

There had been many celebrations in the village over the centuries, but none as joyous and glorious as the celebration that started that night and continued for the next several days. For the two of them had been lost ... but were found.

A More Quiet Mind

For if you remain silent at this time,
relief and deliverance will arise for the Jews
from another place and you and
your father's house will perish.
And who knows whether you have
not attained royalty for such a time as this?
Esther 4:14

Once upon a time, there was a homeless man who lived in New York City.

He managed to sustain himself by playing his violin on street corners and in Central Park during the nicer times of the year and down in the subways on the coldest days or when there was too much ice and snow. He had been classically trained when he was young and for a time had lived a life of great promise, but then it all took another turn. He had started with much but ended up with only a violin, the clothes on his back, and the spare change that had been tossed into his violin case over the last hour.

He called his violin "Dorothy, Sweet Dorothy." There was a reason for this, but it was one he could not remember. There were few places where he felt normal, but a busy street corner in Manhattan was one of them.

The man heard many voices in his head. Some of them he recognized, and some he did not. Some of them were friendly, and some were not. Some of them were real, and some were not. More importantly, he was not sure which were which. But in New York City on a busy afternoon, he could speak to the voices he chose to, ignore all the rest, and still fit in quite well. As long as he continued to play and did not bother anyone, he was well regarded, a bona fide member of the community.

And from time to time, a symphony musician, or even a violinist, would happen to walk by, and they would almost always stop dead in their tracks and listen as long as they possibly could, even longer, putting off getting back to work or whatever happened to be next on their calendar. They wouldn't be able to help it. Sometimes they would swear they were listening to an angel from heaven.

Every once in a while, a regular person, like you or me, would react the same way, but usually not. Most of us do not have a discriminating ear when it comes to the violin. But if you are a professional, if you have heard some of the greatest violinists of all time, you know when you hear something special. And some of these musicians, especially in a big city like Manhattan, would hear this man playing his violin, and they would immediately be transported back to a time when they had heard this exact same sound in a music hall, or possibly on a recording.

In case you didn't know, instruments have voices, not unlike our voices. The sounds a violin makes can vary widely from one violinist to another. And this man on the street corner made unique and exquisite sounds with his violin, at least on those days he was able to find his old self. Back in his day, he had made quite a name for himself playing his violin. And then, from one day to the next, no one ever heard of him again. The rumors were he had become ill, gravely ill. They were not untrue.

There has always been a debate in the medical and psychological world about "crazy" people, about why they are crazy, about what happens to them that they become so, for they are not born this way. And with all the advances in knowledge and some advances in treatment, even among mental health professionals, there still may not be a better word to describe these people.

Sometimes one word in particular possesses a great deal of descriptive power. "Crazy" is one of those words. Everyone knows exactly what you are talking about when you use it. Crazy people are often crazy because the boundary between inside and outside just picks up and moves on them when they're not looking. It picks up and moves further in, and they feel crushed and violated, sometimes to the point they forget who they are or even lose themselves altogether. Or it picks up and moves further out, and life becomes a fairy tale, or worse, a nightmare in which almost anything is possible.

It is impossible to imagine being crazy if you have not experienced anything like it. Historically, about 1 percent of the population can have these kinds of more severe mental and emotional conditions. Many prefer to believe it is genetic or a chemical imbalance, and there is some evidence for those things. But there are also cases where it is obvious that a whole lot went wrong in the lives of these individuals, where they experienced trauma far beyond what most of us have ever known, to the point anyone could understand why they just might want to give up or at least check out. There are simply some things that can happen in this life that are beyond comprehension, that leave us scratching our heads, that make you wonder how anyone could ever come to terms with . . . *that*?

The homeless man had a name that he had not used in years. Horace. He had never liked his name when he was young. He even complained about it and wanted his parents to call him something different when he was just seven years old, but they told him he should be proud of his name. He had been named after his father's father. The first Horace had been a strong but gentle man, "a rare combination," his father had always said. "Something to strive for." And so Horace continued just to be Horace.

As he grew older, he recognized the strength in the name, in the sound of it. He looked the word up to see what it meant. He found his name came from the Greek word, "hora," which meant *a certain time of the year or season, the daylight hours of the day,* or *just any definite time, point in time,* or *moment.* I would imagine that "hora" is the root for our word "hour." Horace remembered being disappointed by what he'd found. He had hoped his name would mean something more, something more specific, something that might give him direction.

He found this direction, however, when he began to play the violin in fifth grade. He had wanted to play the trumpet in band class, but there were already too many trumpet players. His band teacher suggested the violin. Horace thought it was a girl's instrument, but he tried it anyway. He had never been so wrong about anything. It was almost as if the instrument had been made for his hands.

Horace's life started like many others. He had parents who were not perfect but loved him, a brother and a sister, friends he cared about, and a growing love affair with his violin. His life was not that different until one afternoon in seventh grade, he arrived home to find his aunt Betty in the kitchen, for his mother was lying down in the bedroom. He was told that his father had had a heart attack that morning at work, and by the time he arrived at the hospital, he was already gone. He was only thirty-eight years old.

That day Horace really lost two parents, for his mother was never again the same. For the first year or so, she could hardly speak, and Horace, his brother, and sister gradually began to do most things for themselves. Relatives disappeared after the first month or two—everybody had their own lives—and Horace and his siblings were old enough that no one was that worried about them. They should have been.

Horace's mother functioned better over time, or at least seemed to. She was a gifted seamstress and took in more of this kind of work to support the family. It was also something she could do at home. Horace, however, could never remember having another normal conversation with his mother after the day his father died. Not really.

She would pretend to be present when you talked to her, but the greater part of her had been buried in the same casket as Horace's father and never found its way out. It is all such a shame. A part of it is understandable when you lose someone you love so much, and are so dependent upon, so unexpectedly at such a young age. But the other part of it is not that understandable. There can always be more to life; there are always other people who depend on you and others, who in some ways can take the place of the person you lost. But you have to believe in that for it to come true. Horace's mother somehow never could.

And over time something else crept into her mind and hid behind her sad eyes. Something much worse. Strange thoughts. Weird thoughts. Crazy thoughts. There's that word again. I can't help but use it. It all came on very slowly but over time dug in and formed a beachhead that seemed impossible to penetrate. Horace and his brother and sister should have never been left alone with her for those last several years. They tried to do the right thing, to do more and more for her when she did less and less. And they never spoke of it out loud or especially to anyone else, for they felt ashamed. Ashamed, as if somehow her illness was their fault, their doing.

Horace's mother did not have many close friends before his father died, but the few she had lost touch with her after a year or so when she never called them back. Aunts and uncles would drop by but only for a few minutes at a time, and no one was observant enough to realize something more was wrong. So Horace and his brother and sister just kept quiet, relied on themselves, and hoped she would get better one day. They didn't know what to make of her talking to herself, the mumblings they couldn't understand, and the nightmares that would sometimes awaken her, screaming at the top of her lungs.

Horace had very much enjoyed playing the violin when he was younger, but it became something altogether different when his father died and his mother withdrew from his life. Horace's heart was so broken that he was not even able to put it into words. But he didn't have to, for the violin spoke for him. He would practice long into the night in his room, trying to play quietly, trying to be respectful, but also hoping his mother and brother and sister could hear him, at least faintly. He was playing for all of them, for all of their grief, giving voice to everything that none of them could.

And they all did listen, each and every night. Countless tears were shed listening to the hauntingly beautiful music, somehow so sad and yet so unbelievably soothing at the very same time. It did not take long for the violin to become Horace's best friend. No one knew him as well. They had already been through so much together.

Horace and his siblings finally knew they needed help with their mother when she wouldn't eat anything and had already lost twenty pounds. Before long she was admitted to a state hospital, and she spent the remainder of her life there, all twenty-two years of it. Horace's older brother was just old enough to live on his own when they first took her away, and Horace and his younger sister lived for a few years with Aunt Betty. For several years they would visit their mother, but as she deteriorated more and more and became almost catatonic, it was too painful. Eventually she was not responsive to anyone. She had fully retreated into the privacy of her own internal world, her own internal, crazy world.

When Horace was fifteen or so, something miraculous occurred in both of his hands, and he began to play his violin in a way that few people ever have on this earth. His band instructor at high school was leading the class through a piece one afternoon when he noticed this miracle. The instructor was so mesmerized that his hands stopped moving from one moment to the next, and he just stood there completely still. The rest of the class was so surprised and confused by this that one by one they all stopped playing. All except Horace.

He was so lost in what he was playing that at first he didn't even notice everyone else had stopped. And then he could feel everyone's eyes on him, but especially the teacher. For the very first time in his life, he experienced that feeling down deep in his soul, the feeling he would get when the music he played took people to another place, to another world, a better world. Horace played all the way to the end of the piece that day. He looked up when he was done, and everyone was looking at him like he was a god. He never again doubted what he wanted to do with his life.

There have to be a good number of excellent music schools in the world, but there is only one that most of us have heard of. Juilliard. Horace was able to get a partial scholarship to attend there but had never wanted to go anywhere else. There were many famous violin instructors at Juilliard, and before long one of the instructors and Horace began to spend more time together.

There is a long history of such mentoring relationships in academia, whether the subject is philosophy, religion, business, or even music. We are relational creatures, and something special happens when two people share their love for something privately, spending many hours together, as the older master slowly but surely passes off the torch to the younger. For Horace it was particularly life giving, for this man became a father figure for him. Horace needed him to be. He had never been able to resolve his grief; it was just too enormous.

Horace's two years at Juilliard would go quickly, and a promising musical career was never in doubt. To begin with, it was impossible for his mentor to not be happy for Horace—he was such an astounding talent and such a nice young man. Horace's mentor had made quite a name for himself during his own musical career; very few people qualify to be instructors at Juilliard. But before long it became apparent Horace would not only be successful but possibly one of the greatest violinists in the world. Pride lives inside us all, and the instructor's pride felt more and more under siege when it became apparent Horace's skill would not only surpass his mentor's but surpass it by a great distance.

For their relationship to continue, it would have to change, slowly at first, but eventually a great deal. There would be less and less the mentor would be able to offer Horace, but he could always offer his friendship and guidance. And this would have been fine with Horace; he would have treasured it no less. Horace had benefited a great deal from this man's musical instruction, but in the end, Horace desired this man's companionship and even his love more than anything else, for this was what he needed. It was unfortunate for Horace this gentleman was not able to view it all the same.

In the end, Horace's awe-striking success was just too much for the old man to take. And as usually is the case, he was never able to say the first word to Horace about it. He could not talk about it like you and I are right now, for pride and its relatives and the evil they wreak are much more comfortable in the dark.

From one day to the next, just like that, this man stopped talking to Horace, as if he had done something wrong. As close as they had become, as much as Horace wanted to believe this man would continue to be a significant part of his life as though he were part of the mentor's family, he learned just how wrong he was. Horace found himself alone . . . again. It was a different demon this time, a more wicked one in a way, but the result was the same. Horace was left with only his own thoughts and questions and a deep and relentless aching in his heart. Why did the people in his life most important to him all seem to disappear, and so suddenly?

Because of this Horace walked with a limp for some time but tried not to show it. He had made several good friends at school and continued to go through the motions with them, but his mentor had always been more important, for he had never lost his brother and sister, but his mother and father. After a few months, Horace began to feel better and was also looking forward to his last year of school. The year would include more competitions and contact with symphonies for whom he might want to work after graduation.

There were a couple of other instructors who offered their time to Horace outside of class and could have become mentors, and Horace was appreciative of this but kindly refused. He was not strong enough to try again. And then he met Angela.

She worked at a coffee shop close by the school, where many students hung out. Horace had had a girlfriend for a brief time in high school but had always been more of a loner. Angela was friendly and even bold, and Horace was attracted to this. They say that opposites attract, and it is not untrue. She had to ask *him* out on the first date; it would have taken him too long.

She had been raised on Long Island, the daughter of working-class parents. Her mother had been a waitress at a diner, and her father a mechanic. They had met at the mother's restaurant, and Angela loved the thought of this and told Horace so. She loved music a great deal but had never played an instrument. She wept the first time Horace played for her, but you might have as well if you had been there. She had never heard anything as heavenly on earth. And she continued to dream she would find something to do with her life that she was passionate about, but as Horace and she fell more and more in love, she began to believe that his passion might just be enough for both of them.

Horace's last year of school turned out to be a happy one. He had fully come into his own on his instrument and was pleased with this but had actually begun to tire of all the attention he was receiving. When he played, he wanted to be as good as anyone who had ever played the violin, and that did take a great deal of self-discipline and practice. But when he was done, he wanted to leave it snugly and securely in its case and live the rest of his life, especially being with Angela and doing all the things they loved to do together in the city. The other people in his life had great difficulty separating him from his instrument or talking about anything else. And so over time, Horace spent less and less time with people from school or other musicians and more and more time with her, which was fine.

They decided to go ahead and get married in the spring. Horace had already received offers from smaller symphonies here and there in the US but was advised to be patient and to even devote more time to learning and practicing. The school had also offered him a part-time job as an assistant professor in the fall after his graduation, which he accepted. It provided a decent income yet gave him a good deal of time every week to practice.

Angela and he planned to stay in Manhattan indefinitely and moved into her apartment, which was a little nicer than his. They were perfectly suited to each other, almost never had a disagreement, and both could not have loved their life any more. By the time they celebrated their first anniversary, they were mature enough to realize just how fortunate they were to have found each other, but especially to have the life they had and a future with such promise.

And Horace spent the next several years continuing to practice his trade, teaching classes at Julliard, playing in more international competitions, and eventually playing professionally as a featured soloist. His virtuosity spoke for itself, and as a result he never needed to join a symphony, even as the first violin. He skipped right to the top.

Angela and he loved Manhattan so much they could never imagine living anywhere else. They purposely waited to have children, but after five years could not wait any longer. The birth of a child can often be the most beautiful and awe-inspiring experience of any in this life. We all know it will be a very significant event, but most of us are still surprised by just how deeply it touches our souls when our first child is born. The physical process itself is so incredible. The way the female body is able to first conceive and then feed and nurture this child as it grows inside. The way the body is able to accommodate it, to grow and stretch as much as it has to, but even more amazingly, to stretch again so that the child can be born.

And then, after all of that, return to its original state. Although many women would quickly claim "not quite." But it is the spiritual aspect of the birth that can really take our breath away. Even though men and women participate in the birth of their children, they are no more responsible for the creation of this new life than the farmer who plants a seed in the ground is responsible for the plant that bursts forth. The mother and father and the farmer know what they have to do, but the creative genius is not their own.

None of them could create matter out of nothing or program living cells on the molecular level so that they could create new versions of themselves when just the right conditions are met. We seldom think of life in this way, but the truth of it is, we all kind of "woke up" from one moment to the next, having no idea where we came from, how we got here, or how any of this was made. And ever since, our greatest contribution has been to discover how things *already* work. I would imagine that unless God spoke to Adam and Eve explicitly about their bodies, they likely had sexual relations for another reason altogether and then were very surprised over the next several months when Eve's belly grew, and even more surprised sometime later when, lo and behold, Cain emerged.

Horace and Angela's baby was a girl. She was named Dorothy after Angela's grandmother who had died a couple of years earlier.

When Dorothy was five or six years old and able to watch *The Wizard of Oz* with her parents all the way through without being too terrified of the flying monkeys, her name took on a new significance. She loved the song "Over the Rainbow" and would sing it over and over, and sometimes Horace would accompany her on the violin. They were quite a duo.

She loved to pretend that she was Dorothy from Kansas, who had all the amazing adventures with Scarecrow, Tin Man, and Lion. When her parents were able to find her little Wizard of Oz dolls, she played with them for hours and hours, reliving all their adventures in Oz and making up many new ones.

As Dorothy grew older, it became clear she was a dreamer, not unlike the Dorothy from Kansas. The hurtful things in this world would so easily break her heart, and there is much of this to be seen in Manhattan: so much impatience, so many angry voices, and so many homeless people. But one homeless man, in particular, Dorothy could never forget. She saw him one day while running errands with her mother. The poor man had both his legs amputated, but just a few inches below his hips, so that all that was left of him was barely two feet tall. He lived his life on a little pallet with dolly wheels, far below everyone else but right at eye level with Dorothy.

It was a sight that no little child really needs to see and one that made many adults squirm. Sometimes it takes something this extreme for us to want a song like "Over the Rainbow" to be true. For there to be a place, another land, high in the sky, beyond it even. Where our troubles vanish, the sky is always blue, and we have the courage to dream, for they really will come true. And for us to want, even more, to be able to go from *here . . . to there*. For if the birds can fly there, couldn't we too?

Horace and Angela tried to have more children but were not able. They thought of adopting, but Dorothy was such a joy and so full of life, they decided to be content with what they had been given. Horace's career continued to blossom; he was far too gifted for it not to. Before long he was considered to be the most gifted violinist in the world in his generation, and depending on whom you spoke to, possibly of the twentieth century. Horace continued to receive all of this adoration with appreciation, but he never felt comfortable with being famous and still preferred when he was finished with a performance to get back to his family as soon as possible.

He continued to teach at Juilliard part time and had a number of students he spent more time with, but one in particular whom he mentored. He promised himself when this relationship started that nothing in the world would cause him to abandon this young man. He would be available to him as long as the young man desired. Their relationship lasted for ten years, until the time Dorothy turned fifteen.

Horace was at home that day when he received the phone call. Angela and Dorothy had gone to visit Angela's mother, who still lived on Long Island. On their way home, they had been in a terrible accident. A large semi-rig going in the same direction had lost control and slid sideways. Angela and Dorothy were right behind, and she tried to avoid running into the truck but was not able to. Neither were several other cars behind that piled into them one by one. Many people were hurt, but only Angela and Dorothy died. They were pronounced dead at the scene. There was little left of their car.

Horace did not learn any of the details or that they were both deceased until he arrived at the hospital. It would seem that public officials have learned the hard way not to give such bad and final news over the phone, and so they just say, "They have been injured. That's all I can say at this time. We just need you to come down to the hospital." You would think that most arrive at the hospital fearing the worst.

Horace had come very close to going with them that day. At the last minute, he had remembered some errands he needed to run, and Angela had convinced him to stay behind. The last thing he ever heard her say, laughing, was that "the three girls" just might have a better time without him.

Horace had never really attended church but had always believed that God was a loving God. But after leaving the hospital later that evening, having identified both Angela's and Dorothy's bodies, Horace believed, *If there is a God, He has to be a cruel one.* After all the loss he had already experienced in his life, this last blow was by far the greatest, beyond all comprehension.

It is a shame that over time our culture has more and more emphasized the needs of the individual over that of community. More and more of the real community people had with each other for centuries has been lost. Everyone is so busy with their own lives and schedules these days, many families do not even eat dinner together. Horace's brother was ill himself with some chronic health issues and lived in upstate New York, too far away to help much. His sister was doing well, married with kids, but lived on the West Coast. They both came to the funeral, or the funerals, which were held together. I don't know if you have ever been to a funeral with two caskets, but it is disturbing.

Horace's brother and sister stayed a few days more with Horace, but as he said less and less and then stopped speaking at all, they feared the worst. They all had seen this before. As they said their goodbyes, they were both quietly hoping and praying he would pull out of it. His sister kindly offered for Horace to come live with her, and he should have taken her up on this, at least for a time. But he did not. He did not even answer her when she asked him about this, but stared off into the distance.

Horace had a few friends who tried to help out that first week or two, but they had not been that close to him before all this and felt no real obligation to go out of their way now. And so no one did. We don't have enough real community any longer for there to be at least a few people willing to go out of their way when something like this happens and someone desperately needs them to. And there, for sure, is not enough community for a number of people to come around someone, maybe for an indefinite period of time, when the needs are very great.

Horace wasn't reading the Bible, but never have a few verses more applied to someone and their situation: "Two are better than one because they have a good return for their labor. For if either of them falls, the one will lift up his companion. But woe to the one who falls when there is not another to lift him up" (Ecclesiastes 4:9–10).

Within a month or so of the accident, Horace was hospitalized. To begin with, he seemed to be severely depressed. He never tried to harm himself but was mute and ate little. At times he had to be fed intravenously. After six months with no improvement, Horace had several rounds of electroconvulsive shock. It is used as a last resort but has sometimes been a great benefit when nothing else has worked. It seemed like Horace was improving for a time—he was eating better and talking some, although he was still unable to function.

But then it slowly began. Strange thoughts. Weird thoughts. Crazy thoughts. In the beginning, Horace kept his strange thoughts to himself, mostly because he was paranoid. But self-control is not a strong suit of crazy people, and before long, he was found out. And as odd as it might sound, although Horace was getting worse, not better, at some point it was clear he was no longer an immediate danger to himself, so he could not be held against his will.

Horace was finally released from the hospital, and his sister made the trip from the West Coast to see if she could help him settle back in at his apartment. She had been the trustee of all his assets and re-sources during this time and had kept the apartment, never thinking almost two years would go by in the interim, but it did. She had not seen Horace in some time and was surprised to find him as he was. He would talk some, but it was often inappropriate. Horace didn't want to stay indoors and would quietly sneak out. After spending the greater majority of two weeks frantically looking for him, find-ing him wandering on Manhattan streets and escorting him back to the apartment, only for him to disappear again the next day, she finally consulted an attorney.

After taking Horace to a public outpatient clinic that worked with the chronically mentally ill and setting him up with a case-worker, she made the hard decision to return home to her family and leave Horace in God's hands. As much as she wanted to believe Horace would improve over time, and possibly even have a normal life again, they had all wasted many long years wishing and hoping the very same thing for their mother and, in the end, had been incredibly disappointed. It just might be easier to try to forget about Horace altogether.

Horace still had some money and gave his consent for his sister to keep custody of it. She would wire him some every month. It wouldn't last forever but would for several years.

One day Horace happened to be passing a pawnshop and saw an old and distressed violin in the window. It was in such bad condition you would wonder if it could still be played. Someone had found it in the attic of a relative who had died and did not bother to ask anyone who might know if it was valuable. They simply took it to the closest pawnshop, whose owner was just as shortsighted, and it was placed in the window with a $100 price tag.

When the violin was made, there had been a label identifying its maker, but that label was gone. Horace walked into the pawnshop, and the owner started to ask him to leave, as he was clearly homeless and probably just looking to get warm. But Horace just kept looking at the violin and then asked if he could hold it. Most pawnshop owners are not that concerned about their fellow man, but for a moment, this man actually was. He almost told Horace to just go, and that he was not going to sell the violin to him even if he could produce the money. But then something in his heart changed. Something prompted him to go ahead and grant Horace's wish. And so he handed the violin to Horace.

It is thought that there are only 650 Stradivarius violins in the world, none made after the eighteenth century. Well, maybe 651. Horace was crazy, but not so crazy to open his mouth and reveal what he knew about this violin. It was in poor shape, but after holding it for a few moments, he knew it was structurally sound, and with new strings would play well. Very well, in fact. And Horace even offered the man ten additional dollars. The man accepted the offer, and Horace began his musical career again, first for himself but then more and more for the pedestrians of Manhattan.

The young man from Juilliard who Horace had mentored was named Jordan. Jordan had done everything he could to stay in touch with Horace from the day Angela and Dorothy had died. He came to the funeral. He obtained Horace's home phone number and address from his sister and called to no avail in the weeks after the tragedy. When he heard Horace had been hospitalized, he tried to visit but was turned away because he was not family. He fully expected, like everyone else, Horace would be back at home before long and at Juilliard as well, and he would see him then.

But when several months went by and neither of those things happened, he began to drop by the hospital again. After several attempts to see Horace, one time even lying and saying he was a nephew from out of town, one of the nurses finally took him to the side. She told him Horace was not doing well, that no one ever visited, and it would be beneficial if someone did, regardless of who they were. Jordan revealed his true identity, and the nurse wisely did what she needed to get him approved as a daily visitor. For the last eighteen months Horace was in that locked psychiatric unit, Jordan had visited him several times a week.

For the longest time, Horace would not talk to or even look at Jordan, but Jordan continued to come anyway. The shock of losing both Angela and Dorothy in the very same moment, the two people he had come to love more than life itself, that he had dared to love after being so devastated by the sudden loss of his father, his mother, and his mentor had driven Horace to block out all memory of his previous life.

For a time in the hospital, Horace did not even respond to his first name. There was a part of his soul that felt if he more fully acknowledged this last tragedy and allowed himself to feel everything he would have to feel, the consequences would just be too horrendous—he would never survive it. There was the sheer pain of the loss of *both* people, so precious. A woman who had loved him so much and so well he had finally been able to grow into the man he was supposed to be but had been too afraid to become. And a child whom he had loved in a way he never thought possible, so precious that he would easily come to tears, and so innocent that he would go the lengths of the world to provide for her and protect her, always.

And if the pain of the loss of all of *that* was not enough, we need to add the pain Horace had felt for many long years and had barely been able to keep at bay—the pain that *he*, somehow, was not good enough, or special enough, or *something* . . . for his parents to love him well and always be there for him. With his father, the pain was a more confusing one, since his father did not choose to die. But with his mother, the pain was more acute.

Why had he and his sister and brother not been important enough for her to be able to rise above all her pain and care for them the way they so desperately needed? Were they not *worth* it? With this pain in his gut, Horace had managed, somehow, to keep his head up and persevere. And then years later, the heavens just seemed to open up, and he was so blessed, first with Angela and then with Dorothy. After so many years of living in an emotional wilderness, his life suddenly turned into the most beautiful and wonderful of fairy tales that came true. And it lasted for many years. But then, all too soon, in a moment . . . it was all gone. How are you supposed to come to terms with something like this? Would you not even wonder if God was playing a very sick joke?

Close to the end of Horace's stay at the hospital, he began to talk to Jordan but would not call him by name and would still not refer to anything in their prior lives together. Jordan learned to gladly accept any interaction at all and did his best to respond to Horace, talking about the weather, or the awful pictures on the wall, or the smell of the hospital, or anything else.

After his discharge, Jordan would drop by Horace's apartment, but he was seldom there. Horace did have particular street corners he would frequent after he had purchased his violin. He began to play at those corners, and Jordan would commonly check on those when he had time and would usually see Horace at least once every week. Sometimes Horace would even allow him to buy him a cup of coffee and a bagel, and they would sit on a bench together. After a while Jordan tried to engage Horace in conversation about his violin and about particular pieces, and it would go well as long as he never referred to anything from their prior lives.

After a year or so of playing again, Horace began to write some of his own music, and it was very, very good. Jordan was amazed at this man, who might not be able to pass a mental-status exam but was writing music for his violin on par with some of the greatest composers of all time. Horace would also mention under his breath that he had written other parts too. "Maybe one day there will be other musicians to play them."

One day out of the blue, Horace announced he had given his violin a name. He had named her "Dorothy, Sweet Dorothy." Jordan was caught off guard but quickly responded, "What a beautiful name." Maybe it was a sign that something in Horace was coming back to life, wanting to come back to the real world, willing to try one more time.

After another couple of years, Horace's money ran out. He lost his apartment, and his sister came to town to try to get him situated in some public housing, but Horace was not cooperative enough to make it happen. She left town frustrated and worried, the thought of Horace being on the street being so painful, so unacceptable. But Horace was making a decent income playing his violin on the street. He just couldn't hold on to it or save it, and his mind was still too disorganized to be responsible for anything else. Jordan was able to encourage Horace to stay in touch with his caseworker, and she was able to get him medical treatment from time to time when he needed it and a cot to sleep on during the colder winter times.

We all have too many voices in our head, calling out to us, tempting us, condemning us, telling us that some life other than our own would have to be better. We all struggle to find a more quiet mind, a heart at peace, and a soul at rest. This was just more true for Horace. He knew that something was terribly wrong with him—he just couldn't put it into words. He might be crazy, but he knew down deep he had not always been homeless, that he must have had another life. He just could not remember it. Jordan's visits were his only anchor, his only connection with the rest of the world. At some point something in Horace knew that Jordan might be the key, that through Jordan he just might be able to find his way back. *What had happened?* he wondered. Why could he not remember?

As talented as Jordan was on violin, after graduation from Juilliard, he decided he did not want to be a professional musician. His family had owned a business for several generations, and he would try to find his place there and have a more normal nine-to-five life. He continued to practice and play his violin a good deal; he loved it and always would. But he did not want it to control his life.

The business was in Pennsylvania, but Jordan was able the larger part of the time to work remotely from Manhattan. He wanted to stay in the city for many reasons, but one of them was Horace. He had not given up on him—he still held out hope that Horace might come back to the real world. Jordan did not usually keep up with the plays in town; he was not a big fan, and there are so many in the city. One day, however, he heard there was a new production of *The Wizard of Oz* off-Broadway, not something new and different, but as it was originally written.

Horace had spoken to Jordan years ago of Dorothy's love for the movie and especially for the song "Over the Rainbow." Jordan wondered if Horace might be ready for something like this, to participate in a normal activity once again, to be around other people in a structured setting and to have the self-discipline to sit through it. But more importantly, would he be ready to let something like this prompt him to remember his previous life?

Jordan consulted with a couple of psychiatrists for their opinion. He was told it was not a bad plan but that it could backfire. It might be too painful, and if so could result in Horace retreating more fully into his own private world. And if that happened, he might have to be institutionalized again. But his life the way it was did not seem like a whole lot to risk.

On the other hand, Jordan was mature for a young man his age and knew he did not have the right to play God, nor did he want to. But he had also started to think that maybe, just maybe, it wasn't an accident he had met Horace at Julliard when he was a student, that it wasn't an accident he had asked Horace to be his mentor, and even more, maybe all of this had been set in motion a long time ago with the present situation very much in mind.

Jordan had grown up in church and could not help but remember the charge that Mordecai had given to his cousin Esther: "For if you remain silent at this time, relief and deliverance will arise for the Jews from another place . . . and who knows whether you have not attained royalty for such a time as this?" (Esther 4:14). Jordan might have been even more convinced if he had known the meaning of Horace's name, that it just might be the very "time" for Horace to be saved. After giving it all a little more thought and consulting with his pastor, Jordan decided to go ahead. He prayed more than anything for God's merciful and compassionate hand. The first hurdle would be to talk to Horace about the play and see if he would even consider it.

Jordan saw Horace a few days later, and after listening for a while, invited him for another cup of coffee and a bagel. Horace was quiet, as usual, and Jordan asked him about his music. "You played something new today. I don't believe I have ever heard it."

"No one has," Horace replied.

"Well, I really liked it. I think you have found your own voice. I am not sure if anyone has ever written quite like that."

"You are just trying to flatter me," Horace said matter of factly. "Do you *want* something?"

"Well, no." Jordan laughed. "I was just being honest. It is incredibly good and very unique. And I think that *you* know that even better than me. But I did want to ask you something. We have never really done anything together. I heard there is a new production of *The Wizard of Oz* off-Broadway. I wanted to go see it. I thought you might want to see it too. What do you think?"

"Maybe," Horace replied softly.

"Well, think about it," Jordan said. "I don't think it will be sold out—we should be able to get tickets most any night." Jordan thought to push a little, but something in him told him not to. That was enough for now. Give him a little time.

Horace felt something move in his heart when he thought of going to see the play, but did not know why. The choice to go mad is not an easy one, but like most other things in the heart and mind, at the time seems to be the best path, the lesser of two evils. But there is always a price to pay for such absolute concessions. When you think of it, it has to be quite challenging to completely block out certain thoughts and memories from consciousness when they are intertwined with so many others.

Horace did not have difficulty allowing himself to remember *The Wizard of Oz*, in general, but it was quite an amazing feat to remember it—to remember Judy Garland and Dorothy and the Scarecrow, the Wicked Witch, and especially the Yellow Brick Road and that song—and at the same time *not* to remember his childhood, his parents, the sofa he was lying on in the den when he was six years old and watching that old black-and-white TV, completely mesmerized, lost in the whole incredible story, the thought of being whisked away to this fantastic place by a tornado that just picked up your house and *took* you there!

And Dorothy. What little boy didn't have a crush on Dorothy or on Judy Garland, the way she looked, the way she talked, the way she *sang*? But somehow Horace was capable of this, of remembering the movie in general and not remembering all the other personal associations, including his daughter, Dorothy, and just how much she loved it all.

After Jordan and Horace said their goodbyes that afternoon, and Horace went back to one of his corners and started to play, thoughts of the movie kept creeping back. His mind would drift off to something else for a while, but before long he would find himself thinking about the story again, and then finally he found himself humming the melody to "Over the Rainbow." He started thinking of Judy Garland and how she looked when she sang it, how she looked up into the sky.

And then Horace thought to play it on his violin. Why not? He was so gifted and had such a good natural ear, he could play a song like this from start to finish without having to find it first on the strings or remember it from the past. On most days people would stop and listen to Horace, sometimes creating a little bottleneck on the sidewalk. That was not that unusual. But this afternoon was different.

Most of us have good memories of *The Wizard of Oz*. It is from an innocent time of our lives when we still believed the world was good, that people were good, and everything would work out in the end. Many of the people who stopped that day to listen to Horace play "Over the Rainbow" were spellbound and simply not able to continue on their way until he was done. And Horace could *feel* the crowd too. As a matter of fact, crazy people can be even better at this than the rest of us. About halfway in he could tell it was touching many in the crowd, even bringing tears, and so he purposely made it longer, much longer, about twice as long as normal. And he added a particularly intense solo in the middle, improvising off the melody. There was quite an ovation when he was done, and more tears and many donations.

Jordan made an effort to stop by and see Horace about every other day after their conversation about the play. He mentioned the play a couple of other times, and Horace would reply with the same "maybe" but seemed to be warming up to the idea.

"I'm definitely going to see it—do you want to come along?" Jordan finally asked.

Horace looked down at the ground for what seemed like an eternity, lost in his thoughts.

Jordan was aware of the significance of this moment, of the potential for a breakthrough.

He felt as if he were standing on holy ground, as if he had just asked, "Do you wish to get well?" just as a crippled man had been asked a very long time ago. It may be the most astounding question that has ever been asked. Why would anyone who is seriously ill not *want* to get well? But it seems there is more to our infirmities than meets the eye, more that in one way or the other involves choices. Choices we may not be aware of, but choices we made nevertheless.

"Yes" broke the silence. "Yes, I do want to go," Horace said emphatically.

"Well . . . great!" Jordan replied. "How about tonight? What if we meet right here at six thirty? I could bring you a sports jacket. Is that all right?"

"Yes, that is fine. Thank you."

"We can take a cab or just walk if you prefer."

"I think I would rather walk," Horace replied.

"Very good. Well, why don't we meet at six then. I am really looking forward to this," Jordan added. "Have a good rest of your day." He turned to walk away, not wanting to give Horace any time to change his mind.

That night, in that little theater off-Broadway, a miracle occurred. The kind of miracle that countless doctors and therapists and nurses and family members have wished and prayed for over and over again for the chronically mentally ill patients they care for and love but seldom see. Most of the people who retreat into the depths of their internal worlds never come back, not completely. The forces at work are so mysterious but also so powerful and so poorly understood. The play that night was extraordinary, but not by accident.

The gentleman behind the production loved the story and spent an extraordinary amount of time casting all the parts, creating all the costumes, finding just the right musicians, designing and building all the sets, and practicing over and over again until he felt everything was just right. I wish I could tell you for sure what happened in Horace's heart that night from the moment the curtain rose to the time it fell, but I can't, for I really don't know.

But I do know that one way or the other, through the passion of the actors, and the magic of the story, and the loyalty and love of his friend Jordan, and especially the power of God, Horace found hope again. He found *hope*, for that was what he had lost. Hope, that as painful as life can be, as mind-bending and heart-wrenching and crazy-making as it had been for him, as long and as dark as the night had been, there can always be a new dawn. A new dawn where love is stronger and deeper than anything else in this world, in this universe even.

Horace cried so many tears that night during the play that the front of his shirt was wet. He walked out of that theater with Jordan, and all the voices in his head were finally quiet. He walked out of that theater as sane as he had ever been in his life. He turned to Jordan and asked, "Can I come to live with you for a short while until I get set up somewhere else?"

"Of course," Jordan replied, with the biggest smile on his face. "Nothing else could make me happier."

That night Horace finally found himself again and found the strength and courage once again to dare to dream.

Before All the Streets Were Paved

*Thus I considered all my activities which my hands
had done and the labor which I had exerted,
and behold, all was futility and striving after wind,
and there was no profit under the sun.*
Ecclesiastes 2:11

*Let them give thanks to the Lord for His lovingkindness,
and for His wonders to the sons of men!
For He has satisfied the thirsty soul, and the hungry soul
He has filled with what is good.*
Psalm 107:8–9

O nce upon a time, there was a boy who grew up in the country, but on most days, he could not remember it, so let me tell you his story.

He grew up in a beautiful part of the country with green pastures and grazing cattle as far as the eye could see. Majestic white oak trees reached far up into the sky. The soil was fertile and good for corn, tomatoes, green beans, and anything else you wanted to grow. A large river ran all the way through that broad valley, surrounded on both sides by gentle rolling hills.

A number of farms were situated in the valley, and one of the nicer ones was the Morton farm, where young Tom grew up. They had dairy cows, and this provided the bulk of their income, but they also grew crops and raised horses, and they never lacked for anything.

I never saw the garden of Eden, but it would be hard to imagine a countryside more beautiful than the place where Tom was born and raised. Six generations of Mortons had lived in this place. Tom had heard many stories of his ancestors when he was a child—of Old Man Morton, who first came to this land from England in the mid-eighteen hundreds; of his great-great-grandfather who had the first dairy cow; and his great-grandfather, whom even Tom had known for a while because he lived to be ninety-eight.

Tom's father was a man's man. He had been tempted when he was younger to take off and become a mountain man, for the girl he loved had run off with his best friend and broken his heart. But as painful as that was, it caused him to grow up and grow stronger, and he gave romance another chance. He was the kind of man who could do anything in the wild, like start a fire in the middle of a rainstorm, build a shelter out of nothing, survive on roots and berries for months on end, and kill any wild animal you could think of and know what to do with every part—and that was only the beginning of his résumé.

Tom felt a little inadequate growing up in his father's shadow, but that was not his father's fault, for he was the sweetest and humblest of men and a great father, an encourager and teacher. Tom's gifts were different. He was always better with numbers than people. Sums are much harder to do with people—they don't add up so easily. And numbers for sure didn't have flavors, but people sure did, as many as you can think of. Numbers were plain and simple, no exceptions. Tom had a black-and-white soul but had been born into a world that on many days was gray.

Tom loved helping out on the farm as a young boy, playing outside and especially in the barn loft. He had four siblings, two brothers and two sisters. He had come right in the middle. His life growing up was truly perfect. His mother was sweet and lovely but never minded hard work, and she adored every one of her children. She made the best meals each and every day and loved to play outside with the children when she could. Tom's father would do the same, and the whole lot of them would often pack up the picnic baskets and walk down to the river to have dinner or spend all of Saturday there swimming, fishing, and having a great time.

A dairy farm is a constant and consuming business, but Tom's father was both wealthy and wise enough to hire hands, so the family did not always have to work and could enjoy other things. Looking back, Tom could not remember one thing about his childhood that was hard or challenging. At some point in time, he just began to get bored. Somehow, someway, he wanted something different, something more. And Tom began to think there could be more. But wait. We are getting ahead of ourselves.

Tom never minded working hard, but even as a child he could tolerate only being so dirty. His brothers, in particular, would poke fun at him for this, for they could not understand it. They all seemed to feel better the dirtier they were, or maybe they just had such a good time getting that way. Regardless, it would not occur to them to bother to wash up. But when they all returned to the house after hours at play, Tom would always head straight for the bath. His mother would have to make his brothers do this, but never him, not once.

By the time he was twelve or so, it became clear that Tom enjoyed school and wasn't just putting up with it. His brothers and sisters didn't understand this either. At fourteen he would bring up different subjects for conversation at dinner, from politics and world affairs to geology and even astronomy. His siblings would roll their eyes at him when he would start with one of his questions, and his youngest sister would always say he was just showing off, but he really wasn't.

Tom thought about other things a lot of the time, of other places, and even other worlds. Many times these conversations would end up between just Tom and his parents, for his brothers and sisters had little to offer and even less interest. It didn't take too long for his father to realize that Tom's horizons just might be further off in the distance than anyone else in the family. And he was fine with this. He didn't really understand Tom, but he was a wise enough man and father to know that nothing would be served by trying to change him. His job as a father was not to make little replicas of himself but to help his children find themselves. He would be doing his job as a father when he helped each of his children to first discover and then develop the gifts and talents God had given them—the gifts that helped to make them who they were.

Long before Tom had graduated from high school, he began to talk about going to college. His parents did not object to this, but they were a little surprised. College was not that common in those days, and no one in their family had ever gone. It wasn't the pros or cons of college that was the issue but that life on the farm had always been so full of every imaginable thing that had value. Why would you ever choose another life?

First and foremost, they had such close relationships with each other and with all their relatives and best friends. They couldn't imagine life without this. And the children all looked forward to growing up, finding a wife or husband, and settling down on their own piece of land in that lovely valley. They looked forward to continuing with the life they had always known—raising crops and animals and waking up every day to the glorious beauty that surrounded them, a life they participated in so intimately.

Most regular folks don't give it much thought, but farmers feel incredibly privileged to be able to work with the ground. That's right—work with the dirt. Dirt is quite an amazing substance, if you think about it. Most people don't.

Soil is composed to be sturdy enough to support the roots of the largest hardwood trees so they stand firm, but soil is not too sturdy or hard for the most fragile sprouts to break through. The ground is porous enough to allow most rainwater to run right through and feed an expansive underground river system. But the ground holds on to just enough of this moisture so the plants and trees can drink and is full of all the minerals that most plants and trees need to thrive.

The ground just looks like dirt, so ordinary and plentiful that everyone knows exactly what you mean when you say something is "dirt cheap." But we need dirt to be just as plentiful as it is. We need it for life itself. So I guess it's not so ordinary after all.

And consider all the different types of plants and trees in this world. Humankind didn't know it for a long time, but we finally discovered that humans and plants have an air exchange of sorts with each other. What one needs, the other breathes out; and what one breathes out, the other needs. And think about all the plants and trees and how they know just the right time in the spring to grow and bloom, often down to the very day. Every plant has a little clock in it, but each species is set to a different time, the perfect time for that kind of plant to sprout, grow, and flower.

And think of all the different types of animals in this world, but just to mention a few: the cows that so generously share their milk; the horses, donkeys, and beasts of burden that help us with our work or provide an exciting ride through the meadow; the sheep for their wool; and dogs for their companionship and incredibly cheerful spirits, but also for their watchful eyes and ears and their loyalty, to the death, if need be.

And finally there is the very precious and even holy connection we have with all of nature. Adam himself was literally taken from the ground. This world was made for us to watch over, to use for our own needs, to create with, to make new little worlds. In our modern world, we can easily forget about the natural world. Some people can go weeks on end without spending any time outdoors besides for the few moments it takes them to jump into their car (if they don't have a garage connected to their house), another few moments to walk from their car to their place of work, and then just the opposite at the end of the day. People can be surprised when they happen to spend a few extra minutes outdoors and realize how nice it is and how refreshed they feel. We lost a part of ourselves and did not even realize it.

Tom loved his family a great deal, but the day came when he said goodbye to them and left to go out into the world. He shed a tear or two, especially for his mother, but his grief was brief. He was very much looking forward to his future: going to school, learning new and exciting things, and especially finding the right occupation that would satisfy his appetite for new adventures. Tom dove into his advanced math education. He loved the purity of it, the lack of mess.

But over time he wished for something more concrete, more practical, something he could gain more praise for. He started with engineering but ended up with architecture. He first designed new and improved houses, but then moved on to creating large buildings. They were called "skyscrapers," they were so tall. And finally he designed special-use buildings, like museums and stadiums. Tom believed he was going to create a new world, a better world, a more civilized world.

Now, I am sure there are some of you who are reading this and think I'm being a little too hard on Tom. You are reading my words and can hear my tone and implication that Tom had already begun to lose his way, and you don't really see it. What can be so bad about wanting to be educated, about wanting to learn at the most advanced levels, and about creating things that have purpose and serve great numbers of people? Are all things modern bad just because they are modern?

Some of you may believe that most people always lived a rural life in the past because they had to. They had not learned enough or discovered enough to do anything more. Why on earth would you ever want to work so hard if you didn't have to? And as soon as man *did* learn more, as soon as he invented things, mechanical things that made work much easier, he did not hesitate to do so, and the industrial age was born. People left the countryside in droves and went to the cities to work in factories, where many of them thrived. And I could say a whole lot more, but I will not.

I will simply say there is a very particular belief embedded here, a belief in man's knowledge and wisdom. A belief that man, through the development of machines, and today we would use the word "technology," can make the world a better place. I believe this belief is *so* embedded, so subtle, that most of us do not realize it is a belief but simply a fact. In truth, we are talking about something much more subjective, an opinion, an assumption we have made that might be right or could be wrong.

And I think the thing that makes all this much harder is that there really isn't anything wrong or bad in the development of technology, per se. Many good things, many heroic things, even, have been achieved in this modern world by technology. Just take medical science as an example. This is clearly why people are living longer. But you see, this is another example of just how subtle and difficult all this can be.

Most of us think that people who refuse modern medical treatment for any reason are nuts. In most cases that might be true. But if you ask the broader question, if humanity is truly better off because of the advancement of medical science, I believe the answer is not as clear. Are we living happier lives now simply because we are living longer? Most people do live longer these days, but that does not necessarily make the quality of their lives any better, and in many cases, it is worse. We all have stories of elderly people who have subsisted interminably in very poor health and in a very depressed state of mind, all because medical science has been *able* to keep them breathing.

Or think about this. I remember someone who addressed this subject differently. He said that when he looked back over the history of man, all the way up to our present modern time, the only thing he could see that mankind had truly become better at, more proficient at—was *killing people*. I remember just how stunned the rest of us sitting at the table were that morning when those words left his lips. None of us could really disagree. The same technology that can be invented to do good has also been used to do immeasurable harm, and even evil. Does the whole equation not cancel itself out?

Another example: I recently heard that in just the few square feet of the former Los Angeles County/USC Medical Center Emergency Room, more people, mostly trauma victims, had died than in *any other* space that size on earth. On the other hand, more lives had been saved in that very same space than any other place on earth.

All this being said, maybe the answers to the biggest questions humanity has been asking for millennia are no more obvious now than they ever have been. While there is much to suggest that we have been getting smarter these last couple of centuries, especially the last couple of decades . . . are we really? How do you define smarter? How could we know?

But I digress. I was telling you about Tom.

Tom was so successful as an architect and enjoyed his work so much that he stayed very busy for many years. He became fairly well known in the architectural world and made more money than he knew what to do with. He stayed in touch with his parents as they grew older and with all his siblings, who each found a mate before long, settled down in that same country, lived the life they had always loved, and raised their children to do the same. Besides for Tom, the whole extended family were involved with each other on a daily basis and especially during all the special occasions and holidays. Over the years, Tom visited less and less but still wrote. After a while, he wrote less and less but still thought about them. After a while longer, he would go for extended periods of time without even thinking about them at all. Until one day.

Tom was just approaching his fifty-eighth birthday and was in the middle of another large project. He had married when he was in his thirties, and his wife had really wanted to have children, but they were unable. She had broached the subject of adoption, but Tom could never really get his head around the idea. The truth of it was, he was so committed to his work that he had never been that excited about having children to begin with or anything else that might take up too much of his time. And adopting children, children who were not his own flesh and blood, just seemed to be going too far, trying to make something fit that really didn't.

Tom also knew that children who are adopted can be a good deal of work. This is usually the case because of the instability of their past, but even when they are adopted as infants, they struggle later on to reconcile in their minds and hearts why they were "given up." And Tom never had a big enough place in his heart for any of this, so he never consented, and his wife finally gave up on the idea.

She had been a workaholic of sorts herself when she was younger and an attorney, but deeper down she really wanted to have a family, and especially a husband who cherished her more than his nine to five. Or in Tom's case, his seven to seven. She tried to accept things the way they were, but she eventually became so depressed, she had to do something. She asked Tom if he would go to counseling with her. She had already been going herself for over a year and hoped he would begin to understand her and begin to pay her more attention. But Tom never got it. He didn't want to. He still wanted to save the world. It never occurred to Tom that it was he himself who needed the saving.

And so after fifteen years of marriage and all of her efforts to get

Tom's attention, she finally gave up on him too. Something he never understood but something that was largely his fault.

Tom had always gotten a great deal of satisfaction from completing a project. You could even say he got a high from this that would last for weeks. He could even get little highs from completing significant steps within a project, but finishing it, that was really something. And Tom had always awakened every morning excited to go to work. Until one day.

At first he wondered if he were ill or coming down with a cold. After a week or so of waking up every morning and not looking forward to going in to work, and on some mornings even experiencing a vague sense of anxiety, Tom began to worry. Was something wrong with the project he was working on, he wondered? He racked his brain but could not come up with anything. Not regarding the details of the work itself or any of the people he was working with this time around or anything else. Everything seemed to be going fine, just like always.

By the end of the week, Tom dreaded going to bed at night. At first he thought this was odd, but then he realized the whole problem was how he felt or didn't feel when he woke up in the morning. It made sense he didn't want to go to bed—he was already dreading opening his eyes in the morning. But then Tom had a dream.

In the midst of the dream, Tom woke up in sweat. For a brief time he just sat up in bed, trying to gain his bearings. The dream had occurred in ancient times. He remembered everyone was wearing loose clothing and sandals. There was a large contraption of sorts, made mostly of wood. It was circular in shape and had a number of large handles that protruded out from the side. This piece of machinery, for lack of a better word, was ten or twelve feet high and at least that size in diameter. There seemed to be six or even eight of these handles evenly distributed around the circumference or outside of this contraption, and Tom and some other men each had hold of one of these handles. They were each pushing on their handle, pushing this contraption around. Over and over again. It must have been some sort of mill.

It was hot in that place, so hot the men were dripping wet. And then Tom remembered the rest of the dream. He was a prisoner. No, that wasn't quite right. He must have been a *slave*. That was at least the way it felt. There were other men there too, dressed differently, with more elaborate leather garments and helmets. They looked like soldiers. A few of these men had bullwhips, and they used them to make sure the men kept pushing this contraption round and round at a steady pace. The devise was enormously heavy, and the men had to push hard at all times to keep it going at the rate the soldiers wanted. Round and round, all day long.

Some of the men collapsed from exhaustion. They would be dragged away without the slightest regard and replaced with another man. Tom could never remember feeling so tired in his whole life. What a terrible dream! At first he didn't want to go right back to sleep; he was afraid the dream might pick up where it left off. But after a while he lay back down and finally drifted off. The dream did not continue.

After this started, Tom tried his best to delve into his work and find himself again. This seemed to help for the first week or two, but as the beginning of each day continued with no change, as he continued to wake every morning without the same excitement he had always felt, this became increasingly difficult. After a couple of weeks, Tom was hoping he had some kind of low-grade virus and all of this would pass. But after a trip to the doctor revealed nothing, and week three and four came and went with no improvement, it all affected his demeanor during the day.

And then one night he had the dream again. It was similar to the first time, but now one of the soldiers got in his face and threatened to whip him if he didn't pick up his pace. And then he whipped him anyway. The pain of the whip on his back was so intense, even in the dream, that Tom physically recoiled in his sleep, and it woke him. He had to get up and walk around the house for a while to get the dream out of his head.

The next morning it took him until lunch before he felt better. Tom often ordered something in for lunch so that he could work through it. On this day he ordered from a new restaurant that had opened nearby. When his food arrived at his office, it was in a paper box that was beige in color and had been woven together to look like a picnic basket. As a designer, Tom appreciated the thought that had been put into this; he had never seen anything quite like it.

And then his thoughts drifted, and all of a sudden he remembered the picnic baskets his family used when he was a child, when they all went down to the river. It had been years since Tom had thought of this. Some five minutes later, Tom discovered himself sitting in his chair looking out his window with his sandwich in his hand. He had not taken the first bite. In his mind he had gone back home, to the river, with all his family.

Tom's coworker Roger, a draftsman, had tried to form a friendship with him over the years. Tom had managed to hold Roger off at a distance, like everyone else.

It wasn't that Roger needed any more friends; he was just a good fellow who thought that Tom might. Most of the employees at the firm were a little intimidated by Tom—first, because he was one of the firm's major producers, and second, because he was so standoffish. Tom had always been quiet and reserved and usually did not speak unless spoken to.

Roger would strike up a conversation with Tom from time to time and had even invited him out to lunch many years ago, not long after his wife had left him, and Tom had actually accepted Roger's invitation. Tom never mentioned the separation that day to Roger, but it made him feel better to have lunch with someone.

Over the last few weeks, Roger could tell that something was up with Tom. He definitely seemed more preoccupied, if not depressed.

"Tom. How are you doing this morning?" Roger began.

"Oh ... okay, I guess. I've been trying to finish some of the preliminary drawings on that Center City project we're bidding on next month. I might actually like your feedback on a few things. You have a good sense for aesthetics, and there are a few details here and there I am having trouble visualizing."

"Well, I'd love to help if I can," Roger replied. "What if we talked over lunch? It would be nice to get away from the office. It might even help our thought process."

Tom didn't respond right away and was staring down at his desk.

It was as if the dentist had just told him he needed a root canal . . . that afternoon. "Well, maybe," Tom replied. "Let me think about it. Can I let you know, say . . . by eleven?"

"Sure," Roger replied. "Your choice. I'll just wait to hear. And if not, let me know when we can talk more, in your office or mine. Okay?"

"Yeah, okay."

That morning Tom went back and forth over Roger's lunch invitation. On the one hand, it would be nice to break up his routine, to get out and talk about the project. On the other, spending too much personal time with anyone made Tom feel a little anxious.

Tom and Roger bumped into each other that morning several more times—once in the men's bathroom, once in the break room getting some coffee, and once walking from here to there. Roger thought this was a little odd, as days could go by in the office without them seeing each other.

On the third occasion, Roger thought to say something more about lunch, to press a little. He wasn't sure exactly why, but a small voice told him this could be important, that Tom might be in some real trouble but didn't know how to ask for help.

"Tom," he said as they approached each other. "Let's do lunch out for sure. I really need to get out of the office for a while. It's spring, and it's just so nice outside . . . okay?" This caught Tom off guard, so much so he didn't have the time to come up with a reasonable excuse.

"Okay, we can do that," he replied, already angry with himself he had consented.

"See you at your office at twelve? We can decide then where we want to go," Roger said.

"That will work."

The two left the office at lunchtime and decided to walk for a few blocks to see if they could find something new. They came to the place that used the paper picnic baskets for takeout. Tom had not known where this place was. One of the ladies in the office had mentioned it and that they did delivery.

"Oh, this is the place I got takeout from the other day. It was really good—what if we eat here?"

"Sure," Roger replied.

Tom and Roger looked over the menu, which contained a wide array of sandwiches and salads. When their orders came, the waitress brought them in the paper picnic baskets. "Our dishwasher broke down late yesterday—we still haven't caught up," she explained. "So we're serving in these takeout containers. Hope you don't mind."

"No problem," Roger replied.

Tom just stared at them for a moment and didn't say anything.

"So tell me about the project," Roger started.

And Tom began as they ate their lunch.

It was a big project with several office buildings, large public spaces, retail, and even a performing arts theater. The other principals at the firm had all discussed the overall concept and came to an agreement on the basic design, but as Tom had fleshed it out, there were some things he was not happy with. He felt some of it could be better, especially more creative, more unique. The two spent thirty minutes or so talking about the project, and Tom was right. Roger did have some good ideas.

Roger and his wife still had two kids in high school, and they were all going camping that weekend. He mentioned this with the thought in mind to see if he could coax Tom into saying a little more about his own weekend plans or his personal life, in general.

"So anything you're doing this weekend?" Roger asked.

"No, not really. I come into the office most Saturday mornings, sometimes till early afternoon. You know, I don't have any kids, and my wife and I divorced eight or nine years ago. I kind of like peace and quiet on the weekends. I lay around a little, watch some TV, sometimes work in the yard.

I do enjoy planting a vegetable garden every year. Just broke up the ground again, getting ready to plant some seeds and seedlings. I grew up on a farm as a kid. Learned a whole lot about growing things," Tom answered.

"Wow, I didn't know that. I wouldn't have guessed it either. You definitely seem like a city boy."

"Well, I think I'm more comfortable in the city now, most days at least."

Roger took a chance and dove a little deeper. "Ever think you'll get married again?"

"Uh, I don't know about that. Maybe. I've gotten pretty used to being on my own at this point. The first time around turned out to be pretty painful. It definitely left a bad taste in my mouth." As soon as those words came out, Tom could not believe they had. It wasn't his way to share what was going on in his heart. He didn't even like sharing it with himself.

"Sorry to hear that," Roger said, with a great deal of tenderness in his voice. "Relationships can be hard. My wife and I have had to work a great deal on our marriage, or we might not have made it. We've spent a good deal of time over the years with a counselor at our church."

"I wouldn't have thought that," Tom said. "You are so easy to get along with. You seem like nothing bothers you."

"Oh, I think we are *all* something of a mess. We don't like to admit it, but we are."

"Maybe you're right," Tom replied, "but I've never really thought that before."

Tom felt an urge to say more, to say more about himself. He considered how out of sorts he had been the last several weeks, and then for some reason, remembered his dream. And then he just began to talk. "You know, I had the strangest dream recently. Twice actually."

"Yeah?" Roger replied, purposely waiting.

"It is one of those really weird dreams, like some kind of strange movie or something. Have you ever wondered where dreams like that come from? All dreams, really? They can be so real."

"I *have* wondered that," Roger replied. "So often they seem like nonsense, but I really don't think they are. Some people think the things that happen in dreams are symbols, almost like code, for something else. I believe that sometimes. But I believe they are very personal too, almost like we are talking to ourselves, trying to help ourselves with things in our lives. Real things. Or *someone* is."

"Like *God*?" Tom asked.

"Well, yeah, maybe so."

"I've never believed in a God like that," Tom said. "Or maybe I've never really believed in God at all." Tom again couldn't believe how much he was saying. And then he realized that a lot of this was . . . Roger. He was so easy to talk to. It almost seemed like he had known Roger well for years.

"Well, I lived most of my life without thinking about God that much," Roger continued. "It was my wife who wanted to start going to church and take the kids. It took a while, but it all really began to make more sense when we had our own struggles and we were in counseling. I had never wanted to take a serious look at the things I said or did or even thought about, not really. I played a good game, but at some point, the things my wife was complaining about made sense. Not that she was always right—she wasn't—but she was more right than I had ever wanted to admit.

There were a lot of things I was selfish about that had hurt her, *really* hurt her. It took a while—it wasn't the easiest thing—but talking to that counselor was the best thing we ever did. I have a different view of people now. We are all screwed up. Admitting it is half the battle." Roger almost jerked after those last two sentences. He hadn't meant to be that forward, to say anything that might cause Tom to feel he was being examined or judged. But it must not have been that forward, for Tom continued.

"In my dream I think I was a slave in ancient times. There was this huge contraption, like a mill of some type. We were pushing it round and round. There were soldiers there, forcing us to work all day long, whipping us. I have no idea how I got there, how they captured me, or how I became a slave, but it all seemed right out of a history book. Other workers were dropping like flies, and they just dragged them off, replaced them with others, and, I imagine, just let them die."

"Golly, that sure sounds intense," Roger replied.

"Yeah. It actually scared the crap out of me. The second time I had the dream I wasn't quite the same until the middle of the next day." Tom was tempted to say more, to tell Roger the dream had not been the only thing on his mind lately, how he was really struggling every morning to feel normal, to be excited about coming into work, but could not bring himself to say more. But then he did. And he wasn't even sure where it came from.

"You know, I have always wanted to believe that I am making a contribution, that somehow the work I do and my life in general is making a difference. I would think we all want to think that. That it all matters. That *we* matter."

Roger leaned in just the slightest. His intuition had been right.

"Why doesn't anyone talk more about stuff like this?" Tom added. "What are we thinking? That it's all going to work out by accident?"

"Well, Tom. You're asking some pretty big questions now. I have had similar thoughts before."

"To be honest, I don't think I have *ever* thought of any of this before. Not before this very moment. But I sure am thinking about it now."

Tom's eye happened to catch Roger's paper basket on the table. He smiled to himself. "Maybe God is trying to speak to me."

Roger couldn't believe his ears but could not help but smile. "How so?"

"It's like I lost my way but never realized it. It's like I took for granted the things I learned when I was a child, so many of the things we had when I was growing up." He looked at the picnic basket again.

"You know, my parents took us to church and we talked about God, and as I look back, I see that they lived godly lives. They were humble, always grateful, incredibly loving, and just enjoyed being able to participate in the lives they were given.

And that is definitely how they looked at it. They were stewards, never owners. They lived it out, we lived it out, but we almost never talked about any of these things. But it should have stuck. I think it did with the rest of my siblings. But it didn't with me. Somehow I lost hold of it.

'And without any clear vision of a life-giving way of life, I began to turn, first in school and then at work, to one task after the other, doing as well as I could but never really certain about what doing things *well* would look like.''

You know, sitting here now talking with you, for the first time I can see that's what I have always longed for—to live my life according to what is true and good. But I have never had a clear idea about *what* that is. How crazy is that?"

Roger didn't say anything, again on purpose.

"It all makes my head spin to the point I wonder if I'm losing my mind," Tom added.

"Oh, I don't think you're losing it," Roger replied. "I think you are right. You just may be gaining it. You know, I was listening to a song the other day. Do you ever listen to bluegrass? It was by a guy named Peter Rowan. The title of the song was 'Before All the Streets Were Paved.' It came to mind again as you were talking about your parents, growing up on a farm, about 'progress,' as we now think of it. The song really provoked me. I checked online to see if I could find out more, what Peter Rowan might have been thinking when he wrote it, although the song really speaks for itself. What I did find were the words of someone else. I can hardly believe now how much they sound like the words that just came out of your mouth. It struck me so much, I wrote it down. I have it in my wallet. Let me find it. Here it is:

> As a species we crash heedlessly into a future we refuse to anticipate clearly, leaving behind a past we fail to value. Sure, there are those among us who see some unfortunate and perhaps irreversible consequences to the pathways down which we allow ourselves to be led, as there are those among us who do greatly value the more cohesive aspects of our history. We laud technology and religiously keep faith that it will save us from ourselves. Yet in the midst of our amazing material wealth, we have people enough without homes to constitute whole cities, while throughout the US much housing remains vacant.[2]

Now, that guy didn't have to use such big words, but it is easy to understand his drift," Roger said.

"Wow," Tom could only say. They sat in silence for a few moments. "Roger, can we do this again? Can we get out of the office and have lunch together again sometime?"

"Of course. That would be great."

Endnotes

1 Craig Dykstra and Dorothy Bass, *Practicing our Faith: A Way of Life for a Searching People* (Minneapolis, MN: Fortress Press).

2 Hank Alrich, Armadillo Productions, notes on *Before All the Streets Were Paved*, http://www.armadillomusicproductions.com/notes/Streets.html.

Everybody's Favorite

Charm is deceitful and beauty is vain,
but a woman who fears the Lord,
she shall be praised.
Proverbs 31:30

nce upon a time, there was a young girl on whom it seemed heaven had just opened up and poured its blessings.

She almost never cried or fussed as a baby, slept through the night early, and enjoyed being alive. Which was a good thing because everything remaining equal, the sixth of six children, everyone was excited about her birth, but that was about it. But very little was ever equal about this young girl.

Her name was Leah, a name with a soft and beautiful sound, but a name that means "weary," reminding those who know Bible stories of the Leah who was the elder daughter of Laban. Laban fooled Jacob into marrying Leah, his older daughter, instead of Rachel, with whom Jacob had fallen in love. Rachel is described as being "beautiful of form and face," while Leah is described as one whose "eyes were weak." Everyone has always assumed that the Leah in the Bible was not attractive, not attractive at all.

I do not believe Leah's parents were thinking of the Bible when they named their daughter; they just liked the sound of the name. For there was nothing about this baby that was like the other Leah. And maybe there was even some eternal game going on here, some great irony, a rebalancing of the universe. Maybe baby Leah was meant to rise up and redeem the Leah of old and allow her to exchange places with her sister, Rachel, as the beautiful one, the chosen one.

For you see, baby Leah was never going to be second to anyone. Ever. Her big blue eyes could take your breath away even when she was an infant. In fact, many people would comment that she *was* the most beautiful baby they had ever seen, not that she "may be." And her looks grew even more striking when she was a toddler and then a preschooler and then a talkative first grader. Leah was such a beautiful child that people who didn't even know there were beauty pageants for children would say that there *should* be just so she could enter, because she would win. And guess what? She did.

From the beginning, Leah was received fairly well by her five siblings but took all the usual battering and disregard that came her way for being the youngest. The mother of the family was a stay-at-home mom, and a good one at that. But one day, it occurred to her that Leah could be a child model. After some research, she learned about beauty pageants for little girls and was surprised to learn they actually had pageants for girls of all ages, from 0–11 months, 12–23 months, 2–3 years, 4–6 years, and so on. Leah was already four and had missed three whole categories.

Leah could be a child model and make some good money, but there was something more alluring about the beauty pageants to her mother. Before long she started buying Leah outfits for the pageants, learned of the events in their city or close by she could enter, and prepared for the beginning of Leah's "career."

You might be surprised by this, but it's not uncommon for some parents to live vicariously through their children. In the more common form of this illness, it is a passive thing. The child has a talent or ability or is just a good student, and the parent gets more satisfaction out of this than the usual amount of pride. Eventually they mention the child's achievements to others and, ultimately, have trouble talking about anything else. It is pretty clear their child's achievements have taken on more importance than they were ever meant to, with the parent very much sharing in the credit. The child's notoriety has somehow become a part of the parent's own self-image as well.

But then there are those situations where a parent is involved in the child's choice to become engaged in a certain activity to begin with, and maybe even a career when they are older. The more typical example is a father who was an athlete himself in a sport he very much loved. He pushes his son hard to compete in this sport, often coaching his teams when he is younger and always in the stands when he is older.

Some of these fathers can be obnoxious spectators, sometimes screaming obscenities at the referees and even their sons. It's clear that something selfish and narcissistic is at work—this is really more about the father's self-esteem and self-image than anything else, especially the son. For the son, it is a demand he perform, and if he does well, he is a success. But if he does not, he is a disappointment.

It was just this important and selfish for Leah's mother, although she tried to hide it, and the pressure on Leah very great, although it seemed much easier for her because she was always so successful.

There is no reason this phenomenon cannot happen with almost any activity that can be measured or is competitive. I read Andre Agassi's autobiography, in which he details his bitter relationship with his father, who abusively pushed him to become a competitive tennis player. It makes you wonder if Andre didn't need to write the book to help him come to terms with it all, like a war veteran with PTSD might be compelled to write about their war experiences.

People even live vicariously through their dogs, for crying out loud. If you have ever seen a dog show, especially the better-known ones, it is obvious that the whole performance is more about the owners than the dogs. I don't believe there has ever been a single dog who wanted to be a show dog or chose to be one. I might be wrong, but I don't think so.

Enter little girls' beauty pageants, vicarious living on steroids. Little girls enjoy wearing clothes and looking pretty, no less than boys like playing sports and getting dirty. But no little girl would have ever thought to make this into a serious competition and to look like a grown woman, including the full complement of makeup that would only be worn to the most formal of occasions. But their mothers thought of it.

Leah's mother was not an unattractive woman, for Leah had gotten many of her features from her. But she was not Leah. No one was. What woman does not want to be regarded as breathtakingly beautiful and stunning, the kind of woman who turns every head when she walks into a room? By the time Leah was twelve and looked sixteen, this fantasy had become Leah's life.

It is one thing for a good number of the men in a room to look at an attractive woman when she passes by. It is another thing altogether when every single *woman* in the room cannot take their eyes off her, all their heads turning in unison as she makes her entrance. They may even be so mesmerized by her that they don't notice their husbands are looking, too, and can't stop. Or maybe, for once, they finally understand.

Leah's mother might have left her in the beauty pageants for longer, for she enjoyed them so much herself, and Leah never lost, not even once. But modeling agencies approached them, at first for ads for local department stores. But it did not stop there. By the time Leah was eight years old, her mother was approached by national agencies looking for children for major advertising campaigns for well-known brands. The money was just too big to ignore. And you might have guessed since Leah was such a striking beauty, the opportunities just continued to get bigger.

By the time Leah was thirteen, you might not have known her name, but you would have likely recognized her face. Her career had clearly arrived when her picture graced the cover of *Cosmopolitan*, something that happened when she was eighteen. Several years earlier, the magazine had been very tempted but were concerned they might be accused of over-sexualizing a fourteen-year-old young girl. Imagine that. The editors themselves would not have lost any sleep over this—they just didn't want any undue publicity.

Everybody loved to use Leah; they could not help themselves. Sadly, it took Leah a lot longer to figure this out.

Can you imagine what it would be like to be a "star"? A star ... of some type or another? It is actually an interesting word, is it not? It is thought the term was first used to describe an English stage actor name David Garrick in 1779. He was, evidently, such a great actor that his performance diminished the performances of the other actors in the play. It brought to mind the image of his "light" being so bright that it diminished the "lights" of the other actors. Later the term was used for actors in motion pictures, and it especially took off when the studios in Hollywood began to market the actors and not just the pictures themselves.

It is quite an interesting image, is it not? Your light being *so* bright that it actually diminishes the light of others around you, the way the full moon makes most of the stars in the sky seem to disappear. And with that image, you get a sense of just what Leah's life had become—of just what it might be like to be her.

Have we all not wished we could be a star? It all started when we were young and began to understand there were certain people others especially admired. I wish I could go back in time to when I was five or six years old and hear my parents talking about movie stars and other famous people. I wish I could watch myself and see the expressions on my face or hear my thoughts when, for the first time, I heard the distinctions that were being made, the use of unfamiliar adjectives. *How could someone be that special?* I must have wondered. *And how on earth did they ever become that way?*

And when I was a teenager struggling to feel comfortable with who I was and who I was becoming, or to have any stable sense of self whatsoever, oh how my thoughts and fantasies must have run rampant! And if any of us were fortunate, by the time we were young adults and were working and maybe had kids, we had begun to feel more secure with who we were, or at least could anticipate a time in the future when we would. Hopefully, by the time we were twenty-five or thirty, we were not spending so much time fantasizing about being *someone else* but were mostly comfortable with ourselves.

But life is rarely a black-and-white thing, and most things are relative. And I believe our thoughts and feelings on this subject are

115

relative as well. Most of us continue to struggle with how we feel about ourselves to some degree, still having some way to go with liking ourselves as much as we could, and may still spend some time believing we would be happier if we could just be someone like . . . Michael Jordan or Clark Gable or Elizabeth Taylor. This must be why the idea of being a star has so much allure, so much draw. Such a strong statement would erase any doubt, would it not? Those who are really famous receive almost constant attention everywhere they go. It is almost like they are being worshipped like gods.

You know, there may be other things like this, aspects of our human nature that are so common to everyone and so compelling, so filled with conflict, so pushing toward some type of resolution. But maybe not. Maybe there is nothing quite like this. It is almost as if we are *all* participating, one way or the other, in a great drama. There may be a few wise old souls here and there who are completely on the sidelines, but I doubt it. We all so much want to feel good about ourselves and, if it could ever happen, to be a star. And we all so much don't want to feel bad about ourselves or, at the very worst, to feel like a reject. My, that is an old word. How about the word "loser"?

We all spend far too much time with thoughts and feelings like these bouncing back and forth in the backs of our minds and hearts. Most of us never feel we could be on the main stage, in the spotlight, but we still have trouble dismissing the idea altogether. If, by some miracle, our name was actually called and we could run up there and be a star, many of us would not hesitate. But most of the time, we at least find it hard to resist the temptation to look up to someone who has made it on one stage of the world or another. Someone begins to talk about a movie star or a professional athlete or an immensely successful entrepreneur or maybe even a politician, of all things, and our ears perk up.

If you could hear our thoughts and listen carefully to the words that came out of our mouths, you could tell we have completely bought in to the belief that there are a few people here and there who are different than the rest of us. Better. More special. We all participate in this great drama in one way or the other, either in giving our approval to the chosen few who have taken to the stage, or in turning our thumbs down to those who never could, or in deciding when the time has come for a star to fall. A little overdramatic? I think not.

And there is another side to this great drama. A dark side. For the very reason that so many of us desire to be in the spotlight if we could, that we value it as much as we do, it can be hard for us not be jealous of those who are. From the very moment Leah stepped up onto the pedestal when she won a beauty pageant as a child, she put herself squarely in the sights of all the other mothers and daughters who lost, but especially the one or two who just might have won if she had not showed up.

Was this not even the very reason the first murder in this world occurred? Abel brought an offering to the Lord, the firstborn of his flock of sheep and of their fat portions, and Cain did too, an offering of the fruit of the ground. "And the Lord had regard for Abel and his offering, but for Cain and his offering he had no regard. So Cain was very angry, and his face fell. The Lord said to Cain, 'Why are you angry, and why has your face fallen? If you do well, will you not be accepted?'" (Genesis 4:4–7 ESV).

Cain was jealous of the accommodation that Abel received from God when Cain received none. And God even commented on this, implying Cain's anger was unnecessary. For you see, herein lies the distinction. God's regard, His love, is *not* conditional. It is unconditional. God loved Cain just as much as He would ever love Abel. Abel had just brought a better gift, a gift that came more from the heart. God just wanted and hoped that Cain would choose to do the same in the future. But Cain could not see that—for him it was more personal. The gift defined the giver. His gift had defined him. And the attention and regard that Abel received *made him* into a bright, shining star. At least to Cain.

As a result, Cain decided that the best way for him to shine was to put out this other light. And many of us have been doing similar things ever since . . . hopefully not murdering anyone, but spending far too much of our time and energy wanting to be in the spotlight, feeling we need to be in order to really succeed, and being jealous, even angry, toward those who are in the spotlight instead.

All of this brings to mind a moment during my adolescence, when in the throes of passion and jealousy, I was overcome by one of the strongest temptations I have ever felt—a great desire to do bodily harm to a rival. I am not being overly dramatic. It may have been fatal if I had given in to my first impulse. Looking back, I don't really understand how I was able to control myself; I'm just glad I did. My life could have taken an abrupt turn if I had not resisted, just as Cain's did. There may have been an angel present that day standing between the two of us, holding me back. If so, I thank that angel now.

Before Leah finished high school, she had no desire to be the queen of the prom or to receive any other accolades from her peers, for she had no real friends. As a matter of fact, she had become so well known by the time she was sixteen, it made more sense for her to go to a private boarding school. From her earnings, she could have paid for it ten times over. Her mother enjoyed the status of her going to such an outstanding institution and especially enjoyed telling everyone about it. But Leah more enjoyed the privacy of it, if you can imagine that. Her fame had already begun to wear on her.

She enjoyed the attention, to begin with, especially when she was very young and had no real way to understand it or put it into perspective. It is very hard as a little child not to light up when others notice you, and notice you a lot. But you don't have to be that old when you become as famous as Leah, even at the age of twelve, before you begin to tire of it. Other people have difficulty talking of little else, especially when they first meet you. It is as if you have this special power, and if others get close enough to you and spend enough time speaking to you, especially if they have your undivided attention, they believe *the power*, this life-giving force, can be passed to them.

As a teenager, Leah could not give voice to it, but she had already felt it. And to her credit, she had already sensed that none of this had anything to do with her. She was just being *used* as a vehicle for it. The real story was about something much greater. It was about the power, the power of stardom. She just so happened to have it or to have come upon it. It was the *power* that others wanted, that some people believed they could get a little taste of if they got close enough.

Others did not want to warm up to her. They just wished they had it themselves and would have stolen it from her if that were somehow possible. She sensed more and more in the back of her mind and down deep in her heart that none of these people cared for her. They never had. It was all about the power, nothing more.

As it turned out, boarding school was the best thing that ever happened to Leah. Truly. Her mother would call her almost every day, but at least Leah did not have to constantly be in her presence. She began to feel like she could breathe, at least a little. And she found two or three girls who were able, most of the time, to just treat her as a regular person, as just a girlfriend.

But her greatest hope came in the form of a young man named Victor. It would be the most unusual of romances.

Victor had never had a girlfriend and was a bit eccentric. Enormously bright, he was the only child of a mathematics professor who had won the Nobel Prize in mathematics for things I will not bother to explain, for I am not able. Everything about Victor was peculiar, even his sense of humor. He was not outspoken but from time to time would offer his thoughts on this or that.

He would commonly use words that even bright people did not use or did not know. But it was more than that—it was the way he explained and described things, the way that he saw the world. Victor had a unique perspective, to the point where those listening were often at a loss as how to respond. It was like when someone tells a joke and no one gets the punch line, there's that lingering and awkward silence. Many of Victor's interactions with others went this way. Let us just say he was an acquired taste.

But although Victor was difficult to understand, he was easy to be with. He was comfortable with people, regardless of whether they understood him or not, and even more importantly, whether he understood them or not. And Victor had no interest or taste for anything that might be vain or bring attention to himself, things of pride, which is where Leah enters in, for her whole life up to that point had been defined by things that are vain and, if we can just be honest, narcissistic.

At first Leah took no notice of Victor, though she did get his jokes more than the others and could not help but laugh under her breath at them. But the first time she did notice, and everyone else, was in eleventh grade when Victor was walking up to the front of the class to write out a math equation on the board. The teacher asked if Victor could write it out and explain it as he went; maybe that way the rest of the class might understand it better. To Victor it seemed like child's play, but to everyone else, it was as dense as the thickest fog.

Victor was thin, and he paid little attention to his clothes or how they fit. He had been in such a rush that morning, he had failed to completely fasten his belt. As he was walking between the rows of chairs up to the board, his belt came all the way loose, and his pants, which were a couple of sizes too large, fell all the way to his ankles. It is hard to describe what happened next. To most of the class, Victor just disappeared from one second to the next, doing a face plant on the floor. For those sitting right there . . . there he lay, tighty-whities and all. At first Victor tried to pull up his pants without standing all the way up, but after a moment he stood and yanked them up.

Some laughed so hard they couldn't stop, and others were struck silent and dumb by the sheer shock of it. But the reason Leah noticed Victor on this day was not any of that but just how obvious it was that Victor was not embarrassed. Not embarrassed at all. He didn't blush, and he wasn't tempted to run out of the room. He just shrugged his shoulders, smiled, and walked up to the board and began to write out the equation.

He tried to, that was. He had started laughing so hard, he had to stop to gather himself. Victor had never taken himself very seriously, but this instance proved without a doubt he simply did not have a vain bone in his body. He had never felt that tempted to put on for others or worried that much about what anyone thought about him. To Leah, it was deeply attractive, but even more, a lifeline. She had never realized it, but she desperately needed to be rescued.

Leah quickly understood she would have to approach Victor if she wanted to get to know him better. He would never think to approach her, no matter how many hints she gave. And at first that was all she wanted. She had to know what made him tick, how it was, or how it came to be that he was so different, so immune to all the things that had come to define her life. So she decided to ask him if he would tutor her once a week in math.

"What if we meet at Stan's Coffee Shop right off campus on Wednesday afternoons after school?" she asked.

"Well, yes, we can do that," Victor replied. "But are you sure you need that much help? You seem to understand it all pretty well from what you say in class."

"Well, yes. I think I need a *great deal* of help!" And just as these words came out of her mouth, Leah realized what she had said. And she felt a glimmer of hope, the first she had felt in a long time. It is all quite ironic, is it not? Who would have ever thought the famous one would be looking to anyone for assistance, but especially someone like Victor. Poor, awkward Victor.

And that is how it all began. Leah did her best to pretend she really didn't understand the math for several weeks, but after a while that felt dishonest. But Victor was not an idiot either—she could tell he was going to say something any minute. So she fessed up.

"Victor, I need to tell you something."

"Yes?"

"I really didn't need as much help in math as I said. I just wanted to get to know you better. I hope you're not angry with me. I just wanted to be friends and didn't know how else to do that."

"Well, I'm not angry, just a little confused. We *were* friends, were we not?"

"Well, yes, of course. But I wanted to get to know you even better and thought the best way to do that was for the two of us to do something together, like this."

"Well, that makes sense. But *why* did you want to get to know me better?"

Leah wasn't expecting such a straightforward, candid question, but this was Victor's way. It surprised her, and she actually blushed, for she hadn't anticipated feeling more for him, that there could be more here than a simple friendship. Victor was perceptive of some things, but not *these* types of things, and simply sat and waited for her to say more. Finally she was just able to say, "What if we just got together to do things . . . for fun?"

It would not occur to Victor for several more months there was anything romantic in all this, but that probably doesn't surprise you. No one else at school thought so either when they saw the two of them walking together. Leah could have had any young man she wanted and many who were much older. At the age of seventeen, she could have even tempted some married men to leave their wives, as sick and sad as that may sound. But it was Victor she was attracted to. At first for his innocence.

That was the word that came to her sometime later as she was trying to understand it all better, give voice to this quality he possessed that she so wanted to have herself, that she hoped he could impart to her. It was as if the world had not been able to spoil him. Somehow, Victor had been able to put up a defense, an impenetrable defense, or maybe he had some inborn immunity. Regardless, she wanted to learn more about it, why he was so blessed, and was praying she could find it herself.

Before long they began to talk about life in general. Leah told Victor things she had never told anyone, many of the details of her relationship with her mother and her "career." Victor was compassionate and an excellent listener. Leah had never known anyone who was able to be so present with her, right where she was, no matter how ugly or painful it ever became, which only encouraged her to be more forthcoming, and more than once she completely broke down.

Victor had always thought of his life as boring, but the more he heard from Leah, the more fortunate he felt.

His parents were both like Victor, somewhat eccentric, mostly living in the academic world. But they were also like Victor when it came to how they related to others, comfortable with themselves and accepting of others, to a fault. As Leah shared more and more, Victor got a real taste of what Leah's life had been like.

Like the time Leah's mother had one of her temper tantrums, a tirade that was precipitated by a seven-year-old's innocent comment that she really didn't think she wanted to go to beauty pageants anymore. She just wanted to spend more time with her best friend across the street, playing with their dolls and having tea parties. I don't know if you have experienced anything like this. It is particularly shocking to a young child. You say something to someone, and you are just trying to be honest, to share your heart, but they react so violently and so viciously, it literally scares you. Scares the breath right out of you.

And the worst part of it, I believe, is the confusion and anxiety that rises up and overwhelms you. Confusion, because their words are telling you that you have just hurt them so badly, wounded them so deeply, that you were so insensitive, even abusive, when you weren't doing anything but just being honest about what you thought and felt. And anxiety, because there is so much condemnation in their words and anger that you feel incredibly threatened. Will they forgive you? Can what you said *even be* forgiven? It sure doesn't seem like it from the way they are talking, even screaming at you.

And if you are a little child, it is almost impossible to resist the temptation to agree with them, to accept their judgment of you as just that—insensitive, selfish, and abusive. For you are so dependent on them for *everything* in your life. What are you to do? And if all of this is not already so hard, it gets worse. In order to agree with them, it is *yourself* you will have to put up there on that altar and sacrifice. They are pressing you to submit *your* view of what just happened, your view of reality, to theirs. Submit your will to *their* will, or else.

And once you have agreed to do this once, it will be much harder to resist the next time and the next. As a little child, it seems you have no option but to concede, to relinquish your own opinion and judgment to theirs because they are the adult and they must know better than you. Or you could fight back. But that was not Leah's way.

There is a great evil here, maybe one of the greatest, and it has to break God's heart. It most assuredly broke Leah's. But for the first time in her life, she had a friend and confidant she could share her deep and dark secrets with. And the hurt, the enormous pain and hurt. Victor was just being himself; he didn't know any other way.

But just being present with her and giving her permission to be just who she needed to be, exactly who she was, was giving Leah the very thing she needed all her life but had never received. And truly, he gave her back *herself*. The self she had been forced to give away, time and time again, until there was so little left. It was like being born all over again. How can you not fall in love *with that*?

Over time Leah began to help Victor too. He had his own wounds, as we all do. There was safety in being so subdued, in always being so lost in ideas, lost in his intellect. Emotions are a little scary, less predictable. You never know, someone might get hurt.

In time, Leah drew Victor out more and more, and he even began to be a little "spontaneous," something they loved to laugh about and that became a private joke between the two of them. For Leah, it was the opposite in a way. She had always been expected to be *so* visible, so outgoing. She needed to come to believe it was okay, truly, to recede into the background—to step down off the stage and even disappear if she wanted.

She gradually became more and more casual in her dress and eventually tried to go out of her way to look as plain as she could. She would never be able to do anything about her natural beauty, but she did go without any makeup at all on a daily basis, a big deal for her. And she still turned almost every head when she walked into a room, but there seemed to be little she could do about that unless she never went out of the house. Let us just say she was tempted.

It did not take long for Leah's mother to dislike Victor, like right away. Leah was wise enough to not even mention him for the longest time. This may sound extreme, but it really is not. The inmates in a prison clearly know what will be okay with the guards and what will not. The lines are clear and have been for a long time. Leah's mother very much wanted *nothing* to change in regard to Leah's career and her part in it. Any close friend or confidant was a wild card, something she could not control, and the treasure was just too great to risk.

But Leah grew stronger each and every day that Victor was a part of her life. At some point midway through their senior year, Leah was ready to talk to her mother about Victor and was also ready to make the break. Or should we say break *out*? Leah knew it would be black and white to her mother—there would be no middle ground. By the time Leah's mother had heard just how long the two of them had been dating and that they were serious about each other, she had already started screaming and demanding that Leah withdraw from school and return home. Fortunately, Leah had just turned eighteen, and state law was in her favor. Leah had to hang up the phone. And hang up the second time and third.

After that, Leah's mother started showing up at her door. Victor was a great support, but Leah had also begun to see a counselor. She did not want to be such a constant burden on Victor, plus she wanted an objective opinion. It would not be a friendly divorce. After a month or so, Leah's mother backed off, but only after Leah had consulted with an attorney. Leah learned she had the right to fire her old agent and hire a new one, with the understanding this person would work for her, and only her, going forward. She really did not want to continue with modeling, but the money was so great and she was so used to it. It was not that difficult to show up and look pretty, and if she continued with it for another couple of years, she could be set for life. That was the plan, at least.

Victor wanted to pursue math in college and also at the postgraduate level. He wasn't sure what he might do with it, but he loved it so much that he had to take a closer look. His parents would pay for all of that, and there was no reason why he shouldn't let them.

No one would have ever faulted Leah for taking this ride as long as she wanted, but by the time she was twenty and Victor was midway through his undergraduate degree, she had had enough. She had hated being everyone's favorite for all her life and finally found the strength to say, "No. No more." She even fantasized about staging a disappearance, maybe even a drowning, something dramatic, something all the newspapers would love. Plus it would scare the living hell out of her mother. Victor and she had a lot of great laughs over this. The reality did not turn out to be that different. When the time came, Leah had to make more of an effort to disappear into the night than she had ever imagined.

They had a small, private wedding right after Victor's college graduation and decided to live wherever he went to graduate school. In order not to be noticed everywhere she went, she put her hair up into a bun and wore large sunglasses, but the kicker was her baseball hat. There are few things in this world that can erase femininity as quickly and completely as a baseball hat. For a time it became a game she enjoyed, but before long she grew weary of it.

Most of us are so lost in the self-doubt we deal with on a daily basis, trying to keep all the negative thoughts at bay, that we have never even given the first thought to what it might be like if our dream actually came true.

How impossible it could be to do the littlest thing: go to the grocery store, go out to dinner or to a movie, or just walk down a sidewalk without being noticed and people surrounding you to get your autograph. Leah was tempted to become a recluse, but Victor always talked her out of this and was willing to run interference for her in public. As soon as they were able, they moved to a small town and made good friends who, over time, came to understand their need to just be like "everyone else."

And then one day in that little town, Leah finally was able to come full circle, possibly to the place that always been intended for her, she just hadn't known it. It had been such a great blessing to find her freedom, to break off things with her mother, and to work for herself and only herself. And then to quit modeling altogether, to live a quiet, simple life in a little town with the man she loved, the man who had played such a large role in her redemption.

One day Leah met a teenage girl in town who was almost as pretty as she had been at that age—and the girl had a mother Leah recognized as well.

They had been introduced briefly in one of the diners, but for some reason Leah could not stop thinking about the girl, worrying about her, in fact. When she saw the girl in town, she would go out of her way to say hello, and on more than one occasion was able to have some longer conversations with her. All of which was a good thing, for it became obvious the girl was getting thinner and thinner.

Leah tried more than once to broach the subject with the girl. Leah had never struggled with her own weight but had seen the affliction of eating disorders affect many other models. She had read a good bit on the subject of young girls and eating disorders. Before long the girl became so thin and emaciated that she had to be hospitalized to help her turn the corner and gain some weight. It was a long battle, and an even longer story not to be told here. But let us say that Leah began to see a purpose for her life, a real purpose, for the very first time. This young girl became a good friend and eventually came to understand many of the underlying issues:

Low self-esteem

An unrelenting desire to be accepted by others and a terror of being rejected

An obsession that beauty may win one's acceptance

A belief that beauty is defined by thinness and ugliness by fat

A terror of losing control of all this, but especially being vulnerable to others' ability to receive or reject you, and the enormous pain this brings

And I'm just getting started. But isn't all of that enough to make you to want to think of something else?

Before long this girl, her parents, and Leah wondered if they could somehow do more to help other girls with the same problem. Though she hadn't struggled with her weight, the larger issues had all been Leah's curse as well. It occurred to all of them that with Leah's history—that is, her fame—doors would open for them quickly that would not open for others. They created a publicity campaign that warned about the dangers of eating disorders, and it started in their town and the surrounding counties. But it went well, as you might imagine. Everyone really just wanted to see Leah. Again. But that was okay, at least to start out.

Over time they were able to better define the real message, to warn young girls about the enormous pressure our Western culture places on them to feel that they have to be beautiful and thin to be okay, to be accepted, maybe even to be loved. Leah, of course, brought instant credibility to the campaign and an even greater irony. The campaign was a huge success and eventually went national. After several years, Leah had become "famous" again, but this time for a different reason. There could not have been a better storyline.

Who would know all the ups and downs of trying to be as beautiful as you could ever be but the one person who actually had been? And who would know if it was truly as great as it was all supposed to be than the very one who had taken that journey, stood in the spotlight, received all that praise, and been worshipped by such an adoring public?

Leah was eventually able to help many young girls and women to let go of the "dream" to find the freedom they so desperately needed. And many years later, after both of her careers, Leah's face, her beautiful face, was more associated to her latter career than her former. And for this, she was eternally grateful. For no one had ever known just how much she had never wanted to be everybody's favorite.

Mitakuye Oyasin

All my relations, I honor you in this circle of life with me today.
I am grateful for this opportunity to acknowledge you in this
prayer—to the Creator for the ultimate gift of life,
I thank you. To the mineral nation that has built and
maintained my bones and all foundations of life experience,
I thank you. To the plant nation that sustains my organs and
body and gives me healing herbs for sickness, I thank you. To
the animal nation that feeds me from your own flesh and offers
your loyal companionship in this walk of life, I thank you.
To the human nation that shares my path as a soul upon the
sacred wheel of earthly life, I thank you. To the Spirit nation
that guides me invisibly through the ups and downs of life and
for carrying the torch of light throughout the ages, I thank
you. To the four winds of change and growth, I thank you. You
are my relations, my relatives, without whom I would not live.
We are in the circle of life together, coexisting, codependent,
cocreating our destiny, one not more important than the other.
One nation evolving from the other and yet each dependent
upon the one above and the one below. All of us, part of the
Great Mystery. Thank you for this life.[1]
—"Mitakuye Oyasin," Lakota Sioux Prayer, author unknown

nce upon a time, before the interior of this country was ever
seen by a white man, before any foreigner ever stood on its
great expanse, many native tribes lived and thrived. They lived a life
like no one before or since.

It is hard to know how long they had lived in these Great Plains that stretched all the way from Texas north to Canada. From their appearance, these people seemed related to those from the East, some of whom must have crossed the great ocean long ago and then migrated all the way south to their new home.

They were later judged to be "savages" by the white man, who saw himself as morally and culturally superior, although over time, a different story has been told. A story of oppression and usury, of a proud people who didn't want to give up their beautiful life and had every right to it. A people who were slaughtered in great numbers and who finally, in humiliation and against their better judgment, conceded, thinking and hoping the white man could be trusted, that he would allow them to live the life they had always lived. But in the end, they found themselves holding little but false promises. It is one of humanity's sadder and uglier stories. Maybe the Indians' time was only *for* a time. But no story should end the way their story ended. And so this story will not.

This story is not about their end, thank goodness, but about better days. And I would like you to consider something, if you are willing. If you were given the choice to live any kind of life you wanted, across all the centuries, all the lands, and all the cultures, what life might you choose? Do you know? Have you ever really thought about it?

I have. If I could choose to live any life, out of all the possible lives that have ever been lived on this earth, if I could go back in time to any place, or even into the future, I would have to pick the life of an Indian who lived on the Great Plains several hundred years ago.

For modern man, it would be quite a challenge to go back in time, to once again have to do so much work with his hands in order to survive from one day to the next. We have all become so addicted to convenience and comfort, it would be hard to give these up. But these are not the key to life we seem to think they are. If they were, we would all clearly be happier now than we were in the past. But there does not seem to be any evidence for that. In fact, it seems to be just the opposite.

Now, I know we are all different. We like different things and, therefore, might choose different lives if ever given this choice. But consider this. Have you ever imagined what it would be like to ride a horse bareback, a wild horse you had chosen as a youth, a horse you had broken and trained and that had become your best friend? A horse who had clearly been placed on this earth to be the most incredible running machine you could imagine, across any type of terrain, even water two or three feet deep?

Can you imagine what it would be like to ride this beautiful animal on a bright summer day on those expansive golden plains that stretched as far as the eye could see? Can you imagine the warm air blowing through your hair and across your skin? The feel of the soft leather clothing on your skin and even its smell, clothing your wife had made with her own hands, taken from the hide of a buffalo you had killed many summers ago on a very similar day?

Can you imagine your head adorned with feathers and your clothing adorned with beads and colored by natural dyes, for there was nothing in this world or life that was not natural in the true sense of the word? Can you imagine chasing down a buffalo with your great spear, a spear you had made as a teenager, the completion of which was part of your initiation into adulthood? A spear that flew straight and true, whose shaft had once been the great branch of a tree and whose point the breastbone of a buffalo?

Can you imagine the enormous gratitude you would have for everything that allowed this beautiful life of yours—your wife, your family, your tribe, your horse, the great expanses themselves, the rivers, and the rain? And especially the great buffalo, who provided its flesh for your food, his hide for your shelters, clothes, and shoes, and his bones for your tools and weapons? Almost every part of his body was used for something, even his dung for fuel for your fires.

Everything was connected. *Everything*. Everything was part of this grand life, all in harmony, all in unity. The Indians had two words for the unity of everything in the world and a prayer of acknowledgment and thanks of the same name—"Mitakuye Oyasin," pronounced "mee-ta-ki, o-ya-sin."

Now, I am not a fool or an idealist or just naive. Well, I am all of those things, just not completely. The Indian life on the Great Plains was not perfect, and they were not perfect people. Some of the tribes could be brutal; some of them were continually at war with others. I am not sure why. They all had more than enough land, and none of them believed they had a right to permanently possess it, the motive that has started almost every true war this world has ever known.

And so their hearts and their lives were not perfect. But oh, if I could go back, I just might. I would close my eyes and allow myself to drift off from this modern world. And maybe, just maybe I might feel the sun and then the breeze. And I might feel a warm horse underneath my body and smell his scent and notice the texture of leather across my skin. And if I chanced to open my eyes, would I find myself on the edge of a great ridge, looking out over great golden plains, my village set below with teepees and smoke from fires?

And if I looked far into the distance, would I be able to see a great herd of buffalo grazing, hundreds and even thousands of little dots decorating the horizon? Aaahhh! What might it be like to go back and be one of the great Sioux, a young brave right in the midst of his prime, right in the midst of theirs?

His name was Takoda, which meant "friend to everyone, friend to them all." He was born with a smile on his face and joy in his heart and time for everyone. Takoda was just like one of the children you might remember from your youth whom everybody liked. We used to call them "popular." Hasn't everyone who has ever lived wanted to be popular, wanted to be liked? Well, almost everyone?

There are definitely some, from time to time, who seem to do everything they can *not* to be liked. Maybe they want to be popular too, but they don't know how. There are very few people like Takoda. There was something different about him. He had this almost magical way of making almost anyone feel better about themselves. He treated everyone with respect. And truly, if I think about it, he treated everyone the *same*. That is what the rest of us struggle so much to do. It makes you wonder . . . in heaven, will we all be *popular*?

Growing up as an Indian child in the seventeen hundreds on the

Great Plains was quite a remarkable thing. The winters were harsh and still, but everyone disappeared into buffalo furs to stay warm and dreamed of spring. During the rest of the year, they were nomads, following the buffalo herds. The Indians essentially lived outdoors. They were only in their teepees at night to sleep or keep warm.

As an Indian child, you learned very early just how connected you were with everything else in the world, with all of nature. Very much like farmers, the Indians had much to do to fill their days. They farmed some but relied more on hunting buffalo and deer to fill their stomachs. They did not possess anything nature did not provide. And apart from their shelters, their clothes, their weapons, some basic tools, and a peace pipe or two, they had no other possessions. None at all.

They did not have the same desire to possess things as we do, no obsession with ownership, especially with accumulating things. They believed they were partners with everything in the world, animate and inanimate, and that they were just one part of a much larger cycle of life. At the most, they were stewards, grateful stewards, who had been given this life and all of nature to watch over. And so it was easy for them to be nomads and pick up and move, for they never had more than they and their horses could carry.

There is so much variety in nature it almost seems infinite. So much, no one person can know it all. It does make you wonder if it was all made for a different purpose, to express something beyond us. After all, we are not the center of the universe, as we seem to think. Sadly, it seems as we have "progressed," we have lost touch with the natural world. Most people seem to prefer to stay indoors these days, even when the weather is perfect. We seem to like everything constant and the same. Weather is our enemy and the thermostat our friend.

The people who love the outdoors these days, who seek it out on their days off, are a small group. There are even specialty stores for these folks to purchase items for their "hobby." Takoda and his childhood friends would have scratched their heads over this. The outdoors was their whole world, their wonderland. They had chores to do, helping their mothers and older siblings gather wood for fires and other simple tasks, but they also had time to play. They pretended to go out in parties to hunt buffalo with bows and arrows and spears, taking turns being the hunters or the buffalo. They pretended to ride their horses across the great plain. And they painted their faces for make-believe celebrations and danced around make-believe bonfires.

Takoda loved the Great Plains. He could still remember the early days of his love affair. When he was two or three, he would spend hours introducing himself to the world around him. His mother would be busy cleaning a buffalo hide spread out on the ground or making some clothes, and he would wander from one thing to the next. He remembered the first rock he took the time to make friends with. It was about half as large as his little hand and mostly beige, with reddish streaks. He was amazed by how hard it was and wondered how it could have been made.

He was beginning to understand that babies came from their mother's stomachs. Could this rock have come from its mother's stomach? Did it have brothers and sisters? He looked around on the ground to see if he could find any just like it, but he could not. He kept his friend for a time, even sleeping with it, but it was left behind by accident when the tribe moved a month later. He missed it a good deal but soon found another rock to make friends with.

There were not that many trees in the Great Plains, but they did flourish alongside the rivers, which was often where the tribe made camp. Little boys and sticks have a special relationship. Primarily because sticks are so easy to envision as weapons but also because they are easy to throw and so good to beat on things. Takoda would use one longer stick as a bow and a shorter one for an arrow. It took him a while, but in time he learned to hold both of them in one hand, the arrow set, ready to fire. And once in a while, he would find a larger and longer stick and would tell himself it had been a brave's left behind from a great battle. Takoda would spend all afternoon throwing that spear, trying to launch it farther and farther. He would pretend that a small boulder was a buffalo and see if he could hit it.

Takoda could also remember the first time he noticed just how incredible an oak leaf was. Its shape and texture, its color, and even the little veins running through it. His mother told him it was alive, just like him, and pointed out that he had little veins running through his arms too. He glanced at her in amazement and then back at the leaf and then again at his arm. It was . . . *wonder*. That is what children have that we have lost. Wonder for everything, but especially for all of nature. Wonder, for all the beauty and all the complexity and all the wonderful things in this life. Wonder, for all of this great mystery.

Takoda had to be taught a certain respect for some things in the natural world. For certain spiders that were not to be touched, for ticks that needed to be discarded, and especially for types of snakes that could bite you and make you very, very sick. The snakes of different colors that made the rattling noise with their tails were the most dangerous. Takoda almost stepped on one when he was three. The rattling noise is what saved his life. It startled him and caused him to stand still, but it also alerted his mother, who did not waste any time in killing it with a rock. They said a little prayer afterward. No life in this world could be taken without deep respect.

Takoda could still remember asking his mother, "Why is the snake mean, and why did it want to hurt me?" He remembered that faraway look on her face as she gathered her thoughts, and then after a few moments, she said she did not believe it was mean. It was "scared." He was surprised by that answer. It sure hadn't looked scared. His mother told him that the snake did not know any better since people were so big and it was so small. It was afraid he might hurt it, maybe even kill it. It was just trying to protect itself.

"But you did kill it, Mother," Takoda said in return.

"Yes, I did. I could not let it harm you. I could not take that chance—you are too important to me. I wish the snake could understand our words, and I would have talked to it and told it we meant it no harm. But it does not, and so I could not."

Takoda was confused just enough to not ask any more questions, but he liked the fact that his mother loved him so much. Even so, he still felt bad for the snake lying dead on the ground.

There was a great, great love between the members of Takoda's tribe. They lived in such close proximity to each other and participated together in almost every single thing they did. Many in the tribe were related to one another, but all the rest felt related. Every adult believed they should play some role in the development of every child, and every child was respectful of each and every adult but also open to their guidance and wisdom. And everyone respected those older than themselves. The little children deferred to the older children, the older children to the adolescents, the adolescents to the young adults, the young adults to the middle aged, and everyone to the elders, especially the holy men and the chief. They were all one large and happy family. Well, almost.

As Takoda grew tall and became a young man, he began to think more seriously of whom he might marry. There was a girl he had felt close to since they were young, but a child's thoughts about marriage are just fleeting, only a game. When Takoda began to think about her on a daily basis, he knew he was no longer a child. Her name was Ichante, pronounced, "ee-chan-tee." It meant "from the heart." Sometimes things are just meant to be.

For her to be his wife, her father would have to agree. Marriages were, in many cases, arranged, determined by the wishes of the father or the father and mother. But if the father was a good father, if he understood his daughter deserved to have a say in this most important decision, he would involve her. They would discuss it privately and ultimately agree on who to encourage and who to discourage. It all could become complicated, but often it would work out just as it should.

Ichante did have another potential suitor, a brave named Kangee, pronounced just as it is spelled. His intentions were only known to himself, however, as were his thoughts on most subjects. He had always been quiet and serious. His mother had died when he was young, and he was raised by an aunt and uncle who loved him, although he always struggled to fit in. His father continued to be involved in his life and later remarried, but he died when Kangee was a teenager. He was killed during a buffalo hunt when he fell off his horse and was trampled by the herd. The other children had always been nice to Kangee and tried to include him, and he usually came along, but before long, he would be off to himself. Most of the time, he just felt more comfortable alone.

Ichante had caught Kangee's eye over the last couple of years, as she grew taller and especially as her beauty blossomed. Kangee was not the most intuitive fellow. It was not that easy for him to read others' thoughts, for his own were often very different. But even he was able to notice something stirring between Takoda and Ichante, and he was bothered by it. He quickly began to doubt himself, that he would never be able to match Takoda's joy and peace and his ability to engage Ichante in conversation. And he was right about all of that—he never would. But Kangee could have risen to the challenge nevertheless and done his best to surrender himself to Ichante's decision or to her father's.

How would he know if he did not try? And no one in the tribe would fault him for trying either, win or lose. Everyone would have respected him a good deal for deciding to enter the battle. But Kangee was never able to think of it this way. And he had great difficulty seeing the larger picture as well.

For instance, there were many other girls coming of age in the tribe whom he could pursue, and several who would be more responsive. And all of them would also be watching to see if he chose to pursue Ichante. Who knows—one of them might be so touched by his bravery in this regard that she would find herself falling for him.

And as we all know or have learned, this is often the way things in the world work best. If we could only be more patient, over time things can fall into place in a way we never would have imagined or in a way we would have never chosen ourselves. Almost as if someone is watching over us, taking care of all the endless details with such care and precision that it all works out just perfect in the end.

Kangee didn't know it, but Ichante would have never been well suited for him. He had no idea what was best for him. We often don't.

Well, that is the way things *could* have been if Kangee was not so bound by self-doubt. For when something is desired so much but at the same time so far out of reach, so unattainable ... there is seldom a happy ending.

It had been some time since a buffalo herd had come close enough to the tribe to make a hunt feasible, but one day this finally changed. A scout out on a day's journey had felt the whole ground tremble underneath him. There are few things in the animal kingdom as incredible and as powerful as a large herd of buffalo running at a full clip. There were millions of buffalo in the Great Plains hundreds of years ago, and there could be tens of thousands in any one herd. The Indian riders had to be careful to stay alongside the outer edges of the herd and not get lost in the haze of dirt that was kicked up by the herd as the buffalo ran.

It would be safer to pick some of the herd off from the back, but that was the very place it was hardest to see. And so most braves did their best to pick off a buffalo on the edges, but from time to time the herd would change direction and these boundaries would shift back and forth. You had to be careful or you could quickly be overcome by the herd, horse and all.

On this day, the hunt was a glorious one, and all the braves brought down at least one great buffalo for their family, and some two or three—all except for Takoda. About midway through the hunt, he was positioning himself to throw his spear right through the neck of a buffalo. This might not sound that difficult, but you have to remember the buffalo were all were running at full speed. If he missed, he would likely never use his precious spear again, for it would be trampled to bits by the herd.

Just as Takoda rose to throw his spear, another buffalo just behind the one in his sights stumbled in a small divot in the ground. It lurched forward and to one side before regaining its balance, but not before it bumped into the side of Takoda's horse. The horse mostly absorbed the impact and also managed not to fall. But this all happened at the very moment Takoda had risen to his highest point and was least secure on his horse, his spear high above his head, his torso twisted to gain as much leverage as he could. The impact caught him by surprise and threw him to the ground.

It is a traumatic thing to fall off a horse when it is running at full speed. Fortunately, Takoda was thrown away from the herd and fell just outside their path. He was stunned for five or ten seconds but had presence of mind enough to know he had to get up immediately and get farther out of the way. Just as he took his first few steps, one of his legs gave way, and he fell back to the ground. The leg was not broken but had been severely bruised in the fall and suddenly cramped up.

As fate would have it, Kangee was not far behind in the chase and, within a few more seconds, noticed Takoda on the ground about fifty yards ahead of him. A brave's duty was to protect his brother's life as his own. For a moment, Kangee was resolute in purpose, just as he had always been taught. But then another thought came into his mind, a foreign thought, a wicked thought. On this day, most of the braves were riding along the other side of the herd, more than a hundred yards away. There were only a few braves on this side of the herd, and the others were farther ahead, all except Takoda and Kangee. And much of the hunt was concealed in all the dust in the air.

What if he pretended he had not seen Takoda? What if he turned his head toward the herd and veered off to pursue another buffalo? What were the chances the herd might continue to drift back and forth and just so happen to trample Takoda where he lay? No one would ever know the difference.

It is a remarkable thing how much can go on so quickly in our minds and hearts at just one moment in time, often beyond our awareness. It all seemed to fit together too perfectly in Kangee's heart. He had never fully recovered from the loss of his father to a herd in full flight just like this one. His father, whose death had been the last in a number of insults that had kept Kangee off balance most of his life. What kind of eternal math was in play here? One herd years ago that had taken a life and hurt him so deeply . . . and another herd today that could take another, but a loss that would be a gain to him, that would erase his greatest adversary, the one person keeping him from his greatest happiness? Could fate finally be leaning in his favor?

As Takoda tried to get back up, his head turned in the direction from which he had come. He saw Kangee. Their eyes locked for a second. The air had been hazy, but right at that moment, and just for a moment, it cleared. And Takoda's heart sank as he saw Kangee turn his head back toward the herd and then turn his horse as well.

Nothing in Takoda wanted to believe this was possible, that any brave would so forsake his duty. He could only surmise that Kangee was just that selfish and didn't want to be distracted from the hunt. Or worse, he was a coward and afraid that he might be hurt or killed in doing his duty, in getting off his horse to help Takoda to safety while the herd was still running a few paces away. There was clearly a risk in helping Takoda, but a brave's duty was clear and his honor greater than all. But Takoda had no time to waste in thinking about this now. He was able to stand, and dragging his bad leg with him, he made it to safety.

Before long the hunt was over. The women and children caught up with the braves and the buffalo they had killed, and everyone celebrated but also started the work of dismantling the great beasts part by part. Takoda had been massaging his leg over and over. It responded, and he was able to walk. He was angry but had always been wise beyond his years and found enough self-control to not say anything to anybody. He did not want to act rashly, although he was sure of what he had seen. He needed more time to think this through. His actions needed to be measured and prudent, as a brave could be exiled from the tribe for such a thing. And that would be equal to a death sentence, for no one could survive for long in the Great Plains by themselves, not in those days. You wouldn't wish such a fate on your worst enemy.

Takoda's pride was hurt some by the fact he did not make a kill, but he was not married and did not have a family to provide for. There were many others generous enough to allow him to come alongside and benefit from their kills. After he explained how he had fallen, everyone was happy he was okay, for they all knew he could have been killed.

Takoda purposely avoided Kangee; it would be difficult to hide his feelings completely. He did notice, however, that Kangee was often nearby and seemed to be watching him. Takoda wondered if he was worried. He should have been. But after a few days passed and Takoda had not confronted him or talked about the incident with anybody else, Kangee drifted into the background. He must have concluded he was in the clear.

Takoda considered going to the holy men and the chief to ask their advice, but if they felt the situation was serious enough, they could take action on their own. He did not want that. He respected their judgment, and truly he always deferred to them, but something deeper in his heart told him to remain silent for now. Takoda would spend some time alone to work it out in his mind.

From time to time, a brave could go off by himself for several days for a little sabbatical, for lack of a better term. It could be because of a great loss, a death, or any big decision that had to be made. Takoda had to ask for the permission of the elders and let them know his destination in case he did not return at the appointed time. Takoda told them that all was not at peace in his heart over his fall during the hunt, which was true, and that he needed some time to put it behind him. The elders simply thought his pride was still hurt, which was understandable and exactly what Takoda wanted them to think. They bid him farewell and expected to see him back in three days.

Takoda had traveled over large expanses of the plains, several hundred miles in distance from east to west and almost as far from north to south. There was one little place about half a day away to the southwest that he loved. Takoda would first come to a small tributary of a river, which softly bent back and forth as it coursed its way through the plain. As he followed it upstream back to its source, he would climb through some hills. Eventually he would come to a large meadow, which in wetter years would serve as a floodplain. The ground there was fertile, the grass stayed green most of the year, and many varieties of trees grew and thrived. A nice breeze blew through this little valley and rustled the leaves of the trees, a novel sound in that part of the country.

And Takoda loved the sound of the water rushing over the rocks in the stream. As a matter of fact, he never felt more alive and at peace and connected to all of life than when he lay on the bank of this stream. Feeling the sun on his face; hearing the breeze in the leaves and feeling it move across his skin; listening to the multitude of sounds coming from the stream all blended together in one great voice; taking in the smell of the water and the earthen banks; and allowing his eyes to experience the great range of colors—from the browns and brilliant greens of the landscape to the dark blues and blacks of the water to the breathtaking blues of the sky and the soft whites of the clouds. *My, oh my*, he thought. *The Creator had one glorious day when he made all of this.* It was a perfect summer day, and Takoda allowed himself the luxury of enjoying it all on his first day.

On the morning of his second day, he permitted his thoughts to run deeper. How could he understand what had happened during the buffalo hunt? He tried to put himself in Kangee's place. It was hard. He had never understood this man. He was so quiet and so odd. He had tried to reach out to him in the past, many times.

From time to time, Kangee would respond to his graciousness, and they would have a more normal conversation. But they had never made a lasting connection, never formed a friendship. Kangee seemed unable to take Takoda's kind words and gestures and use them to build a foundation from which something more substantial could grow. And everyone else in the tribe had the same experience. Kangee did not have a real friendship with anyone, and everyone had come to expect very little from him, for he had never given any more.

What could have gone through Kangee's mind during the hunt? Takoda wanted to give Kangee every benefit of the doubt, and so even though he did not want to, he took some time to recall everything that had happened that day, to consider if there was any way Kangee might not have seen him lying on the ground. When Takoda had first seen Kangee, he'd been fifty-odd yards away. But it was one of those moments you didn't easily forget, one of those moments that is so surreal that time seemed to come to a stop. Takoda wondered why.

Was it that he knew in his heart those seconds lying there on the ground could have been his very last in this world? That made sense. But it felt like there was more. Takoda closed his eyes and asked for the Great Spirit to take him back to that moment and help him see the truth. There was a sudden silence in the trees for ten or fifteen seconds, and then the breeze blew again. Takoda felt resolute. He knew in his heart Kangee had seen him and had purposely left him to fend for himself. But why?

Kangee *was* different. There was no doubt about that. Could he have been so taken up in the hunt, so insensitive to everything else, to *everyone* else, that somehow it did not occur to him that Takoda was in danger? This was how self-absorbed he was most of the time. No one ever expected Kangee to be the first one to extend a helping hand or to share an encouraging word. There had been many times a situation would warrant he do this or that for someone, but he rarely did.

And truly, everyone felt sorry for him, for the loss of his mother when he was just six years old and for that lost expression that had been fixed on his face for years afterward. He could have thrived as part of his uncle and aunt's family, but somehow never did. And no one knew just how much the death of his father impacted him, for Kangee never spoke of it to anyone and by then was becoming a young man and better at hiding the things in his mind and heart.

As hard as he tried, as much as Takoda wanted there to be some reasonable explanation for what had happened on the plain that day—something that would excuse Kangee from being guilty of a much greater, deliberate, and malicious act—he could not come up with anything. Kangee lacked the compassion he should have as a man, but he had still been taught all the same things as the rest of them. Everything remaining equal, he would want to do what duty required. He would want to avoid the shame of falling short of his calling as a brave. He was not crazy or mad—there was no evidence of that. And so there had to be something else, some specific motive, something powerful enough to cause him to risk the shame of forsaking his duty. But what?

Takoda enjoyed watching the stars that evening as he kept warm by his little fire, but as he drifted off to sleep, he was still troubled. That night he had many dreams, some good and some bad. As he woke in the morning, however, one dream was particularly clear. A dream about a badger and a snake.

Badgers were common in the plains and known to be about as vicious an animal as the Creator had ever made. They preyed on many smaller animals but were the particular nemesis of rattle-snakes. But in Takoda's dream, the badger was not vicious at all, just out on a stroll, enjoying the day. As the badger walked by a boulder, he surprised a rattlesnake lying on the ground just behind it.

The rattlesnake immediately struck out, trying to bite him, but badgers are quick, and he jumped back out of the way.

"Well, my, my," the badger exclaimed. "Here I am, out on a stroll on a beautiful summer day, minding my own business, not meaning you any harm. I didn't even know you were lying there behind that boulder, and you didn't even greet me or ask my business but just tried to bite me with those nasty, poisonous teeth of yours! That wasn't nice! No, it wasn't nice at all."

Now, Takoda thought the dream was odd, for in real life it was always the badger who was the predator with the worst of intentions. And not many people feel sorry for rattlesnakes, but if you have ever seen what a badger will do to one of them, you just might. In his dream, it was the badger who was nice and unassuming, a gentleman even. The snake was the aggressor who did not hesitate to strike out.

As his dream continued, the snake snapped, "Oh, don't you give me that! You want me to feel sorry for *you*? You are ten times bigger than me and have teeth that might not be poisonous but are much bigger and longer than mine. How am I supposed to know you mean me no harm? If I wait to find out, it might be too late!"

"Well, I have to say I can see the logic in that," the badger replied. "I am a very nice badger, but you have no way of knowing that. As a matter of fact, all the other badgers think I am too nice; many of them will have nothing to do with me. They think I give badgers a bad name. They also think I will go hungry. But they are wrong about all of that. I try to be a friend to everyone I meet. But you have no way of knowing that, for you have never met me. But now that you have, if we ever happen to come across each other again, you will know that I mean you no harm. And maybe, just maybe, we could be friends."

"Well, I don't know about that," the snake replied. "Then it would be all the rattlesnakes that were doing the talking, about me, if they knew I had made friends with a badger. But I do believe you, and I am happy you do not want to eat *me*. Maybe we will see each other again one day."

And right then, with those last words still echoing in Takoda's mind, he awoke from his sleep. He had to laugh about it. It made him think of stories from his childhood, the kind adults love to tell that are so often about animals who talk like people do. And he thought, *Dreams can be so strange. Where do they come from, and who makes them up?*

He made a fire to warm himself from the chill of the morning air, and as he did, he remembered again why he had come to this place and hoped that today would be more fruitful than yesterday. The conversation between the badger and the snake came back into his mind. And as it did, he had the oddest feeling, one of those feelings you can't put into words. You don't why, but something deeper down inside of you says you need to be paying attention, for you just might be getting ready to hear something important. *Could there be something more to this dream?* Takoda wondered. *If so, what could it be?*

As the fire burned and he warmed his hands and feet, Takoda let his mind drift. He thought of badgers and remembered the times he had seen them. He had never seen one kill anything but had heard many stories. And he also thought of snakes and even rattlesnakes, and all of the sudden, he remembered the time when he had almost stepped on one and his mother had killed it. He remembered being sad she had killed the snake but also that he felt very loved after she had explained why. "You are too important to me," she had said, for she was worried the snake might harm him.

And then Takoda remembered the thing his mother had said

that surprised him. The snake was not mean, like he had thought. "It was scared." And he realized this was identical to what the snake in his dream had said, the reason he gave for striking out first. And Takoda was transported back to the plain where the hunt occurred. He saw Kangee's face again, right when their eyes met. *He was scared*, Takoda thought. "But scared of what? I was the one in danger, not him."

Takoda made himself something to eat for breakfast and then took a walk along the bank of the stream. He continued to let his mind wander in the hope that all of this would make more sense. Maybe the Great Spirit would speak to his heart. Just before lunch, he was returning to his camp, and a conversation he had had with one of his better friends came to mind.

His friend had just married and was teasing him about Ichante. "When are you going to make your intentions known to her father? Everyone can tell how much you love her, how sweetly you talk to her, and how much your face lights up every time you see her."

"Is it that obvious?" Takoda had asked, blushing.

"Yes, it is. To everyone."

And with those last words, Takoda thought, *To everyone? Even to Kangee?* And he never would understand it, understand why he just so happened to have the very next thought, but he did. *What if Kangee is interested in her too?* Passion is a great motive, maybe the greatest of all. Could this be why Kangee abandoned him on the plain? Could this be the answer he had been searching for?

Takoda wanted to be patient and not rush to conclusions; if there was something else important, he wanted to know it. He gave himself the rest of that day and stayed for the evening just as he had planned but had no further insights. He woke the next morning, made himself some fish from the stream for breakfast, and then headed back home.

The plains were something to behold in early summer, with the grass so tall and full and golden yellow. He was still angry about what had happened on the plain—he had to be, if he were honest with himself—but fortunately, there had been no tragedy. He was so grateful for the disposition he had been born with. He truly was a "friend to all" and had always wanted to be.

He recalled his dream again and thought about the hard and cold fact that the animal kingdom is not a kind place. Many animals have to be incredibly vigilant just to survive from one day to the next. Their life is often a story of predators and prey, fear and death. *There has to be a better story than that,* Takoda thought.

And people liked to think they were so very different from their more primitive cousins, but Takoda knew better. Humans are capable of the same kind of brutality, even worse and on a much larger scale. Takoda wanted to know the whole truth of what happened that day during the hunt, and his thoughts ran deeper. And as they did, he realized his dream was not only about Kangee but about himself. The dream was not only about why the snake had struck out but, even more, why the badger *had not.*

"Why did I not see it until now?" Takoda said out loud.

He could speak to the elders and let justice take its course, and no one in the tribe would think ill of him. But how much of this might also be driven by his desire for revenge? And in that moment, the Great Spirit allowed Takoda to see his own heart more clearly than he ever had in his whole life. He still had great difficulty imagining what it would be like to be Kangee, to do what he had done that day on the plain. But he knew there was evil in his own heart as well—it just might take something more to cause it to rise to the surface. The badger in his dream could have killed the snake, and no one would have faulted him, but he spoke to the snake instead, to try to make friends with him, and in so doing forgave the snake for striking out before the snake had ever asked to be forgiven. With all this clear in his mind, Takoda knew exactly what he needed to do and exactly how to do it.

It would be a gross understatement to say that Kangee was surprised by their conversation later that day after Takoda returned to the village. His face went white when Takoda asked him if he had feelings for Ichante. But Takoda just continued on. He did not even give Kangee the time to speak. He told him he believed he knew the truth of what happened during the hunt, that Kangee had seen him on the ground but then decided to abandon him. Kangee's face turned even more pale.

And then Takoda said, "I have no desire to ever speak about this again. I have not mentioned it to anyone else, and I have no intention of ever doing so, especially to the elders, not even to Ichante. I am not holding this against you, and I am not angry about it anymore. I am deciding to act as if it never happened, and I am hoping you will do the same. I will never understand it, but that is okay. I completely forgive you. If you ever want to say more about it, I will listen, but if you don't, that is okay as well. Most importantly, I hope we can be friends, even very good friends. Maybe, just maybe, this is why all of this happened. Maybe it was the Great Spirit's way of bringing you and me together as brothers, as real brothers."

Kangee struggled to hide it but could not. Tears filled his eyes and then flowed down his cheeks. He did not say anything. He simply nodded in affirmation to Takoda, turned, and went on his way.

And guess what? It took Kangee a while, for it had always taken him a while for everything. But as the days and weeks went by and Takoda behaved exactly the way he had said he would, Kangee came to believe it. For the first time in his life, Kangee felt a longing in his heart to be the best brother he could to another brave. And everyone else in the tribe was amazed as well, for they never knew why or what on earth could have happened to change Kangee, but something clearly had. And for the rest of their days on those beautiful and expansive plains, Takoda and Kangee were the very best of friends.

Endnotes

1 "Mitakuye Oyasin" means "we are all related" and is a Lakota phrase that reflects interconnectedness, according to Mary Black Bonnet, an enrolled member of the Sicangu Lakota Nation, "Mitakuye Oyasin—We Are All connected Star Stuff," JamesMilson.com, https://jamesmilson.com/about-the-blog/mitakuye-oyasin-we-are-all-related-by-mary-black-bonnet/. The prayer is found all over online but is not attributed to an author.

Nowhere Man

(For Alex)

Once upon a time, there was a blind man.

He believed he had been blind from birth, for he had no memories of ever being able to see or any real conception of sight as you and I know it. He grew up in a large urban orphanage, and his earliest memories were in that place. He could not remember anyone ever telling him how he came to the orphanage, so when he was older, he believed he must have been left there at birth, or soon after, by his mother. For one reason or another, she was not able to care for him.

He did live his later childhood years in a home for blind children, where he at least learned some practical skills. He had been out on his own in the world since he was eighteen, when by law he was required to leave the second institution. You probably haven't ever thought of this, because I never had, but orphanages have the unusual responsibility of naming an infant who has been abandoned on their doorstep.

Our little man was given the name George Thomas, a name he never particularly cared for but not something he ever questioned. He had many other things on his mind, growing up as he did, and it never occurred to him until just before his eighteenth "birthday" (something else given to him) that his name was not a *real* name like yours or mine, given to him by his real parents, and given with an inherent blessing. As a young adult, he finally dispensed with the name "George" and began to go by the name "Nowhere Man," refusing to be addressed any other way. A little odd, I know. But if you knew him better, you might not think so.

In the city where Nowhere Man lived, he had come to be fairly well known. To most regular folks, he appeared no different or better than the rest of the homeless people. He spent most of his time on the street, dressed poorly, and was clearly blind, carrying a long white cane with a red tip. If you observed closely, however, Nowhere Man seemed to be quite familiar with his surroundings. He would hold out his cane as he walked, which alerted others to the fact he was not walking as rapidly and should not be expected to react as quickly either. But his cane rarely touched anything, which you would think was its whole purpose.

They say that people who lose one sense, or have never had it, develop their other senses to compensate. Maybe this was why Nowhere Man seemed to know just where he was walking so much of the time, even in the midst of the city with all the pedestrians and cars and intersections. The other homeless people and the police assumed he was homeless, although no one could ever remember seeing him bed down for the night on a sidewalk, or in an alcove, or down an alley, or in a shelter like the rest of the homeless people.

But each and every day, he would be on the streets again, just like all the rest of them. He never begged either, which many of the homeless did without shame and sometimes took in so much they should be paying taxes. No one else knew this, but Nowhere Man could have been receiving a monthly disability check from the government for the rest of his life, but he did not because he refused to use his legal name. No one knew who Nowhere Man was, not even the government. He must have had some other source to draw on, for he never seemed hungry or weak or fatigued.

The homeless people who knew Nowhere Man considered him somewhat of a sage. The more disturbed individuals were a bit afraid of him. Not so afraid they would go out of their way to avoid him or refuse to talk to him, but they were more self-conscious when around him—kind of like some of us when we are around a policeman.

From time to time, you would see Nowhere Man talking with someone, either walking with them or sitting with them on a bench in the park. Sometimes he would chat at length, but usually it was the other way around—the other person did most of the talking. After observing him for a while, you might wonder if he had a counseling practice of sorts, although he never asked for a fee. He drew people to him in this way, but usually one at a time.

At other times, you might find him sitting in the shade with a group of others, but he usually said little unless spoken to.

If you think about it, if Nowhere Man was a counselor, he chose a good place to locate his practice. Any of us can have problems. All of us have more than we will ever admit. But the people on the street are often the worst of the worst. Some of them came from nothing, got used to nothing, and believe they will always be nothing. Some have stories to tell that will do more than break your heart. Their hearts have been so shattered, broken into so many pieces, that it reminds me of Humpty Dumpty. You have to wonder if they could ever put all the pieces back together again. But this was Nowhere Man's business. He was a cardiologist of sorts, a heart man.

The homeless situation in this country has clearly become a greater problem. Current numbers put the homeless in the US at roughly half a million people. Most live in the cities, where it's easier to ask for spare change, find something to eat, and find a shelter to sleep in at night. Some believe that a major policy change at the federal level regarding the treatment of the chronically mentally ill in the 1970s is one of the reasons the homeless population exploded around that time. This policy led to a reduction of the populations in many long-term facilities, based on the belief these folks would have more meaningful lives if they lived in a real community. But this assumed they could adequately be treated as outpatients in those communities or live in halfway residential programs.

And those assumptions sprang from the more basic assumption these individuals could live relatively independent lives, which for the most part was not true and the reason most of them were in long-term institutions to begin with. It may have been a noble vision, but it was at best unrealistic, and at worst, irresponsible. A more sinister view is that the policymakers in our government were tired of paying the much-higher cost of running these long-term facilities and were determined to find a way to empty them, even if that required embarking on an unproven strategy.

No one had ever wanted to assume that a person who had developed more severe emotional or psychiatric symptoms would not get better. Everyone hoped they would. Only after years of protracted illness, or at least interminable reoccurrences of severe symptoms, did a person ever get a chronic diagnosis. Long-term institutions were rarely a good place for anyone, but being discharged and sent back to the real world was an even worse idea. Many of these people could not care for themselves or hold down a job and, at the very least, needed a caseworker to make sure their basic needs were met. But that would also cost a lot of money.

And in the last several decades, there has also been a new type of homeless person—people who fell into a terrible financial position and found themselves living out of their cars. It would seem this became a phenomenon for the first time in a new age of credit, in which lending institutions were willing to lend large amounts of money to people who were not the best risks. But our culture had more and more filled their heads with the lie that they would never be happy without a new car and a new house. Many of us would now cite the significant homeless problem in this country as one of the more painful reminders this world is definitely broken, but we are not sure, at all, what to do to fix it. It is particularly ironic that in this country such homelessness coexists with the most affluent population that has ever lived on earth.

And so, you see, there may have not been a better place to set up a counseling practice than exactly where Nowhere Man set up his. He did not take appointments ahead of time—first come, first serve—and appointments could always last as long as they needed. You never knew how long it might take to talk someone off a ledge. At any point in time, he would have several regular customers. Most recently one of these was an elderly woman who had been homeless longer than she could remember.

That was actually her main problem, her memory. She had dementia and severe short-term memory loss as a result. Most of us have never thought about just how dependent we are on short-term memory to function. This becomes obvious when a person begins to lose it and has trouble completing tasks because they forget what they are doing right in the middle of it and find themselves staring off into space. We don't realize how almost everything we do is sequential, how almost everything has a beginning, a middle, and an end, even this little story. And since dementia always progresses, at some point the person loses track of who they are—for our sense of ourselves, our very identity, exists in time and over time as well.

This lady's name was Mary, and her story was a sad one. She ended up homeless and forgotten because there was no one left in her family who cared enough to stay in touch and make sure she was okay. Her husband and one of her two children were dead. She had no grandchildren. And her other child, a son, was so irresponsible that he'd decided it was easier to pretend his mother was no longer living than to try to see to her needs from two thousand miles away. There were no other relatives who cared enough to ever check on her. How pitiful is that?

Mary could remember much of her childhood and other past experiences but for whatever reason could not remember any of her family. Sometimes God is gracious in the midst of our greatest storms. Much of the time Mary spent with Nowhere Man was used to help her remember who she was, that her name was "Mary," and that her life was there on the street, plus reminding her of the people she knew in the present. Nowhere Man knew that just reminding Mary in that moment would not make Mary's memory better—in fact, her memory would continue to worsen. Deep in her heart, Mary knew this too. It was just too terrifying to consider. What Mary really needed was time with a loving friend, the reassurance there would be people there to assist her when she needed it, and more than anything, that someone else was looking after her, someone who could do the job.

"He is, you know," Nowhere Man said to her, over and over. "He's watching over you, even right now."

"I know. I know He is," she replied. "I just love to hear you say it," she added. "And you know, I am thinking this might be the last time I see you. I am thinking He is going to take me away very soon. All of this struggle . . . will finally be over."

"You might be right about that," Nowhere Man replied.

And Mary leaned a little closer and whispered something in his ear. Nowhere Man smiled. She gave him a big hug and didn't let go for some time.

"Thank you for all you have done for me. I can't remember much of it, but I know you have done a lot. I don't know what I would have done without you here to help me."

"You are very welcome. That is why I am here." And they parted.

Mary was right. Later that night, she calmly went in her sleep, all wrapped up in several blankets inside some large cardboard boxes that another homeless man had, some months earlier, put together for her using duct tape. That same homeless man would check on her every morning and throughout the day. He found her that morning with the most peaceful look on her face.

Nowhere Man heard the ambulance arrive with its sirens blazing and stood there as it quietly pulled away. He raised his head as if looking up into the sky, although you and I know he couldn't see anything.

"You give her a very special place, okay? I'm not kidding! And *thank You* for letting me know her. I will miss her."

"Who are you talking to?" asked a short, disheveled, frightened man who came up from behind Nowhere Man.

"I don't think I have ever met you, have I?" Nowhere Man replied.

"No. You haven't. I have just been in this section of town for the last couple of days. Came from across the river, heard that things might be a little better over here."

Nowhere Man could hear the man trembling as he spoke, not an uncommon thing for homeless people. Sometimes it was the result of chronic malnutrition, but it was also not uncommon with schizophrenia.

"You hear voices, do you not?" Nowhere Man said out of the blue.

"How . . . how . . . did you know that?" the man said, barely able to respond.

"I can't really tell you how I know that. I just do."

"You can't see, can you?"

"No, I can't. Never have."

"Never?"

"No, never."

"Are you some kind of . . . *spiritual* man?"

"Well, I am not really sure what you mean by the word 'spiritual.' People use that word freely these days."

"Can you tell the future?"

"It depends, but usually not."

"Then what *can* you do?"

"I can do all sorts of things. What is it that you *truly* need?" And with those words the man stared at him in disbelief. Within a matter of seconds, his facial expression vacillated from being contorted, because he was so terrified, to more relaxed, like he was thinking but curious, back to contorted.

"Do not worry," Nowhere Man said. "I will not harm you. I am only here to help."

"Okay . . . I hope so," the man replied. "My name is Daniel."

"Daniel is a strong name. Very strong." Ever so slightly, Daniel smiled from one side of his mouth. The bond had been made.

Many doctors in mental health facilities will spend weeks and even months with people like Daniel and not be able to make the connection that Nowhere Man made with him in these few short minutes. It takes a sort of magic to break through the thick walls a person like Daniel has had to construct. They are so terrified of what might get in but even more terrified of what might get out. But Nowhere Man found a way.

"You can call me Nowhere Man," he said to Daniel.

"Nowhere Man? Like the song? You're kidding, right?"

"No. I would never kid about something as sacred as a person's name."

Daniel and Nowhere Man walked for the rest of that morning around the five-block area that was their home. Nowhere Man pointed out various people and things to Daniel: the store owners who were more tolerant, the ones who were less tolerant, the ones who were kind, and the ones who were cruel.

There was one storeowner who had actually beaten two homeless men to death behind his store in the alley, each on a different occasion. No one knew who was to blame for these murders. No one except Nowhere Man. The men were beaten so badly, it was obvious they were murdered.

"Stay away from *that* man," Nowhere Man said, holding up his stick and pointing at the store owner across the street, who was arranging his wares on the sidewalk.

"That man there?" And as soon as Daniel said this, he realized his error, that Nowhere Man could not see like he could. But then he was even more confused.

"How do you know that there is a man standing over there? And how do you know that is the same man you are wanting to tell me about?"

"Well, I can't tell you that. For I don't really know myself. But I am right, am I not? There is a man standing over there. It looks like he works at the store that is right there, for he's rearranging some things sitting out on the sidewalk, and he's very overweight with a full head of black hair."

"Well . . . yes. Exactly that," Daniel replied.

"*Stay away* from him and from his store."

"I will," Daniel said, staring at Nowhere Man.

It was not uncommon for Nowhere Man to conduct orientations like this with newcomers. Most everyone appreciated the time he took to show them the ropes. Most would not continue to speak with him much after that, but a few would. Sometimes a person is ready to hear more, but usually they are not. Sometimes a person knows they need help desperately, but usually they do not. And it takes a particular type of person to have the faith or to be open to the possibility that someone like Nowhere Man could be a help to them, that someone who is blind and homeless and insisted on the name "Nowhere Man" could offer *anything* to someone else. But irony and truth have much more in common than many people think.

There was another homeless man who was different than all the rest. He had been homeless for about eighteen months, though he'd worked at some pretty good jobs at different times in his life. But his life had gradually unwound over the last several years. And then he lost everything. He had never been close with his family, was too proud to ask for help, and did not have any other support system. He lived out of his car for a good while and was determined not to associate with any "homeless" people because he was clearly not one of *them*. His car finally stopped running. For a while he still slept in it, but eventually he left it behind to live on the street.

His name was Saul, a good Jewish name. In looking back at his life, nothing obvious would explain how he started out as a privileged kid in a Philadelphia suburb, the son of a successful accountant, and yet ended up homeless. A multitude of things contributed over a period of time that built and built to the point they would not be denied. Saul, on the other hand, insisted it was all just "bad luck." He'd had bad luck his whole life, as a matter of fact. If you ever wanted a word of encouragement or a little lift to help you along your way, Saul was not the guy. But he would be more than happy to bring you down to his way of seeing things.

Nowhere Man had had his "eye" on Saul for some time. It would not be that enjoyable an assignment, but this was not for him to decide. The first challenge would be to get Saul to talk to him for more than a simple hello and goodbye. Nowhere Man made an effort to be close to Saul so they might have the occasion to speak but made it look coincidental. One time there was a group of men from a church who were giving out breakfast on a Sunday morning, right next to a park where there were benches and other comfortable places on the grass to sit. One of the pastors gave a little sermon while everyone was eating. Nowhere Man sat down on the grass next to Saul. He had asked another man if there was any room on the lawn there for him to sit, and this man helped him get situated.

The pastor had not yet started talking, and some of the others were talking among themselves, but it was fairly quiet. Many of the homeless people there that morning were familiar with each other, but this was not a normal social gathering. They did not talk as much as other people.

Nowhere Man turned his head toward Saul and said, "Your name is Saul, is it not?"

"How did you know my name? Or that I was sitting next to you when you *can't see*?" Tact had never been Saul's thing.

"I heard your voice when you spoke to the man next to you a few minutes ago. We met some time ago on the street. I have a good memory for voices. You have to when you're blind."

"Well, that's quite impressive nevertheless."

"Saul is a powerful name. It means one who asks or inquires of God's guidance. We *all* could use that."

"Well, maybe *you*, but not me. I don't believe in God . . . at all. And I have no problem with saying it right out loud."

"I can see that quite clearly," Nowhere Man replied with an easy smile and no offense.

"They call you . . . *Nowhere Man*? Is that right?"

"It sure is."

"Well, that's got to be the strangest name I've ever heard. Are you crazy? Have you always been? A lot of these people are, you know."

"Yeah, you're right. A lot of them are. But *you* aren't, are you?"

"You never know—I just might be crazy as hell. I just might ..." Saul was going to say more, something more sarcastic, maybe even violent. But then something told him not to. Even he had a little sympathy for a blind man. He thought for another moment and then began again, "How do you know I'm *not* crazy? Some of these people are pretty good at pretending."

"Oh, I just know you aren't. You've done a lot of things in your life, a lot of different things. Most of these people have never been able to do much of anything. Not always their fault. That is just how things have been for them."

"How do you know *what* I've done? You don't know anything about me."

"You can tell a lot from a voice, more than most people think," Nowhere Man replied. "I can tell that you're very bright, that you had a good education. I can tell that you can be a good leader, at least when you want to be. You have good ideas, and you can be self-confident, although that has sometimes led you astray."

"Who the hell do you think you are? Maybe you *are* crazy. You sound like some kind of astrologist, and a bad one at that." Nowhere Man's words had struck a chord with Saul, just as intended, but Saul was always the last one to know this.

Nowhere Man did not want to say anything further—he did not want to scare Saul off. He had wanted to say just enough to prompt Saul's curiosity, and he had done that.

The greater truth was that Saul's "self-confidence" had *always* led him astray. Nowhere Man had a way of saying this that didn't come across as that profound, but it was. Saul didn't say too much more to Nowhere Man that day. All the egg sandwiches were eaten before long, the pastor gave his fifteen minute message, and everyone departed. But it was a beginning. A good beginning.

Several weeks later, Nowhere Man was walking down the street, and Saul was just about to pass him going the other way.

"Hello, Saul," he said just before they passed.

Saul stopped dead in his tracks. "How in the hell did you know it was me?" he yelled.

"Your footsteps," Nowhere Man replied.

"My footsteps?"

"Yes, your footsteps. Everyone has a different gait. The noises that people make when they walk are very different. You probably don't pay attention to that, but I do. And the shoes they are wearing make a difference too."

Saul just stood there and looked at Nowhere Man, not knowing what to say.

"Where are you headed?" Nowhere Man asked.

"Nowhere, really." Saul realized what he had said and had to add, "Just like you, I'm headed *nowhere*."

"Well, do you mind if we head nowhere . . . together?" Nowhere Man asked.

Saul smiled. At least this guy didn't seem to take himself too seriously.

"The weather is still pleasant this morning. It would be nice to walk a bit," Nowhere Man added. "You could help me find my way too."

"I don't know about that—you seem to do just fine. But yes, we can walk for a while."

Nowhere Man turned to walk with Saul.

Saul walked a little slower than normal to stay abreast of Nowhere Man as they made their way down the street. The sidewalks are wide in the city, but there are also a lot of pedestrians on them. Many people moving toward them could see Nowhere Man coming, with his white cane out. Most people stay to the right, but some in the middle go both ways, zigging and zagging. A couple of times, Saul would start to reach out to grab Nowhere Man's arm to keep him from running into someone, but just before he did, Nowhere Man would step to the right or left and avoid them. He started to say something about this but decided not to. Maybe his hearing was just that good, but it was still a little uncanny. It was almost as if he could *feel* the people around him.

"Where do you want to go, Saul?"

"What do you mean, where do I want to go? You were the one

who asked if we could take a walk."

"No, I meant, where do you *really* want to go, besides living here on the streets? Where do you want to be, say, a year from now?" Nowhere Man had broken one of the most sacred rules on the street. No one asked questions like these. No one talked like most people do, people who still had dreams, who still had hopes, who still believed they could actually make something happen in their lives. No one questioned why you were here on the streets, why you weren't somewhere else having a real life. It was just too painful, but even more, there was no point to it. Everyone on the street, at least in their minds, had run out of options. *That* was why they were here. There was no other place to be or any way to get there.

Or maybe it could be said this way. There *were* other options for some of these people, maybe even most of them. But there were no simple solutions. It was a grave insult to suggest that any of the homeless were on the street because they had chosen to be or refused to choose something else. And there was little point in looking back at their past, thinking that something easy could be learned from the errors they might find there that needed to be avoided going forward. Far too much had gone wrong back then, and it was all too convoluted to draw much guidance from it now.

To find and keep a good life, a better life, would take more than perseverance. It would take a good plan and the ability to stay the course through a great deal of difficulty, plus an unbelievable amount of patience and humility and, maybe most of all, others who would lend a strong and helping hand, now and for some time to come. And let's not leave out the merciful and compassionate grace of God. It was possible. It was just hard to see.

Everything we just said and more ran through Saul's heart and mind in just a moment as he was trying to decide how to respond. He started to speak and then stopped. But then couldn't help himself.

"Is this what this is? A counseling session? Do you really think that anything you might say to me is going to make a difference? That you know anything that I do not?"

"I agree with you, Saul. I don't know anything you don't. Like I don't know why your mother started to struggle so much with life when you were just a child, and then one day when you came home from school, was gone. I just know, like you do, how much it broke your heart."

Saul was speechless. But for many long years, anger had been his first line of defense, and he almost struck Nowhere Man. I don't know if you have ever felt anger like that before. It rises up so quickly and is so violent that it can lash out before you even think. Somehow Saul didn't strike out. And for the first time, he wondered if he was in the presence of something else.

How could Nowhere Man know something like that, something that specific? Saul had never been so drawn toward someone yet so intensely repelled at the same moment. Not knowing what to do, he bailed. Without saying a word, he turned around and walked back the way they had come, leaving Nowhere Man to himself.

Nowhere Man had hoped for more, but Saul needed some time to think. That was fine. That was the way it needed to be.

We all have pivotal moments in our lives, many of them. Sometimes there is one moment, however, that creates such a disruption, is so earthshaking, like a geological event, it changes the very landscape on which we live. For Saul, this was one afternoon in November when he came home from school in sixth grade and his mother had deserted the family. He never saw or heard from her again. His father did an admirable job for himself and his three kids, extraordinary at times, but he was never quite the same either. She didn't even leave a note.

To this day, Saul would be a little tormented when the leaves first fell from the trees that time of the year. He was playfully walking through the leaves that had fallen in his front yard that afternoon. They were so thick he was kicking them up as he went, and his heart was particularly joyful as he opened the front door. He went in and called out his mother's name, just like he did every other afternoon when he got home from school.

He had been a little worried about her, as she had not been quite herself in recent months, but sixth graders only worry so much about the adults in their lives. They expect that things will always be all right because they always have. You don't need something like this to happen in your life to struggle with trusting others, but when something like this does happen, especially in regard to one of the two people you have relied on more than anyone else, the effect is always earthshaking.

Saul was the youngest of three children. In just another year or two after that eventful day, he was fine on his own until his father got home in the evenings, which seemed to get later and later with every passing year. They all turned inward, a natural reflex. His father tried to talk with Saul about the whole situation from the beginning. He tried to get Saul to express himself, just like he did with the other two. It was good that he tried, but very little came of it. It would have helped if any of them had known more.

Like, for instance, that his mother was no longer at home because she had become sick with some fatal disease and had died. Or she was no longer there because she had died in a car accident. Or anything else, which would have clearly implied that she never *wanted* to leave or intended to . . . it just happened. But none of that was the case. She *had* decided to leave, to leave *them*. Wherever she went, and why, she had chosen *it* over *them*.

Saul's father never said anything to any of them, but he, of course, wondered if she had run off with another man. More than anything, however, he tortured himself by rehashing all the events of the last several years leading up to that day. Had she been giving him any clues? Had he missed something he shouldn't have? But every time he went through this, he came up dry. And no one in the community ever said anything to make any more sense of it either. They all seemed just as surprised and never seemed to be hiding any information.

After a while, you finally stop limping and begin to walk again in your regular stride, but there is still a pain there that you are hiding. Saul was depressed for a few years, but he seemed to get tired of that, fed up, angry even, and was able to pull himself out of it, but not without becoming an arrogant ass. He tried to hide it just enough that it wouldn't come back to bite him, but he was an easy read. He did well in school and in business and eventually was a successful manager, a vice president even, just like Nowhere Man had said. Although privately, most of his reports did not like him. They didn't trust him. And guess what? He didn't trust them either.

Sometimes people can be very self-focused, and over a period of many years, they give the rest of the world reasons to fail them, but somehow it never does. And sometimes there are other self-focused people, and one day it catches up to them. One day something substantial happens, like a corporate takeover, for example, and that person could very much use someone to do them a favor, who wants to do so, but there is no one there because the person in need has never built those bridges. And most people recover from things like this. They have enough ability or talent or persuasiveness, or something finally falls their way, and they get through it. But some don't. For some, one misfortune cascades into another and another, and before you know it, you're living on the street. Saul never wanted to rely on another person again, so he didn't. And then he didn't have anyone to rely on when he needed someone the most.

A couple of days later, Saul saw Nowhere Man walking across the street. He had continued to go back and forth in his mind about their conversation, angry one moment, intrigued the next. Saul had never been a religious man, and he wouldn't have described some of his thoughts over the last few days as "religious," but they were. For the first time in his life, some part of him was willing to believe there could be a larger story, that Nowhere Man might be playing a part in this story, in *his* story, and that maybe, just maybe, there could be a good ending. Well, that was going a little too far. How about, at least, that there could be a better ending, better than Saul had been able to believe in for a long time.

Saul crossed the street and purposely walked ten or fifteen feet behind Nowhere Man. He wanted to say something to him but wasn't sure what. He wondered if Nowhere Man could already sense his presence, but that thought was absurd. And then he walked up beside him and said hello.

"Well, good morning, Nowhere Man."

"Well, good morning, Saul. I was hoping I would see you today. I wanted to make an apology."

"Oh, yeah? What for?"

"Well, you can probably tell by now that my methods can sometimes be quite provocative. That is not the intention. There is nothing gimmicky about it. I can't really explain to you how I decide what to say at any given point in time, but just that it is given to me. Given to me to give to you. I have come to believe that the timing is always perfect, but that doesn't always mean it is easy for me to say or easy for you to hear. Just that it is best. I hope that makes some sense."

"I understand, I think," Saul replied. "The bigger question is whether I believe it or not, whether or not I believe *you*," Saul added.

"I think you are right. Let me say a little more. Your mother was not well. She was not well at all when she left all of you. She didn't know it then, and she wouldn't know it for many years later, but she finally did. And when she finally realized how distorted her thinking had become and the enormity of what she had done to all your lives, and hers too, she just couldn't face it. She couldn't forgive herself. Several times she came close to contacting all of you, but it never happened. It is all very sad, for she died a miserable creature, very miserable indeed."

Nowhere Man hesitated a moment, wanting to give Saul a chance to end the conversation, but he gave no indication of this. And so he continued. "I am going to say something to you, and it will sound far too simplistic and even trite, but it is not. Please just receive it and let it settle into your soul over time. I believe it will do its magic if you just let it. It is this: It wasn't *your fault* that your mother left all of you back then. It wasn't your father's fault. Nor your brother's or your sister's. It was *hers*. And hers is not a simple story either—it never is—but that is the net of it. It was her fault. Allow her to bear that burden, and then do anything you have to do to forgive her. That is the path back. It sounds simple, but it is not. It will be hard, but it will be worth it. Everything else pivots on this. *Believe it.*"

For once in his life, Saul said nothing in return. He received it all. The cure had begun.

"Are you an angel?" Saul had to ask.

"Now, Saul, really? An angel? A homeless blind man?"

"Okay, I get it. I'll never get a real answer out of you."

And Nowhere Man just smiled and gave a little nod as they continued to walk together down that busy sidewalk.

A Most Unusual Proposition

*Therefore let us draw near with confidence
to the throne of grace, so that we may
receive mercy and find grace to help in time of need.*
Hebrews 4:16

*For everyone who does evil hates the Light, and does not come
to the Light for fear that his deeds will be exposed.*
John 3:20

Once upon a time, there was another world.

In this world, there were people who lived on the surface of the planet, a planet much like ours, with grass and trees, lakes and streams, and air to breathe. And the people lived in families much like ours, some in the country farming the land, and others in towns where rudimentary industries were springing up. It was a simpler time, more like the early eighteen hundreds had been in our world.

But there was something else different about this world. There was another race of people who lived below the ground, far down in caverns, some that were natural and others man made. Very little was known about this other civilization—as a matter of fact, most people who lived on the surface did not believe it existed and thought these stories were myths.

The few people who *did* believe this underground civilization existed had all kinds of theories about its origin. They had found artifacts they claimed had belonged to these creatures and even told stories of "sightings," although these had been few and far between. And some of this might sound familiar to you, like the talk about Big Foot or the Loch Ness Monster in our world. Without some conclusive evidence, it cannot be proven. Evidence, like a clear sighting in the middle of the day by a number of reliable witnesses, or the apprehension of one of these creatures for all to see and examine. Without any of that, the debate or myth, or whatever you want to call it, may continue on for forever.

Two things were clear, however. These cave dwellers, if they really existed, were obviously private and secretive and did not want to be discovered, or they would have made themselves known long ago. And the people who lived on the planet's surface did not have any real desire to solve this mystery, for if they had, they would have gone down into the earth to see if they could find them. But nothing like that had ever been attempted.

There was a great uneasiness among the surface people about the possible existence of these other creatures down below, not a whole lot different than the way little children in our world feel about the monsters that might possibly be under their beds at night. The best they can usually do is to be still and try to disappear under their covers. They almost never find the courage to lean down and look to discover the truth for themselves. And so it was rare this subject would even come up in conversation, as there were only a few odd souls who would ever bring it up, and most everyone else was accomplished at changing the subject. But I will tell you this. Actually, I have told you already. There really was another civilization of people who lived below the ground.

It is hard to imagine two more different places. One, just like the world you have always known with vast continents of dry land and even greater seas. There is a great rhythm, like a divine breath that exhales every morning as the magnificent sun rises and rules and brings so much to life, and then inhales every evening as the lesser moon and the expanse of stars take over the sky while most of the world sleeps. Breathes out. And breathes in. Over and over again, each and every day, for centuries without end.

And there is the texture and smell of the good earth, the endless variety of all green things that grow, the fertile and lush valleys and the majestic mountains of stone. The soothing warmth of the sun on your face, the stiff breeze that invigorates, and the pool of water waiting to refresh your very soul. And we are just getting started, for the world is vast. But any realm below the surface, down deep in the earth, could never have any of these things.

Down below, there is no natural light and little to see but walls and ceilings of dirt and rock. There are underground rivers that can inspire, but they can also kill, as they will rise quickly and unexpectedly. They are fed by the rain from the surface that no one can see or anticipate. The temperature varies little, between fifty and sixty degrees. Without the light from fires and torches, there is nothing but darkness.

The people who lived there had developed a slower-burning fuel from coal they mined and had dug vents up to the surface so that the smoke from fires and torches would dissipate. But they had also dug these vents so fresh air from the surface could flow down so the people wouldn't suffocate. Yes, the cave dwellers knew that the surface existed and had similar myths of a people who lived there. From time to time, some would venture out on the surface at night, but it was rare.

In some ways, the belief of each civilization was a mirror image of the other. The cave dwellers feared the surface, especially the bright light that shone there. They had even heard tales that large monsters roamed the surface and had a particular liking for their flesh. If the people below had not lost their collective memory, they would have known they were much more like the people on the surface than they ever could have imagined. They would have known that, in fact, their ancestors had actually come from the surface hundreds of years in the past.

There was a reason why the first person from the surface decided to go below. You would think there had to be for anyone from the surface to ever want to go under the ground to live, for there was nothing about it that could ever compare to the wonder and beauty of the surface world.

Once upon a time, there were two brothers who always competed a great deal. Some of the time the competition was in fun, but most of the time it was not. This was something their parents could have recognized early on and should have discouraged, but they had no way of knowing how it would turn out. Most young children grow out of sibling rivalry, at least enough to have better relationships as adults. For these two, this wouldn't happen.

The back and forth became more and more personal, not unlike two bordering countries that have a long history of skirmishes and even wars and aren't capable of getting along. At some point, with all the anger, desire for justice, and even revenge, and especially the damaged pride and distrust, striking out again always seemed the best option. "Maybe *he* will get tired of it and stop," one brother would say to himself. "If he does, I will. But I will not allow him to make me look *weak*, to look like a *fool*!"

And guess what? Both of them were thinking the same exact things. Both were waiting for the other to do something different before they changed what they were doing. But neither was willing to do anything different themselves. They were stuck in a cycle that would continue on for the longest of times, unless something new and different occurred.

In their case, it was an unfortunate circumstance. The punch that was thrown that day was no different than many of the other punches that had been thrown on other days. It wasn't even as hard as some. But on this day, there just so happened to be a large rock on the ground behind one of them—the same brother who was hit and then fell. The back of his head landed on the rock. He never got up. The cycle ended.

There were local governing bodies in this world that dealt with criminal and civil issues, but usually with matters that were much smaller. It was for this reason that this incident was so shocking. The name of the brother who was guilty was Brock, and the name of the brother who was unfortunate had been Lane. The local council convened and discussed the matter fully, interviewing Brock and his parents and anyone else who knew anything about the incident.

They debated long and hard, particularly over the fact that Brock had not intended to kill Lane, and to his credit, was honest during the proceedings and admitted to much hatred and resentment toward his brother for many long years. Brock was eighteen at the time, and Lane seventeen.

Partially because they felt the deed had to be punished, but also because of a fear that something like this might become contagious within their community, they banished Brock. He could go anywhere but could never live in their community again. There were areas here and there that were populated, but most of their world was not. Brock had no idea where he would go, but his parents and he said their goodbyes, and off he set.

After some time of wandering, Brock came to a sinkhole. It was so large he could not see the bottom. He had been going back and forth in his mind about what he should say to the people he would meet along the way. He had already come upon several on the road. Most were nice, as most people were in that world.

It was customary to stop and talk at least momentarily, to say hello and to politely ask each other's business. To see if you could help in any way, if you had any provisions the other could use, and things like that. So far all that Brock had been able to say were some white lies about who he was and where he was going, and that all was fine.

As he looked down into the sinkhole, he wondered what he would say to the next person who came by.

Part of him wanted to tell the truth—he would need to if he were to more fully forgive himself for what he had done. But what would people think? How would they respond? Had they ever known of someone who had contributed to another person's death? And someone in his own family, at that? Lane and he had never lost much love for each other, but they still had loved each other. He already missed his brother a great deal.

In truth, Lane had been more vindictive than Brock over the years, usually being the one to take torment to a new and deeper level. Brock had never been able to find the self-control to not respond in kind. They had both thought of themselves as invincible, that no real harm would ever come of all of their fighting. But many teenagers over the ages have learned suddenly and abruptly that all things they believe are not true.

The debate in Brock's mind continued on, however, because there was another part of him that felt so bad about what he had done, he did not believe he could ever be forgiven. He had seen that look on some of the council members' faces that made him feel what he had done was unforgiveable. And as he thought about the people he might get to know in his future, especially the ones he would come to know after he settled down, it was all too easy to think they would be more likely to condemn him than to ever be understanding or forgiving.

Would he not react the same way? If he settled somewhere and was able to put up with everyone's harsh looks and cold shoulders for a time, would it ever get better? After he had been there for a while, might there be some who would be able to see he was not such a bad guy after all? Over time might some come to believe he was truly not that different from them? That he deserved a second chance? That he had really deserved that back home? But he already knew how that had turned out.

In the end, I'm sorry to say, Brock could not get past his lack of faith that others would extend to him the great volumes of grace he would need. In the end, it all seemed easier, much easier, to keep it all a secret.

And you would never think a sinkhole could look that appealing, but given all Brock's options, it drew him. In theory, if we could ever know all our motives at any particular point in time and somehow put them into a sum, we should be able to predict our next move. Going down into the ground and disappearing altogether seemed to satisfy more that was churning in Brock's mind and heart than any other option he could imagine.

And so he took his first step down, just to see if he could see any farther. And then he took another step down. And yet another. And before long he became more and more curious about what he would find if he continued on. At some point he had to climb back out and make a torch so he could continue farther, but he did, and the rest is history.

Brock was the Adam of the underground world. In the end, he chose to walk into the darkness instead of persisting in the light.

At first Brock could only stay below for a few hours before he would feel anxious, even panic, and would have to resurface. But soon he felt more comfortable for longer and longer periods. The sinkhole went a good distance down on its own, but then it connected to underground caverns that went in several directions. For many days, and even weeks and months, Brock explored new areas and found pools of water and even a river, plus much larger areas with high ceilings.

As he discovered these things, his mood gradually improved, and he felt more hopeful. He thought for the first time that life below could be more than just tolerable—it might become a real home. To begin with, Brock had to resurface more frequently to gather food and wood for fires, but he soon tired of this and tasted some of the plentiful roots that grew down below. Some were not so bad when they were cooked, and some he used for fires instead of wood. One day Brock ate some of the insects that were so plentiful down there. It was slow going for a while, but he found some that were easier to stomach, and cooking them was always an option.

Brock even wondered if he might be a true Adam—that was, the father of a whole new race. But he could not fathom how he would convince a young lady from the surface to come live with him of her own free will. For a time it was easier to put this out of his mind. Eventually, however, Brock found plenty of motivation to think further. These motives included the pain of being so alone for such a long time. It had been four years since he first came below. His thoughts also included, if we can just be honest, his desire to experience sex. And possibly the greatest, the mysterious existential anxiety most of us feel about leaving this world without leaving someone behind. That is, if we have children, somehow we don't really die but live on.

The most obvious solution to his dilemma would be to kidnap someone. Not the best way to start a romance, however. And then one day he realized it might not be impossible to find someone who would *choose* to live underground. He had made this decision, had he not? If he could just find someone like him, someone who had experienced some great difficulty in her life, something so difficult that coming down below would feel like the lesser of two evils.

Who could possibly fall into this category? Who might be so dissatisfied with her life she might want a new start? And even more, how would he find her? And then it occurred to Brock he could find someone who was in prison, maybe even for life. In this world, they struggled with all the same dilemmas we have and in most cases had come up with similar solutions. If he could learn of someone like this, he could make her a most unusual proposition.

Brock's underground world was far out in the country, which made it easier for him to go undetected when he surfaced to gather provisions. He had ventured a long way from his home when he had first left. No one in these parts knew the Brock he had been long ago or anything about him. But just in case, he had always explored above ground during the late hours of the night.

This new mission would make that impossible, as he would have to ask questions to be able to find the kind of woman he was looking for. And so he spent time in one of the nearby towns in the evening, trying to blend in. He had washed some of his clothes rather well to get all of the dirt out of them. He had kept some money from his prior life and used this to eat dinner at one of the establishments, then would walk around town, acting like he was one of the regular folks.

Sometimes after he had started a conversation with someone, always making an effort to sound like he was just being polite, the person would ask more about him. They would want to know where he was from and his business in town. So Brock created a false identity, saying he lived far out in the country, which he did; that he was a farmer, which he would have been; and that he was in town getting provisions, which, in a way, he was trying to do.

Before long he discovered there was a sheriff in town and a jail and that at any point in time, there could be as many as three people held there. In most cases the local jail was a holding place until a trial could occur. If the person was then sentenced to prison, they would be sent off to a longer-term facility. There was an alley behind the jail that was closed for normal use but available for the sheriff to come and go with prisoners in a more secluded manner.

As Brock was spying one evening from behind the alley, he saw a back door and three little openings higher up along the rear wall that provided ventilation for each of the three cells. He might be able to pass a note through one of these holes or even have a conversation if the opportunity arose.

Brock did not visit the town too often and always talked to different people so as not to attract attention. As I have said, terrible crimes did not happen often in this world, and so a good amount of time had gone by and Brock had not learned of anyone who might be a good candidate. Until one day.

As it turned out, the head political figure in that town was a man named Ben Johnson. He held a position similar to a mayor, but their name for this person was "benefactor." In Ben's case, this was ironic, for if the people had known the truth, he was not the most honest of men and would take advantage of his position from time to time for his own gain. You could say that the town was more *his* benefactor than the other way around.

Ben also had other character defects, including drinking too much at home and beating his wife. He had a deliberate way of doing this, however, never hitting her in the face or arms or anywhere else someone might see the bruises. This had gone on for many years.

We can all be a little too quick to judge in circumstances like this—that is, why a woman would ever put up with such a situation. I will just say I have come to believe that none of us should judge another person, unless, like they say, you have walked in their shoes for a long time. And since none of us can ever do that . . . well, I hope you understand.

Let us also say, in most cases, someone like Ben Johnson did not accidentally marry someone like Norma Jean Jones. It was as if a part of him planned it all out ahead of time. Not so specifically he wanted to make sure he could get away with beating her. He might have never done that before and couldn't anticipate it. But he at least knew he wanted to dominate her—that was the way he preferred it. And he would end up choosing her as his wife because during their courting relationship he had concluded she would allow this, more than likely, because she already had.

How it all turns out may be another thing. But enough of the time, it turns out just like Ben Johnson was hoping. Norma Jean was a woman who would usually defer to others and could also be critical of herself and get lost in this. She also had been an orphan, raised by some distant relatives whom she had lost touch with. So she had no family or anyone to go to if she needed. She was all alone in the world except for Ben. You see, sometimes predators and prey just so happen to find each other.

Well, you might begin to think a little more of Norma Jean (I've always loved that name) if you hear some more. She had threatened to leave Ben many times, and she had said and done everything she could think of that might make him stop. And then one evening, she overheard a conversation between Ben and another man in their front parlor, talking about a bribe the man was offering Ben for a substantial political favor. Ben wanted more money, and the man did not want to give it. Ben ended up losing his temper with the man. It was his raised voice that first drew Norma Jean downstairs. Norma Jean didn't hear much, but just enough.

Ben and the man were able to shake hands on a deal, and the man left. Later that night, after a few drinks, Ben took out his frustration on Norma Jean. In the midst of it, she told him if he didn't stop, she would reveal the bribe to the whole town and ruin him.

Ben just laughed at her. "If you do, where will you go, and what will you do? You have no one but me!"

Something in Norma Jean shifted. Maybe it was the stark realization that as much as she hated Ben and did not ever want to agree with him, she knew he was right. Her situation was this dire. Why it had never "hit" her the same way until now, she never understood. She never had said anything to anyone about all the beatings, and she had never even tried to walk out. She probably never would no matter how bad he beat her.

But Ben shouldn't have been so confident. He had made it all a little too clear for Norma Jean. For the first time, she saw that things could never get any worse than they already were right at that moment. For the first time, the thought of being completely on her own in the world did not terrify her as it always had. For the first time, finally doing something about it, anything, became the lesser of two evils.

As she stood there, staring at him, being so disgusted with his wide-eyed arrogance and self-conceit, her mind was also working. Ben was a master at disguise, an incredible manipulator and without a conscience. No matter what she said to anyone, even with the bruises to prove it, he would find a way to twist things. He would lie. He would do whatever was necessary to convince everyone in town that Norma Jean and this man who had just paid the bribe had conspired against *him*! They had made it all up. She didn't know just how he would do it this time, but he would. She had seen him do it countless times before.

And then in a moment she would never fully understand, Norma Jean slowly and discreetly reached over to the tabletop by her side, put her fingers around a large silver candlestick, and wiped that conceited glare right off Ben's face. Another whop or two, and he never moved again. She had allowed herself to take far too many beatings herself. There was far too much in her that wanted to set it right.

Norma Jean quietly walked out the door and right to the sheriff to turn herself in. She never said anything in her defense, but only, "I did it." The sheriff thought it odd but would have sworn that Norma Jean sounded proud. It all would have made a great bluegrass song.

Brock just so happened to come to town several nights later, and he didn't even have to start a conversation—everyone in town was still talking about it. The next evening, Brock put a makeshift ladder up against the rear wall of the jail and peeked in to find Norma Jean's cell. He had written a little note and dropped it through the opening.

It read, "I would like to rescue you from your situation. I know what it is like to have killed someone and how much you regret it afterward. I found a new life for myself. I would like to give you the same. I will be back tomorrow night at the same time. We can talk then."

Brock had no idea how he would break Norma Jean out, but he also had no idea just how easy it would be. As I said, people in this world were not perfect, as you can see, but they were usually better behaved. No one had ever heard of anyone breaking out of a jail, so no one took precaution against it. All Brock had to do was to quietly walk into the front door of the jail late that night, make sure he didn't wake up the deputy who was sleeping on a cot, pick up the key lying right on top of the desk, quietly open Norma Jean's cell door, place the key back on top of the desk, and walk out the back door with Norma Jean. He was going to talk with her first but decided not to. He decided she might be more likely to come with him if he just showed up at her cell door. He was right. She did not hesitate but walked right out.

Although Norma Jean knew that Brock's plan had to involve them going to some faraway place, she could have never suspected the truth. She was more than a little shocked when he stepped down into the largest hole in the ground she had ever seen and looked back at her, motioning for her to follow. But follow she did. It had always been her way.

The adjustment to living under the ground took Norma Jean as long as it had taken Brock, about one year. But she did have one thing she had *never* had—a man who fell in love with her and then loved her more than life itself. She had never been so happy. They were, in some ways, more like Adam and Eve than any other man or woman since. It is not so hard to understand that both Brock and Norma Jean doubted they could ever have a normal life among the people they had always known. It is a bit harder to understand how they could ever be content living underground, when you would not think this was necessary.

Could they not go to some faraway place and start a new life? Who would ever know? And yet there was something in both their hearts that couldn't get past the condemnation they feared would inevitably come. Somehow, someway, they believed they would eventually be found out. They even realized this wasn't rational, but they still could not get past it.

But the real problem, the root of it all, was the same thing that had driven Brock underground to begin with. It was the belief, the fear, that they really did not *deserve* to be forgiven, that what they had done was truly unforgiveable. This was what held them captive. Held them captive, in hiding, down below.

Years passed, and then decades. Brock and Norma Jean had children, and their children had children, and a whole new civilization flourished down below. Brock and Norma Jean were so dead set against ever going back to the surface to live that they found ways to instill a strong distaste for it in their children. They didn't like being dishonest, but they concluded that telling some white lies would be best. Brock had forbidden anyone from going to the surface in the daytime so they would not be found out, and he told his children the bright light from the sun was harmful to their skin and could even kill them with too much exposure. He explained to his children that the surface people looked normal enough, just like them, in fact— but they were not like them at all. He told them they were dangerous and you could never trust them. He even told them there had been stories about large monsters roaming the surface that would not only kill you but eat you.

Brock felt a little bad for making up the worst of these stories, but both Norma Jean and he felt that they all would be better off if they were forever separated from everyone up above. And years later, after both Brock and Norma Jean had died, their white lies lived on because no one knew any different. The fear of the surface people and the compulsion to stay below was a strong but unspoken conviction. A conviction that would keep this civilization in bondage for over four hundred years. Until . . .

Until late one night when a group of cave dwellers planned to go to the surface to gather firewood and berries and other wild things to eat. Everyone would go out for a designated length of time to collect what they could and then carry it back to the opening from which they had emerged.

There was a teenage girl in the party named Lily. She had felt a little weak and dizzy after being out for fifteen minutes, and it would have been best for her to cut her trip short and head back right then, but she was too young and inexperienced to think of this. She continued picking berries, thinking the ill feeling would pass, but it did not. She grew faint and then was so tired she had to sit down. Within a few minutes, she fell fast asleep, and when everyone else had returned to their starting place, she was nowhere to be found.

They called out for her and then fanned out to try to find her but had no luck. One or two came close to where she was, but she was asleep and almost impossible to see in the dark unless you walked right over her. The most senior person in the party, Peter, was aghast. Nothing like this had ever happened before. What should they do?

Their orders were to complete their mission within one or two hours tops and return. But in no event were they ever to still be above ground when it became light. They looked for her for several more hours though, until just before dawn. Regretfully, Peter ordered everyone underground to return home. This would have to be a matter for the older men in the community to resolve.

Lily awoke midmorning. As she sat up and opened her eyes, she flinched and quickly closed them again, for it was so bright. Brighter than anything her eyes had ever been exposed to, so bright she could barely keep them open when she tried again. And then she remembered she had fallen ill the night before and had just wanted to sit down for a moment to catch her breath. She must have fallen asleep and had slept until now.

And then it hit her. She was on the *surface* in the middle of the day! Everyone must have gone back below. Her first impulse was to scream, she was so terrified, but she wanted even more to stay hidden, to not be discovered by any of the surface creatures. Within a few minutes, Lily realized just how sick she was. She was profusely sweating and dizzy. She knew she would not last long without water, for she already felt dehydrated. She also did not know which way to go to get back to the hole in the ground.

She sat up and looked over the grass and the shrubbery and thought she recognized the way she had come. She started off in that direction, crouching as she walked, to conceal herself, but was so weak she could only go a little way and had to rest again. Each time she set out, she became winded even more quickly, to the point she was making little progress. In an hour, she had only covered about half a mile. She looked all around now and did not recognize any trees or other landmarks, but she also had more and more trouble thinking clearly. She finally realized she was completely lost.

As the civilization below had continued to grow over the last several hundred years, so had everything above. Large farms had replaced more and more of the wilderness, and as it turned out, that very morning there was a large group of men who began to clear the very land where the cave dwellers had foraged the night before. They were cutting down shrubs and trees and removing boulders.

Lily first heard noise in the distance and what sounded like people talking. She was too terrified to move but could not have gone far regardless. The noises did not fade but got louder and louder until, finally, one of the men walked right up on her. She screamed, and the man jumped back, but then he tried to talk to her. After a few minutes of asking her who she was and if she was okay but receiving only more screams, the man called others for help. After ten or fifteen minutes, Lily calmed down, but it was clear she was not well. All the people below had paler skin, but Lily had lost even her normal color from being ill and looked as pale as a ghost.

No one ever said much about the surface people—almost no one had ever seen one of them, and even then not up close. Lily could not remember anyone ever talking about their appearance and their faces and their skin, much less their culture, or their habits, or their language. She had never thought about any of this. She was a little relieved to see they looked exactly like all the people she had ever known, although they dressed differently.

But as the men asked her questions, using all of the very same words she would have been using if she were speaking to them, she couldn't help but be surprised. Why would they have the same language if they were so different? How could they, without some common ancestry? After a while longer, she calmed down enough to think more clearly and realized she would never be able to escape from the men, not right then anyway. She decided the safest thing would be to do what they suggested but to say nothing. Hopefully, she would feel better before too long and learn more. Then she might be able to plan and execute an escape to get back home. Hopefully, they were not so evil that they would harm her right away.

No one had ever spoken about what to say if you were ever captured by the surface people. Lily knew she couldn't trust them, and they would likely have the worst of intentions. Her worst fear was if she revealed who she was and that a whole civilization of her people existed below, the surface people might kill them all. She was trying to remain calm, but she felt the weight of the whole underground world upon her. At some point, however, she realized the men only seemed to be concerned for her welfare, only curious about who she was so they could assist in getting her home. She couldn't figure out why they were being so nice but thought there had to be some ulterior motive.

Maybe they already knew there was an underground civilization and were purposely being so nice to get information, at least the location of the closest opening to her world. Finally, after the men had made no progress in getting her to talk, one suggested she accompany them back to the farmhouse of the family that employed them so she could lie down if she needed and get something to eat and drink. They had a mule she could ride on as well. Lily was stunned to see such a creature. She saw it was a pack animal, and it seemed to be tame. So she allowed the men to help her up on the mule, and they started on their way.

Little did any of the men know that the virus Lily had was something they should be worried about. Viruses have a way of becoming more or less exclusive among a people group over a period of time. After several centuries, no one above ground had been exposed to this little bug and had little resistance to it. For Lily, it was a bad case of the flu, but for several of the men working that day, and several of the women who cared for her in the days after, it became much worse.

After those first few days, Lily was no longer contagious, but the bug spread to others. To begin with, the surface people's symptoms were similar to Lily's, a fever and fatigue. But many of these people grew much sicker, having fevers that would not break and then developing severe respiratory problems. Before it was all over, three elderly people, two children, and two adults died, one of these the man who'd first stumbled upon her. Lily had found herself becoming attached to this man because he continued to check on her at the end of every day. She had begun to speak after a few days, just to be polite and to make it easier for the ladies who were caring for her. She did not reveal anything, however.

Some had wondered if she had amnesia, but she did not seem confused. And she did not seem simple minded, but she had said so little, they just didn't know. Lily was a little disturbed when she first learned that several people had fallen ill with pretty much the same symptoms as she, and then was crushed when she later heard the first person had died. She did not understand why so many were getting ill, but she still felt responsible. After another week or two, others died as well.

By this time Lily was well but still had no clue what she would do. She could slip off in the night but had little confidence she would be able to find the hole back to her world in a short amount of time. She needed a better plan but couldn't think of one. But something else influenced her as well.

She had been suspicious of her hosts, but after a while realized she had not witnessed even a single instance of ill will. She felt ashamed of her own ill will toward these people, who had only been more than kind to her. Her own mother and father would not have done a better job of caring for her in her illness. But then when the first person died, and the second, her shame overwhelmed her.

At times like these, whether our shame is real or imagined, true or false, we can tend to expect the shame we are feeling to be the very same attitude others will have toward us. That is, we tend to expect they will condemn us just like we are condemning ourselves. But this never happened. In fact, Lily continued to feel like an honored guest. And these people were not ignorant. She could overhear some of the conversations they were trying to keep from her. They were pretty convinced the virus had come from her. In one case, a five-year-old boy had died, the only child of a widow.

Lily could not imagine such grief. And still no one, not even this mother, seemed to feel the least amount of anger or resentment toward her, this foreign girl who had mysteriously materialized in one of their fields early one morning, helpless and ill, and who since had infected so many and still had not been forthcoming in explaining who she was, where she had come from, or anything else.

What Lily couldn't know was that the surface people's spiritual beliefs were different than her own. Everyone she had known held some religious beliefs, but they were vague and not a part of their day-to-day lives. Her ancestor Father Brock had seen to this, deciding to teach his children very little of the religion he'd known as a child. He had concluded it failed him, and so he decided to fail it. Brock and Norma Jean's inability to believe in real grace turned into a form of chronic pessimism, not only toward others but toward life in general.

The generations that succeeded Brock and Norma Jean down below came to believe that most of their neighbors would treat them well enough and go out of their way to help from time to time, but it was not proper to expect more than that. Beyond that, no one believed anyone other than your closest family would want to forgive you for some larger grievance or be able to love you well over an extended period of time. Lily had inherited such a worldview but would not have been able to put it into words. All the cave dwellers saw life as a glass half-empty, and that was on a good day. They tried to be more cheerful than that, but much of the time it was not honest. Any god they believed in was at best a distant and uninvolved father.

And so Lily was not surprised when no one from her world showed up. If they had come looking for her, they had done so under the cover of darkness and were not willing to openly present themselves to the surface people. Not that her parents didn't love her, and not that they weren't very grieved she was lost, but the fear of the surface people was so great, Lily knew it would be up to her to find her way home. And if she did not . . . her life would be a sad but necessary sacrifice.

The surface people had always been religious, but over recent centuries had experienced a revival of sorts that had spread throughout the whole land. They believed in a Great Spirit who was providential, gracious, forgiving, and worked out all things for their good. Not that life was perfect—it was not. Not that the people were perfect—they were not.

But the people had walked a good distance with this Spirit and had always found He was right there with them, in the good and the bad. They did not believe they needed to understand all things, but just enough, and maybe one day they might know more. For now, they knew in their hearts life would work best if they sought out the Great Spirit's will instead of their own and followed it to the best of their ability.

And this is exactly what they had done with Lily. They did for her what they would have wanted someone to do for them if they were in the same circumstance. They were very surprised by how quickly the illness spread and how deadly it was for some but believed they should always consider others more important than themselves, especially those in need. They never second-guessed their decision to take Lily in, trusting in the Great Spirit to work the rest out. Too bad this revival came a few centuries too late for Brock, for he would have received the grace he needed and would have never gone underground.

After a good deal more time and a great deal more thought and deliberation, one day Lily finally found the courage to tell her hosts the real story. They were shocked. At first they thought she was crazy. But as she stuck with her story and continued to tell them more and more and was as coherent and rational as anyone they had ever heard, they came to believe her. They had already told her she could live with them if she wanted, for good. She was tempted. The surface world was so much nicer and more beautiful than underground, the light so much nicer than the darkness. Maybe she could convince some of her family and friends below to come up and join them.

One day she decided she would search until she found the hole in the ground, return home, and give it a try. It was a tearful separation. She wasn't completely sure what she would do if none of her people agreed to return with her, but she was beginning to believe she would return to the surface, nevertheless, and live out the rest of her years. She very much wanted to marry and have children of her own. Oddly enough, there was something in her heart that had become more attached to these people on the surface, whom she hardly knew, than to anyone in her previous life, even her parents. She had found the redemption Brock and Norma Jean had so very much needed but never received. Maybe the bravery and faith of one teenage girl would help some others to find it as well.

A Story for Myself

Love is patient, love is kind . . . bears all things,
believes all things, hopes all things, endures all things.
1 Corinthians 13:4, 7

nce upon a time, there was a young man with a broken heart. That may be one of the greatest understatements of all time. Avery's heart was so broken, he was having trouble with the simplest of tasks. He had decided to take sick days at work for the rest of the week, but he was an attorney and would not be able to neglect things for very long. Today was Wednesday. Or so Avery thought.

That Monday morning, as he was making his coffee, his wife, Ann, walked into the kitchen and simply announced she was leaving him. She did not give him an opportunity to respond. Even worse, she seemed so calm, as if she had only asked him to pour her a cup as well. She did not give any reasons. She wished him well and within minutes was out the door. She had already packed a bag.

It generally took Avery a good thirty to forty-five minutes to wake up in the morning. He hadn't had that much time on Monday. He was not able to collect himself long enough to even say the first word. He just stood there, stunned. After he heard the front door shut, he thought it might be a dream. He was wrong. It was a nightmare.

Avery and Ann had been married for three years after dating for two. They had been talking a good deal about having children over the last year. They had been trying to have one for the last six months. Or so Avery thought. He wasn't so sure anymore. He had been living in one reality from the time he'd met Ann some five years ago. It was the best reality he had ever known. And Monday morning he was abruptly transported to another. He had not elected to take the trip. At least he did not think he had.

Experts have concluded there are four stages to grief: shock, anger, depression, and acceptance. There may be some overlap between those stages as you move through the process, but they usually progress in that order, unless something in your heart does not want to cooperate. But one thing is certain: if the loss is great, the first stage is shock.

The kind of shock we are most accustomed to from a car accident or an explosion or some other traumatic physical injury should not be hard to understand. The physical insult may have been so strong and so violent that it knocked you unconscious. You may have taken a direct hit to the head, which explains why you lost your mental clarity, maybe even your bearings altogether, right when the event occurred. You may have lost your memory for the fifteen or twenty minutes just before. You will likely never get that back. And your ability to concentrate and function normally may be impaired for some time.

But you can also come through a bad car accident and be virtually unharmed and still be in shock. For it happened so quickly, with little or no warning, that you know in your heart and mind you could have easily been hurt, or even killed—but somehow, miraculously, you weren't. This experience in itself can leave you in shock.

In more recent times, the military has come to understand that soldiers can suffer from traumatic brain injury from "only" the concussive impact of air displacement if an explosion nearby is powerful enough. It makes sense now, but many soldiers in the past were misunderstood and mistreated. Many were thought to be cowards who just wanted to avoid future combat, or malingerers who wanted to be discharged.

The emotional complement of shock is not as easy to understand, although I feel it should be, for it is very much the same. The world as you knew it just shifted way too fast. Whether it was the concussive impact of air against your body or everything your heart held dear, it really doesn't matter.

The world, as Avery had known it for the last five years, had been an equation of sorts, a story, which he had believed was real and true. And this story had Ann and him and their love for each other at its center. Their commitment was "to have and to hold; for better, for worse; for richer, for poorer; in sickness and in health; to love and to cherish; till death do us part." Or so Avery thought. He still remembered every word. Ann evidently did not, or at least had decided these were *only* words.

Avery had based so much of his life these last five years on the truth that Ann had loved him ever since their first kiss. To begin with, it was so intoxicating. He took a moment to think, but there was so much evidence that she had been just as crazy in love with him as he with her: all the little surprises; all the little voice messages; all the little gifts; all the little notes; all the little, and big, kisses; all the unbelievable sex; and especially all the professions that their love would last "forever" no matter what.

Professions like these can be made at any time by a lover who just can't contain themselves and in a moment will say the most incredible things.

"I would do *anything* for you!"

"I will *always* be here for you."

"I don't know how I *ever* lived without you!"

"I would *die* for you if I had to!"

And the most famous of all, and most relevant for Avery . . .

"I will *never, ever* leave you!"

Sometimes these professions can come from a feeling of insecurity. One person worries that their lover might not feel the same way or at least as strongly as they do. So they make such a profession, hoping their lover will do the same and reassure them.

And sometimes there can be a big fight and ugly things are said. Sometimes someone is so hurt and gets so angry, they threaten to break up. This most definitely throws the other person into a state of fear, even panic, but it can also scare the one who just made the threat. And this fear can prompt both of them to make up, sometimes only minutes later. And it might be at this very moment that the impulse to make love can be at its strongest, something neither of them can control. And in the midst of it, someone, or maybe both, will passionately confess their undying devotion . . . all over again.

Which should cause us to wonder, should it not? What is this thing we call "love" really? If something is this powerful that we claim will last forever, that we are even willing to *die for* . . . why is it not more stable? Why does something this passionate and powerful sometimes not make it to the next month? Why, so much of the time, does it *not* endure? Is it real or not? And what does that even mean?

Avery was more of a private person, basically an introvert, which meant he was getting ready to torture himself with all this. If he would spend some meaningful time talking to someone else about it, either a good friend or even a counselor, he would give himself the opportunity to hear other perspectives. He would likely be encouraged to think about some of Ann's motives, not only his own.

Without anyone else, however, he would be condemned to go in circles for days and weeks with little time to come up for air. He would continue to search down in the depths, somehow thinking if he just persisted, he might come across a treasure half-buried on the sea floor. A treasure that would explain it all. Like something he had said or done that he never realized was so significant. Or some habit of his that had always bothered her but eventually drove her crazy. Or something she had always wanted from him that he had never been able to give. Something, *anything*, that would somehow make sense of it all. He was more than willing to be the fall guy just to regain his sanity, but also to give him a strategy going forward. If there were specific things she was unhappy with, maybe they could be addressed, and maybe she would consider coming back.

Avery had slept very little the last two nights. He would lay in bed for three or four hours, trying to fall to sleep, and would eventually drift off, even having some dreams. But before long, he would wake and not feel as if he had been sleeping at all. Finally, by three or four in the morning, he would fall asleep more soundly, only to awaken abruptly at seven and not be able to go back to sleep. He would feel sleep deprived the rest of the day.

He also had this acute pain in his gut that accompanied his every waking moment. It was almost debilitating. He was so anxious, so fearful, filled with such dread, as if the sky were going to fall. His thoughts would fly from one place to another and then back, remembering things from the past.

But before long he would be right back in the kitchen that Monday morning, staring at Ann as she spoke to him. He was trying to remember as much detail as possible: what she wore, her facial expressions, the exact words she used, the inflections in her voice, how unaffected she seemed. He was compelled to reimagine this scene over and over again.

It was a crime scene in a way—if only he could extrapolate from her words and mannerisms something meaningful. It would take two more weeks for Avery to realize this exercise would bear no fruit but only cause him to feel even more desperate and alone . . . like a little child lost in a large city.

He didn't want to make it any worse, for he was already feeling bad enough, but it was hard not to wonder *what else* he might not know. Was there another man? In the great majority of cases like this, there *is* another man. Some people are strong enough emotionally to just walk away from someone without any other plans, without another person waiting in the wings. But most are not. Avery didn't know all of this, but he sensed it.

If there was another man, how long had it been? Was he just this stupid, this out of touch, that he never suspected anything? And even worse, did Ann love this other man? Why don't we just go ahead and torture ourselves as much as humanly possible? Feeling betrayed sexually is painful enough, but it is almost unbearable if your lover has fallen out of love with you and in love with somebody else. There are probably no words for this kind of pain. But Avery wished there were, just so he could say them, just so he could try to vomit them out of his mouth.

The phone rang. He jumped. He didn't want to pick it up; he didn't want to talk to anyone. But then he thought, *What if it's Ann? What if she's having second thoughts?* He almost ran to the phone.

It was Ann's best friend, Beth. "Hi, Avery! How come you're home? You're not sick are you?"

"No ..." he barely got out. "I had a ... an appointment near the house. I dropped by here before I went back to work."

"Is Ann there?"

"Uh, well ... no ... she is not. She's out doing some errands."

"Tell her I called, okay?"

"I will."

"See you soon."

"Yeah, you too."

Avery hung up the phone and stood there for several minutes. Beth did not seem to know anything. Avery felt a little better for a moment. If this had been going on for some time, especially if it involved another man, you would think Ann would have talked to her best friend about it. But maybe not. Had she told *anyone*?

It had not occurred to him until right then, but what was he going to say to everyone? Both sets of parents stayed in touch a good deal, and they had several couples who were good friends, but weeks would go by without talking to them. Or, better said, without *him* talking to any of them. Ann talked more on the phone. Most women do. Some of these folks would start calling.

It would be far easier to say nothing for now, to make up little stories like he just had for Beth. Maybe he could say Ann was out of town for a few days. Where would she have gone by herself? He would have to think about that. Maybe before long Ann might call, and they could talk, and she would be open to saying more. Maybe if he just told stories to everyone for a week or two, she would be back, and he would never have to tell anyone the real story. More than anything, he wished he had a story to tell himself.

Wednesday came and went, and Avery slept better but was even more depressed the next morning. He had to call in to work to catch up on a few things and to ask for a few favors. He needed to make some phone calls, to send some emails, etc. Email was still new. Avery wasn't bringing a laptop home and didn't have a smartphone because they hadn't been invented yet.

If he'd had a smartphone, he might have searched for: "Top ten reasons why women leave their husbands." Avery wouldn't have believed in ten years or so you could do that and actually get an answer. Not a good answer but an answer. For the time being, he did not know where else to look.

Believe it or not, Ann did not call, not even once. Avery had no way of getting in touch with her, or he would have. After a while, he was tempted to call her parents, thinking she would have called them and given them the news, at least so they would know where she was. But he could never bring himself to call them. It was just too humiliating.

It would take Avery many more weeks, and even months, but he would eventually come to question love itself. For you and me in this little story, we don't have to wait so long. We can go ahead and consider it.

Some people might think there are other things we should talk about first, other factors that could explain Avery's nightmare, things that are more mundane. They might say, for instance, for a couple to be happy together, they have to be "compatible," whatever that means. Or they at least cannot be *in*compatible. They can't have too many different interests, different passions. Their beliefs about the world and life can only be so different.

Maybe this finally became obvious to Ann, and she realized she needed to find someone more like her. It wasn't really Avery's fault, and she didn't blame him. You could still accuse her of being incredibly insensitive and coldhearted to have walked out the way she did. Or you could say she was just too practical. Okay, maybe we shouldn't give her that much credit.

Avery could not imagine ever doing the same thing to her. How could you be married to someone for three years, and very, very close for five, and just end it from one moment to the next without any explanation whatsoever? How could anyone think that was okay?

And so maybe she didn't love him. But she had decided to marry him. So she must have thought she loved him then, right? Did it change over a period of time? Did she just not know how to explain it?

Avery had dated girls in the past and begun to be interested in them, only to realize it wasn't as exciting as it needed to be, or whatever you want to call that. He would always end it as soon as he realized this. How could he not? It would only make it worse to continue. He remembered once or twice these girls were disappointed. Evidently they had felt more. He remembered not feeling conflicted at all about this, actually feeling quite good he had escaped.

His heart sank. This must be exactly how Ann felt about him, or she wouldn't have been able to do what she did. He hoped there could be some other explanation. Something that would exonerate not only him but her. Something that would allow them both to still have a chance together. But the aching in his gut would not go away.

Many other things came and went in Avery's life for the next several months, but no Ann. He did get a voice message from her one day. She'd purposely called when he was at work so she wouldn't have to talk to him. She had hired some movers to come get some of her things. She told him he could do what he wanted with the rest. She also said she would give the movers explicit instructions, to please let them in and out, but she would not be there herself. The coldness in her voice had become even more natural, almost professional. For the first time, it actually scared Avery.

It is quite incredible, is it not, just how traumatic something like this can be? It shakes you to your very core. You had thought you understood something very, very well. You had thought you had understood this *other person* very, very well, and you could not have been more wrong. It causes you to question your own sanity. What happened to change everything when you weren't looking? Or had you been wrong all along, which is an even worse thought? Because if you were so wrong about this, *what else* might you be wrong about?

And the most painful thing about all of this is that these are not just ideas or concepts. This is about a relationship. A loving, intimate relationship. This is as personal as personal gets. It is a severe and deep betrayal that can cause you to question your own sense of self. It is an assault on the deepest part of your soul.

Avery struggled for a few days after the voice message. He had been doing better. Pain has a way of becoming more tolerable over a period of weeks and months. The body gets tired of it as well and begins to acclimate as best it can. He had become more and more able to get through his day without thinking of Ann every moment, but was still limping. He was just doing a better job of hiding it.

And then one night Avery went to see a movie with a friend. It was the first time he had actually gotten out since Ann had left. It was a war movie. Avery thought he should be safe from anything in the movie that might trigger his emotions. But the movie was waiting for him, waiting to speak to him.

War movies often have a lot of common elements: the backstories of several of the main characters; their basic training and developing friendships; a tough and dedicated commander; their initial battle experiences and growing confidence and courage as warriors; and then, finally, the great battle in which everything in them is tested and some of them are killed. Sometimes the story will continue after the survivors have returned home. They are so thankful to be back with family and lovers once again but emotionally may never be the same.

The movie Avery and his friend saw on this night kept to a similar script. It was about the Korean War, the first war driven by the United States' fear of the spread of Communism. It was the first time jet fighters engaged in dog fights and was a much larger conflict than most people realize. Both Russia and China supported North Korea, and the momentum of the war and the location of the front shifted multiple times over the three years between June 1950 and July 1953.

Avery enjoyed the movie and was able to lose himself in the story, the very thing his friend was hoping for. The movie centered on three particular soldiers who had become best friends, all from different parts of the US. At the climax of the fighting, one of them was badly wounded as they were retreating from some deserted buildings outside of Seoul. The other two did not notice their buddy had been hit until they took up their new position, because he had been in the rear. As the screaming noise of gunfire quieted, they could hear their friend calling out, "I'm hit. I can't move. I'm behind a jeep, two o'clock from your position, about fifty yards out."

The wounded soldier's name was Jed, from Mississippi. His accent was so thick that any Korean soldier who had learned English and could hear him calling out would likely have not understood him. His two friends were Tony, an Italian, of course, from the Bronx, and William, from Nebraska. As soon as Jed called out to them, he felt bad. He didn't want to be responsible for putting anyone in harm's way, but he was only doing what he had been trained to do.

The American military has always been fully committed to every soldier, as they should be. But this takes on a different meaning when you fight in a real war and experience situations you could have never imagined but happen right in front of your eyes. And the most difficult situation of all might be the very situation these three found themselves in.

How do you measure and weigh the value of Jed's life, who is wounded and may already be close to bleeding out, to the value of Tony's and William's lives, who will risk their own in running back to get him? The two of them may be in plain view the whole way there and the whole way back. And getting him back, even with two of them, will cause them to stand up higher and move slower—the two things that will make them the best targets for a Korean sniper.

But the Marines have never cared about any of that, not when compared to the alternative. It is not an option to leave *any man behind*. There might be a better or smarter way to do this. They might need to wait until the barrage dies down. Or maybe they could create a diversion. But they can't wait too long, for Jed might not have that long.

We have all seen movies like this before. In the more common version, just one guy goes back to get his buddy, and he succeeds without being hit. Both live for another day. In some versions, the soldier who goes back gets hit but still succeeds in getting them back to safety, and both survive. In other versions, they both get hit on the way back but both still survive. And in some versions, probably written by depressed writers, they both get shot multiple times before they even make it halfway back, and die immediately. And it is so obvious to the rest of the unit they are dead, there is no further discussion about a rescue.

In this movie, William and Tony both feel compelled to go back. They alternate shooting at the enemy to create cover while the other advances. By this point in the war, they are very good soldiers. They make it to Jed, who has been shot in the thigh. Fortunately, the bleeding is not too severe, but the leg cannot support any weight.

As soon as they get Jed bandaged up, he apologizes for getting hit as if it were his fault. William and Tony each let Jed know that not only is that a bunch of crap, but they are Marines, and that means something. Tony, who is more brash, yells, "So you wouldn't have come back to get *me* if I had been hit? You better have! I'd kick your butt next time I saw ya!"

William simply looked into Jed's eyes and said, "Semper Fi!"

You may not know this, but the motto of the Marines is "Semper Fidelis," sometimes "Semper Fi" for short. In Latin, this means "Always Faithful." Those are powerful words. They may truly be the two most powerful words in the whole universe.

A few tears ran down Avery's cheeks as he watched this scene in the movie unfold. In the moment, he did not make the connection. It is easy to get lost in the details of a story, so much so that the greater message and a connection to our own lives does not become a conscious thought right then. But it always strikes the heart and soul immediately. Our deeper self sees and hears clearly. Always.

The greater message was loyalty, loyalty to the very end no matter the cost. It really doesn't matter if the story happens on a battlefield or in a bedroom. In this movie, there were soldiers who were willing to sacrifice their lives to save their comrade. But many other kinds of stories could have just as clearly taught the same truth:

A business partner who always does his best for the venture, even when his counterpart cannot because of personal and emotional problems that last for years.

A best friend who always chooses to forgive, even when the offender is not able to acknowledge the harm they have done.

And a husband who stays by his wife's side and cares for her for decades after she is diagnosed with multiple sclerosis. He is loyal until her dying breath.

Avery would only make the connection between the soldiers and his marriage later that week, and not on his own. Avery's friend was Tony too, only *not* Italian. Tony had invited him out to lunch on purpose. He had felt the emotion rising in Avery during the scene in the movie. He carefully and quickly glanced over and saw the tears on Avery's cheek. But he purposely waited till now to say something, when they would have longer to talk.

"That movie was really good the other night, was it not?" he started.

"Yes, it was," Avery replied. "It was a great story, and the actors were good too."

"Yes, I agree. You know that scene where Tony and William went back to get Jed? It was quite powerful. It made me think about how brave soldiers can be, about the commitment they make to each other, about how the fighting and the threat of harm causes them to become *so close*. Like true brothers. Maybe even closer than real brothers. Do you believe that?"

"Well, now that you say it like that . . . yeah, I can believe that."

"I could tell you got a little emotional during that scene. I hope it doesn't make you feel uncomfortable for me to say that."

"No . . . it doesn't. You are right. I did." Avery was quiet for a few moments. "It was just the depth of their commitment to each other. It was unwavering. There was nothing, *truly nothing* that could penetrate it, that could ever change it."

"You're right. It was very cool, huh?" Tony was collecting his thoughts before he continued, wanting to find just the right words.

"But why do you think it struck you the way it did? That it touched you so deeply?" And Tony picked up his glass of water to take another sip, looking away, making it clear to Avery it was fine to take as much time as he needed to respond. Tony was hoping, even praying, this conversation would strike the right chord. He had already succeeded in getting Avery to notice the most important thing and to put it into words, very beautifully, in fact.

And right then something happened. At first Tony's question took Avery back to the scene in the movie. He began to think about Jed, about how he must have felt right when his buddies got back to him. How much it confirmed his importance, his value.

Tears came into Avery's eyes. "What must it be like to be *that important* to another person? What must *that* feel like?" And right then the veil was lifted. Avery's whole body quivered. "Oh my God. How did I not see it before?"

He looked up at Tony, who was looking at him intently, with the most compassionate little smile on his face. "Yes ... how *did* you not see it? You have deserved much better, my friend.

I know you are not perfect. You can't be. None of us are. But you did not deserve what Ann did to you. Looking at it from the outside, what she did was inexcusable. She failed you. If she had been Tony or William in the movie, she would *not* have gone back. She would have chickened out. And she would have lived *with that* for the rest of her life. As I am thinking she will."

Tony continued. "The more I think about it, I don't think Semper Fi is just for the Marines. I think we all need it. Somehow, I think we were made to need it. And now, for some reason, it seems to be in short supply. It shouldn't be, but it is.

We all should have more courage. We all should be able to commit more fully to each other, as lovers and friends, as even acquaintances, and keep our end of the bargain when we give our word. Even to the death, if need be. Some might say that is stupid, but I think not. Can you imagine what the world would be like if everyone stayed true to *that*? Stayed that loyal no matter what?"

Avery still had a journey to go on—grief experts are right about that. But he never read one of those books, and I'm glad he didn't. He had another Counselor with whom he began to talk. He had known Him much better as a child. They had to become reacquainted. This Counselor was getting ready to teach Avery much more about Semper Fi, for He knew more about it than anyone else. It had been His idea, as a matter of fact.

Avery's life became more joyful as the months and years went by. He found another wife, and they loved each other very much and were true to each other for the rest of their lives. They both lived until their hair was completely gray and their bodies worn out.

He never did see or hear from Ann again, other than through her divorce attorney. He had to have many conversations with his Counselor before he could forgive her completely. But one day several months after he had seen that war movie, he got down on his knees, and the two of them released her. It was one of the best days of Avery's life.

At different times throughout his life, something would occur that would cause him to think of her. When he did, he would say a little prayer. He would pray that somewhere along the way, she had learned the very thing that her walking out had taught him. And if she hadn't, that she would learn it soon: "There is no greater love than to lay down one's life for one's friends" (John 15:13 NLT).

Soldier

Then Elisha prayed and said, "O Lord I pray, open his eyes that he may see." And the Lord opened the servant's eyes and he saw; and behold, the mountain was full of horses and chariots of fire all around Elisha.
2 Kings 6:17

"Son of man, I have appointed you a watchman to the house of Israel; whenever you hear a word from My mouth, warn them from Me."
Ezekiel 3:17

Once upon a time, there was a little boy named Beau.

Beau had wanted to be a soldier from the time he was three or four, before he could even pronounce the word. He would remind his mother and father at least once every day, and it would be the first thing he would tell every new person he met. "I want to be a soja," he would say. Others thought it was so cute. His mother did not.

She was one of those who wanted to do her part in creating a new world order of peace. Over time she thought her role in this just might be to convince Beau to become a doctor instead. And so she never bought him the toy guns he saw advertised on TV, the ones he asked for over and over again for his birthday and Christmas.

Beau would listen to his mother's explanations for why toys guns were so bad, but at age five he could never quite understand what they possibly had to do with all the men who had died in past wars.

And Beau was industrious enough to save his change and buy a toy gun every time there was a garage sale in his neighborhood. He would hide them for a time and play with them when he thought his mother wasn't looking. But before long, he would be found out, and she would take the gun and discard it, despite his tears. It took Beau some time to learn that the more secret missions had to be fought using guns with silencers.

Eventually he learned to part with his dear weapons more maturely and came to accept he was only to have them for a time. Toy guns died just like soldiers did. And little did his mother know that in the end, it would not matter in the least what she did or didn't do with toy guns. Beau's dream would live on in his heart and one day would come true.

On most days, young Beau didn't need a toy gun anyway. All he had to do was walk out into the backyard and find the right stick. Every once in a while, he would even find a stick that had another little twig coming off it at a right angle, closer to one end, just like the grip on a real gun. And rocks worked just fine for hand grenades. Beau loved to throw them over the fence into Mr. and Mrs. Smith's backyard. It was so much easier to pretend there was a German patrol there when you couldn't see them. It felt a little safer too.

Beau would heave a grenade over the fence and kill every last one of those nasty Krauts. Sometimes he would even run out of spit from making so many explosion noises. Mr. and Mrs. Smith had always been a little annoyed that their backyard was a grenade range, but they also thought Beau was cute. They had overheard a lot of military dialogue over the years, all the rough talk between the American soldiers, the intensity when they were pinned down, and especially those last words spoken at their greatest moment of desperation, right when the last grenade was tossed that would save them all. They didn't mind picking up all the rocks, until the day the grenade didn't kill the Germans as planned, but Mrs. Smith's favorite clay planter. Mr. Smith wondered if it had been made in Germany.

Beau started to read history books on wars when he was in the fifth grade, and by the time he finished middle school, he was an expert on WWII. He grew up in the sixties when times were good and WWII was enough in the past that it was not a common conversation topic. It also helped a great deal that the war had been fought over there and not here.

Those who lost fiancés or young husbands had had some time to piece their lives back together, and most were well into new chapters of their lives. The parents who had lost sons would never be the same, but many had other children and grandchildren they were now placing their hopes in. And there were even more who were wounded, some who recovered their former selves, but some who did not.

The war had become the subject of good television and movies, and if you grew up watching *Combat* on TV, you know what I mean. There had never been good guys as good as the American GIs in WWII or bad guys as bad as those nasty Krauts. Deep in our hearts we know that war can never be this black and white, but we still want it to be.

WWII had such a huge impact on everyone, even more than WWI because technology had come a long way in the short years that intervened. Some believe that mankind has made the greatest progress in modern times with our weapons, in how efficient we have become in killing people. There is no doubt this was the difference between WWI and II, especially with the advent of the atom bomb. For the first time, mankind had developed a weapon that could potentially destroy the whole world. You could almost hear the sound of a collective sigh when the war finally ended, for the good guys had won, and the world, mostly as we had known it, was still here.

There was never a question that Beau would take ROTC in high school. It had been made for him. It didn't bother him that most of his friends said he was wasting his time with something that was "so not cool." Many of the kids Beau grew up with were smoking pot and experimenting with LSD while he was going to ROTC functions. But he never wavered. Something in Beau always wanted to be the hero, although he would not have used that word. It came from somewhere deep down within him. He felt strongly that someone had to be ready and prepared; someone had to pay attention. There were far too many dangers out there and always would be. Many people can be living regular lives and doing regular things, but Beau felt he was called to a higher purpose. He wanted to be one of those watching from the wall.

Beau's parents both had good careers, had been good savers, and planned to pay for Beau and his younger sister to go to college. But Beau thought it would be better if they just kept their money when it came to him and to use it on other things. He planned on enlisting as soon as he was done with high school and thought he would likely never hold another job. But just in case he changed his mind after a few years and wanted to attend college, Uncle Sam could pay for it. It might even make him a better soldier or officer.

The harder decision for him was which service to join. Beau eventually decided on the Marines and ultimately wanted to be in special services, Force Reconnaissance. He set more than one all-time record in the strength and endurance tests. You had to be an extraordinary soldier to even be considered for RECON, and then only 30 percent of these men made it all the way to graduation.

There were not that many men at the end of the day who were capable of all that was required, and even fewer who possessed a spirit and mind capable of withstanding the most tortuous of conditions. They were all proud and capable, but their training purposely forced them to prove to themselves and their commanders just how courageous they would be when faced with the physical and emotional end of themselves.

Beau managed to just miss the Vietnam War by the time he was fully trained; the last units were pulled out in March of 1973. He was disappointed, but he was mostly confused by this unusual time in our history during which we suffered not only our first defeat, but it tarnished our pride and image as well. By the time the war was over, protests in the US were large and frequent. Many Americans had lost their confidence in the government and the military, and many wondered if we should have ever been in Vietnam to begin with.

In one of our greatest disgraces, soldiers returning from Vietnam were screamed at and spit on instead of being honored as heroes.

These soldiers were just following orders, doing what they had to do. But many of them received the brunt of the frustration and anger of a public that would never have the opportunity to confront those who were truly to blame, the politicians and generals in Washington.

Although Beau had always envisioned fighting a regular war on a regular battlefield like in WWII, the world was changing. Vietnam was the first guerrilla war in which US soldiers spent more time looking for booby traps than they fought out in the open against uniformed enemy soldiers. They spent much of the time wondering if they could trust the Vietnamese civilians they thought they were there to protect. Out of frustration, the military resorted to using napalm to burn large areas of the jungle, a humanitarian disaster because fire does not discriminate between the enemy and innocent men, women, and children.

Beau wondered what his first real deployment or mission might look like, if he might ever be the kind of soldier he envisioned as a young boy.

In April of 1975, all of South Vietnam was finally collapsing to the North. By the end of the war, at least one hundred thousand refugees fled from South Vietnam, relocating to many places around the world. At the same time, there was another significant evacuation. There were a number of service organizations based in the West that ran orphanages in South Vietnam. A number of these organizations reached out to Washington in these last days, and President Ford responded. Beau and his unit of nine other men were sent with about a hundred other special forces to assure these children were safely airlifted out of Vietnam. The orphans would fly out on military cargo planes and subsequently find their way to their new homes in the US, Canada, Australia, and France. The mission was appropriately called Operation Babylift.

The first couple of days were spent visiting all the orphanages, consulting with the workers in Saigon and with American defense personnel, and putting together a logistics plan. They would transport the children and the defense workers who were to accompany them by bus to the airport, where military planes would be waiting.

Their best count included at least ten thousand children, many who were very young or even infants. They set up a makeshift headquarters in one of the larger orphanages and planned to move from one to the next until they were done with their mission.

Orphanages can be fairly structured places in more normal times, but this was not a normal time. They were managing but were substantially understaffed. Many Vietnamese workers had left to go home when the ceasefire and US troop withdrawal were announced two years earlier, and even more when it became apparent the North would win. No one had any assurance they would be well treated by their North Vietnamese captors after a war that had stretched on for twenty years.

Beau and his fellow RECON soldiers had been trained to always be focused and serious, but the tough-guy attitude seemed a bit overdone in the midst of the largest childcare facility he had ever seen. There was one little boy who kept peeking into the office they had set up as their command post. Once or twice Beau would catch his eye, and he would disappear, but before long he would be back. Each time the boy would try to be more discreet, hiding more of himself and just peeking with one eye. He couldn't have been more than five or six years old.

Some of these children had American GI fathers but were not children the fathers had ever claimed or even knew existed. This little boy seemed to be of mixed nationality himself. And many of the children had learned some English because of the caregivers from the West who worked there. Beau wondered if the boy could understand what they were saying and if he should worry about this, but he could not help but find the little guy cute.

Little boys are fascinated with soldiers, and Beau and his friends were some of the very best in the whole world. But Beau was thinking that other things were likely stirring in the boy's heart too. He had lived his whole life in Saigon during this war and was accustomed to seeing soldiers and guns and military vehicles. Most things were in good order, but the adults were more nervous now, and the children could sense this. And the children had also noticed that many of the adult workers had left and not returned, which could not be a good sign.

On the second or third day, Beau decided to talk with the boy. The boy's name was Hu'ng, pronounced "Hoong." Hu'ng's English was broken but pretty good. Hu'ng was fascinated with everything about Beau—his uniform, his belt, his pistol, even his boots. Beau could not help but remember himself at Hu'ng's age and how excited he would have been to be this close to a real soldier. Beau made an effort to speak to Hu'ng, to ask him about himself and about the orphanage.

The orphanage had been the only home Hu'ng had ever known. There were so many children at this orphanage, close to two thousand. They were all easy to have feelings for, but there was something different about Hu'ng. There was a little sparkle in his eye that made Beau think that Hu'ng could be incredibly brave. Little did Beau know that Hu'ng's name in Vietnamese meant "hero."

Beau and his fellow soldiers had been given several days to come up with the best plan and to then start the evacuation, which would easily take another several days. During downtime, Beau and Hu'ng would talk and walk around the orphanage. Hu'ng had many stories, some of them the things you might expect from a child but some not. Hu'ng had seen far too many children who were the victims of booby traps or stray bullets. But beyond these more grotesque symptoms of the war, there was also an unspoken but palpable tension in the air in Saigon. The front lines had never been that far away, but now the enemy was so close, the air was thick with . . . fear.

The orphanage was filled with many loving and caring adults, but there was no one in particular responsible for any one of the children. It could never provide the structure and security of a normal home like most of us have known. On its best day, the orphanage felt like a boarding school. Beau wondered how he would have held up under similar circumstances if his first five years had been the same as Hu'ng's. Beau thanked God again for all of His blessings and then said a prayer for Hu'ng and all of the children, that the evacuation would go well, but also that one day these children might have more normal lives. Beau also thought that someday he could visit Hu'ng and his new family, wherever that might be.

Beau's train of thought was cut short by another soldier who reported that the resistance on the outskirts of the city was faltering at a faster rate than anticipated. If they could, they needed to accelerate their plan. After several more meetings, the first flight out was planned for later that afternoon. Beau and the other soldiers filled up six buses with children and the adults necessary to attend to them during the long flights. The city was fairly chaotic, but they made it to the airport in a reasonable amount of time. The large cargo plane was ready and waiting, and after all the time it took to load all the babies and children and get them secured in both the troop compartment above and the cargo compartment below, the plane took off.

Beau and the other soldiers headed back to the orphanage to begin their preparations for the next group that would leave later that evening. On their way back, they received word over the radio that after takeoff, the plane had reported some kind of distress, had made a U-turn, and would land at a military base nearby. Radio contact from the plane had gone dead a minute or so later. After a few minutes, they received another report that the plane had been seen approaching the airport but was flying very low. It was thought the plane might have crashed. Beau and the other soldiers turned around to learn for themselves the fate of the plane and if they were needed to assist. At the very least, they would need to transfer all these children to another plane for evacuation.

As they approached the airport, they talked to several people who had seen the plane fly overhead. Before long they met a woman who told them that the plane did not make it to the runway, and she directed them to a nearby rice field. The buses could not negotiate the soft dirt and mud of the rice fields, and Beau and the other soldiers had to walk over a mile to make it to the plane, which they found in several pieces, some of it in flames. Beau could not believe his eyes.

It turned out that there had been some malfunction in the cargo doors after takeoff that caused them to explode outward. This not only left a large hole in the bottom rear portion of the plane but destroyed some of the hydraulics, leaving the plane disabled. The greater miracle had been that the plane was able to attempt a landing. By the time Beau and the other soldiers arrived, a good number of the men and women, including the pilots, had survived the crash and were doing what they could to help survivors. Those who had been in the troop compartment above for the most part survived, but it did not go so well for those in the cargo department below.

Beau received his first real combat experience that day right there in that rice field. He saw more death in one place than he would ever see for the rest of his life. And it could not have been more depressing, for so many of the dead and maimed were little children, even babies. Between the soldiers and defense workers, they did an amazing job of saving those they could. It was good so many had basic medical training, with all the wounds and burns.

Miraculously, some assistance did come from Saigon to transport those who needed treatment to the nearest hospital. In the end seventy-five children and thirty-eight adults, mostly defense personnel assigned to help with the mission, died in the crash. Just over half of those on the plane survived. Beau and his fellow soldiers felt like they were utter failures even though they had done nothing wrong. They headed back to Saigon with heavy hearts but no time to rest or recover.

The soldiers shared the incredibly bad news with the other soldiers and adult workers back at the command post, but discreetly, so that none of the children could overhear. Everything they had control over had been executed to perfection, and it had all come to naught when the plane malfunctioned. Hopefully, going forward they would be spared all the other forms of trouble they were anticipating: their route to the airport being obstructed, the North Vietnamese breaking into the city and taking over the airport, the US soldiers being targeted by snipers, etc.

The section of the orphanage Hu'ng lived in was included with the next group to go, but Hu'ng did not appear with the other children when they gathered. Beau thought to say something to one of the administrators but was quickly distracted by his responsibilities. This time everything went according to plan. The city was becoming increasingly chaotic, the airport was being flooded with people hoping to find some way to get out, and the soldiers had to use their weapons more than once to create open space for the buses to pass, but did so without incident. The plane took off and within minutes was safely out of Vietnam airspace.

About this same time, workers at the orphanage heard from the hospital that some of the children who had been hurt in the crash were ready to be released and could fly out at any time. And there were others who would be released over the next day or so and could do the same. Those in critical condition would have to stay and would likely miss the evacuation.

After returning to the orphanage, Beau searched for Hu'ng and eventually found him in one of the halls.

"Where have you been? Were you not supposed to fly out with the last group?"

"I didn't want to go without you, leave you behind . . . so I hid. You may need my help!" Hu'ng said.

Beau kept himself from laughing out loud, but he smiled.

"And just *how* might you be able to help?" Beau asked.

"I am not sure . . . but you might need me."

Beau thought Hu'ng's words were cute, but he believed Hu'ng was making it up as he went. He didn't really think he could help; he was only five years old. Hu'ng was just trying to find some way to disguise the fact he didn't want to be separated from Beau, that most likely he felt safer with him close by. Beau understood. He would have felt the same way.

But then Beau had the oddest feeling. It was one of those feelings that washes over you from one moment to the next with no connection to any thought or feeling that preceded it. Usually it is very hard to put into words. And although you might be tempted to dismiss it as a chance association, or a misplaced memory, or even an electron firing by accident . . . you know better. It grabs your attention primarily because it is *so different* from the thoughts and feelings that just preceded it, like it just arrived from some other world.

As odd as all of this sounds, and as surreal as it feels, if you have ever experienced anything like this, there is also something about it that feels so clear and so grounded, that feels *more* real than the real things you have always known. If that even makes sense. It might not.

Beau looked at Hu'ng, and his last words echoed in Beau's mind. "*. . . but you might need me.*"

Maybe, just maybe, Beau thought, *he knows something I don't.*

Another soldier called out to Beau from behind him at the far end of the hall. Beau turned and told him he would be right there, but when he turned back, Hu'ng was gone. "Hu'ng! Where did you go?" Not a sound. "Hu'ng, I have to go back to a meeting. Now, you do what the adults tell you to do, okay? It's all going to be all right." Still no sound. Beau turned to walk away, looking back once or twice as he went to see if he could catch Hu'ng peeking from behind one of the doorways, but did not see him.

On the next trip to the airport, Hu'ng was included. "It is time," he simply said. Beau was happy he was finally obeying.

"Can I stay close by you?" Hu'ng asked.

"Well, of course, young man. I may need your help, just like you said. But if I give you an order, you have to follow it. That is what a good soldier does. Okay?"

"Okay," Hu'ng said.

It would be another several weeks before the city would fall to the North, but small undercover groups of North Vietnamese soldiers disguised as civilians had entered the city (like they always had) and were doing reconnaissance. They had just been given orders to fire upon the enemy if they came upon any high-ranking officers or strategic targets. These would likely be suicide missions, but these soldiers were dedicated.

When one of these men saw the RECON soldiers driving and directing the first few buses, he had no way to know the nature of the mission but thought it must be important. Most of the children were so small they were not visible in the buses from street level. When the sixth and then seventh bus passed, this North Vietnamese soldier could hardly contain himself. He radioed his commander, and they quickly decided to create an ambush several blocks away. There were fifteen of the North Vietnamese, but they did not look any different than any other South Vietnamese civilian. A few of them stayed on the street, but most took up positions inside buildings and on rooftops.

One of the North Vietnamese acted as if he was just crossing the street in front of the first bus, but then abruptly stopped, turned, and faced the bus. He pulled out an automatic rifle from under his coat and pointed it right at the soldier driving the bus. The soldier slammed on the brakes and just managed to stop before running him over. That would have been better. The two of them locked eyes, separated only by a windshield.

The soldier, knowing that the enemy was likely not alone, but having to make the best guess he could, decided his best option was to end it right there. He tried to draw his handgun as quickly as he could but was not fast enough. The North Vietnamese filled the windshield with bullets. Beau drove the second bus, which he'd brought to an abrupt stop just behind the first. He could not see what happened, but he heard it. Then he saw the armed man walk around to the front door of the first bus and kick it, trying to open it.

There were several other soldiers on the first bus, but Beau scanned the streets and was ready to jump out to take matters into his own hands. Before he could, more shots were fired, and the armed man dropped to the ground. One of the soldiers on the first bus took him out. Hundreds of civilians on the street had already scattered, and the street was mostly empty. There were a few cars here and there in between, but all the buses were lined up at a standstill over a block or so. No one expected there to be just one gunman, unless he was someone who was deranged. Until the enemy engaged them again, they had no way to know who to fight.

The driver of the first bus, one of Beau's best friends, was not dead yet but was mortally wounded. Another soldier took his place in the driver's seat, which was soaked with blood. The soldiers talked by radio and decided to push forward. The drivers of the cars in front of the first bus and in between the others all pulled off to the side of the street, parked, and ran for cover. The seven buses rolled forward. But before they moved another hundred feet, gunshots rang out, hitting several of the buses.

The best thing to do would have been to continue on, but with all the panic from the gunshots, several other people had abandoned their cars on the street just ahead of the caravan and blocked it. They would have to fight it out. But first they had to wait. Wait and be shot upon in order to even know where to return fire.

What had been known as shell shock and battle fatigue in past wars became so commonplace in the years just after Vietnam that it finally was given a special name: post-traumatic stress disorder, or PTSD. War is hard enough under "normal" conditions. Having to wait to be fired upon, an order from High Command that all American GIs had to follow, was a death sentence to soldiers and cruel and unusual torture to many souls.

Shots rang out again, and Beau felt the bullets from an automatic weapon stream down the side of his bus, shattering many windows, hitting some of the adults and children. It was hard enough to locate the shooters with buildings so close on either side but even harder from within the bus. Some of the soldiers would have to go out into the street to find the enemy and take them out.

Beau quickly volunteered and shouted at Hu'ng to stay put and stay down. He was sitting right behind the driver's seat. Beau shouted to one of his buddies to close the door after he exited. He lunged out of the bus and crouched down next to a car parked on that side of the street. He was open to fire from behind him but sheltered from everything in front. This was about as good as it would get. Shots rang out and hit the bus, and he could see they were coming from a street-level window about twenty paces away. He did not hesitate but was already moving before the shots ended. The soldiers and kids on the buses were sitting ducks—there was no time to spare.

Beau kept low to the ground and in a few seconds made it all the way to one side of the window. He knew this gunman would never expect anything to happen the moment he stopped firing. Soldiers never do. They are still feeling the rush of having just let loose of so much destructive power. But it is a false notion.

In one motion, just as he heard the weapon pause, just like something out of a secret agent movie, Beau rose to his feet and leapt headfirst through the open window, his automatic weapon blazing. His first rounds did not do the job, and it was his helmet that actually knocked the gun out of the man's hands. Within seconds of hitting the floor inside, Beau finished it.

He quickly went upstairs to see if he could gain a more strategic view from the windows or the rooftop. Several other soldiers took up positions on the street with similar intentions, but they were all at a disadvantage. Another of Beau's buddies was taken out from a rooftop behind him. He had been in clear view of an enemy sniper.

From the enemy's perspective, the safest, and maybe wisest, thing to do was to continue to shoot at the buses from time to time to upset the soldiers and continue to flush them out. If they'd had an unlimited amount of ammunition, which they did not, they might have continued to do this indefinitely. As far as they knew, the cargo could have been the most senior defense personnel still in Saigon. But any time they fired, they also risked giving up their positions. The best tack seemed somewhere in the middle. This could go on for a long time.

The enemy did have some grenades but nothing more powerful. They had been undercover as civilians and had not been able to carry anything they could not easily conceal under their clothes. There were two of the enemy who were less wise, or maybe just more cruel. They decided to open up for a good while on the bus right in front of them. They fired out the windows of a building on the street level.

A large number of civilians had not been able to find any good place to hide when the shooting first broke out and had collected on the sidewalk in front of this same building, crouched against the front wall as low as they could. Beau stayed in his position and listened to the gunfire pelting the bus but could not take it anymore. After going back downstairs, he had to cover about seventy-five feet. He ran as fast as he could down the sidewalk, and several other soldiers from different directions closed in as well. Most of the soldiers, including Beau, had not been able to see these civilians on the sidewalk until they were right upon them. But as soon as they did, their hearts sank.

The civilians were about to get caught in a tremendous crossfire. Beau settled for a few moments in a position behind another car, scanning the rooftops and windows behind him, hoping he was okay where he was. He started to pray the enemy in this building would stop firing at the bus. The screams were at a high pitch now, but the firing just continued. There were two windows from which all the rounds were coming. One of the North Vietnamese saw the soldiers closing in and literally reached out the window and down to the sidewalk and grabbed a six- or seven-year-old Vietnamese girl who was trying to hide with her mother. He pulled her up off her feet into the building and was holding her as a shield in front of him with one arm while continuing to fire his automatic weapon with the other.

I have heard that ethics professors have written about wartime dilemmas like this. I would bet that some generals have never been able to silence these questions in their minds as old men. Situations where multiple things are in play, where the complexity of a situation makes it exceedingly difficult to know the best course of action.

How do you measure the value of one person's life over another? How precious and valuable was the life of this innocent little girl being used as a shield, while every moment she was held there, and no soldier fired for fear of killing her, more children and adults on that bus were dying? The easiest thing to do at this point was to spray the front of the building with bullets. There were several soldiers close by who could do this at the same time and likely eliminate the problem, but some of the civilians crouching there would likely die too. Not one of the RECON soldiers had yet found the heart to open fire.

Beau quickly moved into the storefront in front of him, just one space to the side of the targets. He didn't think the enemy had seen him. He passed by several civilians hiding behind merchandise and exited out the back door into an alley. Then just as quickly, but carefully, he approached the back door of the next storefront. He hoped no one was standing guard, said a little prayer, and quickly moved in.

Beau entered into a rear room filled with boxes, but no people, and fixed his eyes on a closed door in front of him. Behind that door should be the two gunmen. He was resolute on saving the little girl's life but knew there were no guarantees. Beau knew he had to make his move right then, something he would live with for the rest of his life. This coward of an enemy had already decided to use this little girl's life as a shield for his own; he would not change his course midstream.

Beau kicked the door in, surprised the two men, and took out the man on the right who first turned to face him. The other man could not turn as quickly while holding the girl, but seeing his comrade go down, he spun around. The girl was just heavy enough that as he turned, she slipped out of his grasp. Coward that he was, before she even hit the ground, he made his decision. Instead of firing at Beau, he pointed his automatic weapon down at the girl, just before Beau squeezed his trigger. As she hit the floor, the sniper pressed the barrel of his gun to her head and yelled at Beau in Vietnamese. His intent was clear, although his words were not. "Fire at me, and I kill her."

Beau stood there, silent, motionless, for what seemed like an eternity but was only five seconds. He hoped one his buddies would fire from the street and hit this guy from behind, but that did not happen. For the moment all had gone silent; the other soldiers might have thought the job was already done.

And then, out of nowhere, Hu'ng walked up right beside him, looked up, and said, "See, I was right. You did need me." Beau's first impulse was to grab Hu'ng and toss him out of the door behind him, but he was so stunned he froze. How had Hu'ng managed to follow him all this way? How had he found the courage to do so? Beau turned, and the enemy was still staring right at him, his gun still at the girl's head. He was not looking at Hu'ng.

And then Hu'ng said, "Look again at your foe. Are you all alone in this?"

Beau looked back at his opponent and began to see shapes or forms appearing to either side of this man and also above him. At first Beau thought his eyes were failing him or maybe he was becoming faint, but the forms just became more clear and definite. They were in the shape of people, but more like ghosts, as they were partially transparent.

The enemy kept his eyes focused on Beau.

Beau had wanted to be a soldier his whole life. He was finally living his dream. He had never once thought that if he found himself in a moment like this, it would be too much for him, that the stress of it would undo him. Anyone can be wrong about such things, even someone like Beau. And then it occurred to him, maybe *he wasn't* losing his mind—maybe he was being given an opportunity to see beyond this realm.

As he continued to look across the room, the forms continued to become more clear, almost solid now, but the enemy had still not moved his head. There were three forms there, one on either side of the man and one hovering above him. They all had swords: the form above holding his sword in front of the man's neck, the form to the left holding it across his midsection, and the form on the right holding his sword down, on top of the man's arm that was holding the gun.

The enemy should have been able to see these forms, or at least their swords, but apparently did not or could not, because he never lifted his eyes off Beau. And he still hadn't looked to where Hu'ng was standing. And then Hu'ng softly quoted Exodus 14:13–14: "'Do not fear! Stand by and see the salvation of the Lord, which He will accomplish for you today; . . . the Lord will fight for you, while you keep silent.'" And Beau was.

All of a sudden, the North Vietnamese man had a look of terror on his face. It still did not seem like he could see the three figures, but he was frozen. Beau wondered if he could feel the three blades pressed down on him, or maybe he was just struck with paralysis. Either way, it did not matter.

The form to his right moved his sword from on top of the man's arm to behind it and then quickly thrust the sword out toward Beau, ripping the gun out of the man's grasp and onto the floor in front of him. There was no doubt about it now. The enemy was trembling, helpless. Beau thought to go ahead and take him out but paused. He was not alone in this now, and even more, he felt just a little outranked.

He turned to look at Hu'ng, who now looked more like a spiritual form himself than an actual boy. Hu'ng calmly quoted 2 Kings

6:22: "You shall not kill them. Would you kill those you have taken captive?' Bind him and leave him here," Hu'ng said. "And give the girl back to her mother."

Beau simply did as Hu'ng said.

"I know you will find all of this hard to believe," Hu'ng continued, not talking like a five-year-old, "but all is safe now. The other enemies have all been bound, the children and adults and soldiers who were injured or killed have all been made well, and your passage has been cleared to go forward. Go now, and complete your duty."

And Beau did. He bound the man, who was so undone he could not stop crying. He handed the little girl back to her mother. And he turned around to say something more to Hu'ng, but he had vanished into thin air.

Beau lived to be an old man. He learned to only share the story of his time in Saigon with those with more open minds. He made a full career in the Marines, eventually serving in the Pentagon as a top adviser, and he was a wise but cool head when it was most needed.

Before he'd left Saigon, he'd checked the register of names of all of the children at the orphanages more than once but was never able to find Hu'ng listed there. He was not surprised. He'd also asked several of his buddies if they could remember Hu'ng, and especially Beau talking with him, but they'd all said no or just looked at him strangely. Beau was not surprised, again.

Special forces soldiers know just how important courage and confidence are, for they are often sent into the most dangerous of situations. But whenever the occasion arose for Beau to talk to younger soldiers about battle situations, about courage and confidence, he always remembered his time in Saigon. And from time to time, he would share the real events of that day, that his confidence in that moment had not come from himself but from somewhere else. From *Someone* else.

Time Machine

Coincidences are God's way of remaining anonymous.
—Albert Einstein

God is in one mind, and who can turn Him?
His measures are never broken, nor is He ever put upon
new counsels, but what He has purposed shall be effected,
and all the world cannot defeat nor disannul it.
—Matthew Henry, *Commentary on the Whole Bible*, Ecclesiastes 3:1

Once upon a time, there was a man who hoped to change the world.

He was a brilliant scientist with a great theoretical mind. He was born in Germany in 1912, just two years before the beginning of the First War. His father fought in the German army but was killed in 1916, just before his son's fourth birthday.

The man could not remember his father; he was too young the last time he saw him. He only had the pictures his mother placed on the mantel above the fireplace for his memory. The one picture fixed in his mind was taken the day his father enlisted. He was standing tall with a proud smile, dressed in his captain's uniform.

The years after the war were hard. The allies blamed Germany, which seemed reasonable, and punished that nation severely. The treaty the German leaders were compelled to sign required them to pay full financial reparations for the war, 269 billion dollars in present-day currency. The debt was eventually paid, believe it or not, after ninety-two years.

These reparations crippled the German economy for decades after the war and were part of the reason so many German citizens were willing to support a radical new leader named Adolph Hitler. Hitler began his political career in 1919, the year after WWI ended, and for fourteen years, with the help of others, planned his rise to power, which came to fruition in March of 1933.

Our scientist's name was Klaus Richter. This last name in the German language traditionally meant "judge," and in the early nineteen hundreds was still appropriate for Klaus's father, who had been such an accomplished attorney as a young man that he became a judge when he was only twenty-nine. Although his mother hoped Klaus would follow in his footsteps, his passion was always for science. He was fascinated by the sky as early as the age of five. As he grew older, the figure from the past who most intrigued him was Sir Isaac Newton.

Newton's academic world included mechanics and astronomy, and his body of work eventually allowed him to attempt a description of the workings of the universe. To Klaus, whose doctoral degree was in physics, nothing was as important as the concepts and laws that could explain the foundation of the whole world.

It was difficult to be as intelligent as Klaus, to understand some of these things as well as he did, and not feel he was somehow closer to God. He believed there was a greater, underlying reason why he was so drawn to this science, some greater purpose that would manifest one day. He just wasn't sure what this might be.

Newton's theories explained the present motions of objects on earth, the earth itself, and bodies in space. By using their existing motion, their mass, and all the other forces acting upon them, he could also predict their future motions. This was quite an incredible revelation in the late seventeenth and early eighteenth centuries. Newton also believed God was ultimately in control of the universe and that He intervened to assure the continued stability of our solar system.

Klaus was only twenty-six when Hitler invaded Poland in 1939, starting WWII, but was so intelligent that he had completed his graduate studies in math and physics four years earlier. He was so engrossed in his work that he paid little attention to political events, but it was impossible, before long, not to realize there was something different about the Third Reich. His citizenship was not sufficient to assure his loyalty. The SS required him to sign a document that made this absolutely clear.

Using Newton's principles as a basis, Klaus discovered he could "predict" the position of the earth at any time in the past. It was all really Newton's math, looking back instead of forward. Klaus thought more and more of the past itself, not just the past positions of the physical earth and the other bodies in our solar system. And once he started pondering the concept of time, he could not stop. He eventually explored the relationship between mass and time and was beginning to think that time travel, at least to the past, might be possible.

Time is a strange thing, is it not? It is thought that time did not exist in the very beginning. Somehow, God has always been and always will be. He did not have a beginning, and He will never have an end.

And although Adam and Eve were created by God, like all the rest of creation, and so they *did* have a beginning . . . it was not God's intention they have an end. They were to continue existing just as they were, living in an immortal physical universe with immortal physical bodies. God's hope, in the beginning, was that they would continue to exist just as they were, forever.

But since the fall, everything in the physical world has had a beginning and *will have* an end. Now, all matter breaks down. It may have been Augustine who first said God invented time for us, implying that somehow it helps us. I am not sure how. But it sure seems impossible to think of our lives *outside* of time.

When you think about it more objectively, the only thing that really exists is the present moment. You know the past existed, you know it happened, for you can remember so much of it. You remember an hour ago, yesterday, and twenty years ago. But ever since they passed, they only live in your memory, somehow stored in the physical mass of your brain. The past was real, you know it, and there is other evidence of this—all the things that were created or changed somehow at some point in the past that still exist today. But as for the past itself, you can never go there again. Not as it was when it was happening all around you.

And the present moment is only a moment. You remember the beginning of this sentence by the time you get to the end of it ... *right now.* By the time you got to the end of that sentence, the beginning of it was already in the past. And by now, that whole sentence, and everything I have said since, is also in the past ... *right now.* A little mind-boggling, is it not?

The future is very different, but in a way, the opposite. You know it is going to happen, for it happens every day. You wake up and know what a good part of your day will consist of because you have already planned it. You don't know everything you will think and feel and decide to do, and you definitely do not know the great majority of what anybody else will think and feel and do. But most days go by, and you are not that surprised. You could have predicted the day pretty closely but not completely.

Many people have said this because it is true: we waste an enormous part of our lives regretting things we have done or not done in our *past*, and we waste even more time worrying about all the things that might occur in our *future*. But the only thing that is even real, truly real, is this very moment, *right now.*

If we could just free ourselves of our regrets and disappointments from the past and all of our worries about the future and live our lives more fully in the present moment, we would be a great deal happier. And then as soon as I say that, the moment is already over and we have already begun a new moment. What would life be like without time? It is hard to imagine.

As Klaus more and more attempted to understand time and the laws that control it, he began to look at the past as a shadow of the present. There was a dark and noticeable shadow if the past was recent, but a more faded and difficult-to-see shadow if the past was long ago.

Whereas most people seem more intrigued with the future and even the possibility of traveling there, Klaus did not think this would ever be possible. This would require the existence of multiple universes running parallel to each other in some way as if the future already existed in another dimension, and we could go there if we could somehow jump from this "stream" to that. To Klaus, the future was not real, not yet, but only a figment in the mind. It might be more real to God somehow, since He knows and can see all things, but not for us. And so it is not a destination we could ever go to.

But Klaus became more and more intrigued with the concept of time travel to the past and was immersed in this research for several years. He had some breakthroughs, and in 1938 Klaus constructed the first prototype of a time machine. He believed the machine could leave the present and travel back to a certain time in the past. He was also able to preset the controls so that the machine would return to his laboratory at a set time. And his calculations must have been correct, for it did this very thing.

He then began to use primates to take the "trip." The monkey that took the first trip was dead when the machine returned. An autopsy revealed radioactive contamination. He assumed the time travel itself had somehow caused this, though he did not know why. Klaus hoped a suit would protect them from this during future trips.

The second monkey, named Hannah, suit and all, returned back alive and apparently in good health, although she never again spent much time with the other monkeys. Monkeys are social creatures, and it was obvious the journey had affected her. Hannah would stare off into space for the longest periods of time, as if she were thinking about larger things. It was too bad there was not a monkey psychologist she could speak with, for it might have helped. Or maybe she had just decided she wanted to spend the majority of *her* time grappling with the concept of time, like Klaus.

With only primates, Klaus could never insist the experiment had been successful. All he had done for sure was to make the machine disappear when he wanted and reappear at a designated time later.

A person would have to go next if he were to prove the machine had actually traveled back in time.

At some point Klaus's scientific superiors talked of his research to officers in the Abwehr, the German intelligence service, but also to SS officers, who seemed to be involved in everything. By the time word got to Hitler, there was still doubt about the reality of time transportation, but there was also great excitement about the possibility. Klaus needed volunteers, which in normal times might have been difficult, but not in Nazi Germany. Before long dozens of men were reassigned to Klaus's laboratory. He was ordered to interview these men and given the authority to decide the best candidates for the experiment.

Klaus had always been so in love with his work, but for the first time, it occurred to him he was no longer a boy playing with his chemistry set. He could still lose himself in his laboratory, but the risks and the rewards had grown much larger now. He had felt bad using monkeys for the experiments, but not so bad he didn't use them. It was necessary for science to progress, he told himself.

But as he contemplated sending men—men who had no choice in this endeavor and men who might die or never be the same—it all changed for him. He attempted to talk about this to his immediate superior but was cut short. This gentleman seemed sure of the importance of the work to the Reich and especially for the "motherland," but Klaus could sense fear beneath his patriotic words. They could both pretend there was some choice in this. There was not.

Klaus had never hoped for Adolf Hitler to rise to power. He had never wanted to become a member of the Nazi Party. He had just wanted to continue to do the research he was so fascinated with. One day, he hoped his work would change the world for the better. And so he tried not to think about all these other things and to just do his job, but a restlessness grew inside him. There was dread in his heart, a dread of what the world would be like with the Reich in charge.

Klaus was still excited about the advancement of science but could not pretend any excitement for the advancement of the Reich, so he would carefully leave this out in his orientations for the research candidates. He was always surprised when some of the men, nevertheless, would respond with a loud "Heil Hitler." They had been well trained. They had already accepted the fact that their lives were nothing compared to the ultimate objective—the future reign of the Reich over the entire civilized world.

Klaus was not so sure how to pick the best candidates for the machine's next trips. What attributes might be important? They should be in the best health physically and mentally. They had to be able to stay focused at all times and observe and record everything that occurred so that Klaus could learn from this. Other than that, they needed to be brave. Klaus felt compelled to tell them he did not know for sure what the journey would be like, that there could be permanent side effects, and there was some possibility they might not survive.

It was another thing altogether to decide what the time travelers should do when they arrived at their "destination." They needed to get out of the machine and explore. They should find something to bring back that could prove they had gone to the past. A copy of that day's newspaper, still fresh and new, would be the best proof. They could take a camera and take some pictures, but he was not sure if the film would survive the trip unscathed.

And here we come to the one detail that many of us remember from all the time travel stories we have ever known. Time travelers need to be extremely careful with whom they interact and what they do. If it is, in fact, the very same past that you and I had known, they need to be very careful they do nothing to change that past. Any action they take while they are there could have a permanent effect going forward. Anything they say or do that causes someone else to do *anything different* than they would have done otherwise would change the trajectory of the past into the present from the way it *would have* been. People make important decisions every day, but sometimes even the smallest of things can result in something significant.

For example, a young boy decides to become a doctor because he was walking to school one day when he was eight years old and just so happened to come upon a group of people gathered tightly together on the sidewalk. The boy was able to push his way through the people, and when he did, he saw a woman lying there and a young medical student attending to her. The woman had just had a heart attack, and the boy watched in amazement as the medical student brought her back to life. She had stopped breathing and had been dead for several minutes. The boy decided right then and there he would be a doctor, one who, during his career, helped alleviate the conditions of thousands of people and saved dozens of lives.

If a time traveler inadvertently delayed that little boy so that he missed that sidewalk miracle altogether, he may have never become a doctor. What would happen to all the people he had treated in the real past before that reality had ever been tampered with? Would not everything in his life that had resulted because of his decision to be a doctor not just . . . cease to exist? Especially the better health of so many people he had treated and the very lives of those he had been able to save from death, but so many other things as well? Many of them would have just found other doctors, but not all those doctors would have done the very same things he would have done.

And we could go on and on with many other examples when something seemingly insignificant occurred at one particular moment but, one way or the other, led to a particular action that led to another that over time became something significant indeed.

Like two people who met at a party who would have never met otherwise and married two years later. Forty years later, their children and grandchildren numbered thirty people.

Or a seventeen-year-old boy who worked as a summer intern for a congressman in Washington, DC, only because his father knew someone who worked in his office. The young man had never been interested in politics; this was his father's idea. He argued for weeks with his parents about this but finally relented and applied for the position, hoping he would be rejected. He was only given the internship because the five candidates who interviewed better than him took other opportunities. But the experience turned out to be nothing like he imagined, so much so he decided to major in political science in college. He later went to law school. Twenty-two years later he was elected president of the United States.

Or another young man who read Sigmund Freud's *The Interpretation on Dreams* in high school only because the teacher decided to include it on a list of books that could be used for a report. The young man only chose this book because the title sounded less boring than all the rest. He had no idea who Sigmund Freud even was.

But the ideas this young man learned from Dr. Freud introduced him to a secret world he never knew existed and made an impact he would never forget. These ideas influenced the way he thought about people for the rest of his life. They also led to his decision to be a psychologist, which he was for the greater part of his adult life.

And when God finally became important to him later in life, the in-depth understanding he had acquired of the human mind and heart was a great advantage that helped him take leaps and bounds that otherwise might not have been possible. He came to understand the greatest story of all in a deeper and richer way, so much so he could not keep himself from becoming a writer. And who knows, maybe one day some of his words will actually change the trajectory of someone else's life, and their life, someone else's, and so on.

You know, you might doubt the real impact of your life at times, for it can be hard to see concrete and tangible results from most of what we say and do on any given day. Sometimes we are capable of doing great deeds, and the benefits to others are obvious. But sometimes even the smallest of kindnesses we extend to someone else can change the world. Do you believe that?

I do. I very much look forward to being in heaven, for I think we will finally be able to see many of these things that were a chain reaction of sorts: one thing cascading into another, into another, and so on until it finally blooms into full life. From time to time, God may just call our name and ask for us to sit down. He will give us an object lesson, not because we need it any longer but just because He wants to show off. He loves sharing His joy with us.

He will demonstrate one of His greatest attributes: the fact that He uses everything to work for our good. He will direct our eyes to earth and will create a picture show for us of the past, demonstrating to us the most incredible "coincidences," if you want to call them that.

The Lord will start with one thing . . . say, a good deed done by a gentleman who "just so happened" to be walking by a homeless man on the street. The gentlemen stopped because he noticed the homeless man's sign said he was willing to work for food. The gentlemen had just been having lunch with a friend who had a landscaping business, who sometimes hired anyone for a day to give them a chance.

This landscaper usually went to a local intersection in an impoverished part of town where men hung out in the morning, hoping an employer would come by to use them for the day. The gentleman decided to give the homeless man his friend's phone number and told him to call him if he really wanted to work. The homeless man had put those words on his sign only to make himself look better, to encourage some to give him money who wouldn't have otherwise. The gentleman who stopped to talk to him would not have stopped if he had not seen those words. He had never given anything to someone on the street.

This homeless man had an alcohol problem he was feeding. But for some reason he would never be able to explain (and right here, God would show you how at that very moment He reached down and actually touched the man's head with His finger), he decided to dial this phone number the next day. And one day's work led to another, and another, and something in the man's mind and heart changed.

And something began to happen between the landscape employer and this man as well. God was doing many things in the landscaper's life too, but that is another story. But all of our stories intertwine, and the relationship between these two men is an example of that.

The man turned out to be a good employee, and his boss was appreciative of this, giving him more responsibility over time. After working together for several years, the two men became good friends, and the friendship turned into an apprenticeship, which ultimately turned into discipleship. It turned out the landscaper had struggled with alcoholism when he was a young man (which was one of the reasons he'd given men on the street a chance to work) and was able to encourage the man to start going to meetings. After a while, the man became sober for good.

Ten years later, this man, who had once been a homeless alcoholic, became a pastor and had one of the best testimonies of redemption anyone had ever heard. By the time he retired, some estimated he had redeemed the lives of thousands of homeless men and women, most of whom were still leading productive lives. Many would have died living on the street, still addicted, malnourished, and crippled with anxiety and depression.

And what might have happened if the first gentlemen had not decided to stop and talk to this man and given him his friend's phone number? The Lord had seen *all* of it before *any* of it ever occurred. All of these occurrences were like dominos, existential dominos, one falling, hitting the next, and the next, on and on, until it all worked for good.

I apologize—I forgot about Klaus. That happens sometimes. If you knew me better, you would have just laughed out loud. It also pulls back the curtain a little on the fact these stories are not just stories but a vehicle to communicate greater things. Sssshhhhh! Don't tell anyone.

One day, something happened that forever changed the trajectory of Klaus's life, something apparently coincidental. Klaus was contacted by a cousin on his mother's side of the family, whom he had not seen in years. This man was a high-ranking German officer named Armand Konig. He told Klaus a secret, a secret that scared him to death.

The secret was that Klaus's maternal grandmother was Jewish, but she'd died giving birth to twins when she was twenty-three. The twins were fraternal, a boy and a girl. The boy was Klaus's father, the girl Armand's mother. Their grandfather, this woman's husband, was a gentile.

Although Adolf and the Reich were more recent events in German history, Jews had never been popular. The husband had had the means and the connections necessary to essentially erase his wife's Jewish ancestry, something he'd done after her death. He'd had no idea that anything like the Reich was coming, but something inside told him this would be wise.

Armand came forward because of his conscience. He was high up in the Nazi chain of command and had been informed the eradication of the Jews had already begun. His mother had learned of the family secret at some point from her father. She'd kept it to herself but had told Armand on her deathbed. He had kept the secret to himself until now.

When Armand learned of the "Final Solution," as it was called, he felt as if a part of himself was being wiped out. He did not think he would ever be able to do anything about it, but he needed to talk to someone. Klaus was the only one he knew who could both share in his angst and be just as motivated to keep the secret.

Klaus was dumbfounded and terrified. Armand assured him no one would ever learn the truth—it was just as if this ancestry had never existed. For the same reason, Klaus could never prove it to anybody, even if he tried. They decided to meet again and talk further. Over the following weeks and months, they came to believe that maybe 100 percent of their hearts did not have to remain loyal to the Reich. Maybe, somehow, they could do something, anything, that could help their family.

As early as 1932 and as late as 1944, there were at least twenty-two documented plots or attempts to assassinate Adolf Hitler. All of these came from within German ranks. There may have never been a political and military figure as feared and hated from within his own command. A fair number of these plans could have succeeded if some last-minute delay or unrelated change in schedule had not occurred. It is almost as if God was protecting Adolf, or someone.

But there are no documented attempts on Hitler's life as creative as the plan that formed in Klaus's mind. You shouldn't have to think long to guess what he had in mind. The greater question would be *when.* When would be the best time to go back into the past and kill Adolf Hitler?

You could argue the sooner, the better, but it would be hard to murder a child. Hitler was not alone in his fascist ideals, but everything remaining equal, the earlier he died, the greater the impact should be on the Reich, maybe even erasing it altogether. He was the face of the Reich, their trump card. Gaining access to Hitler would obviously be critical, but this would be far easier the earlier it was in his life. As Klaus considered this, he felt a little like God.

What if God questioned something humanity had done that He had one way or the other allowed to happen? If God had created time, could He not just go back in time and correct the mistake? And there was a precedent of sorts for this.

God did very much regret creating man early on because man became so corrupt. He wiped out the whole world with water, preserving only Noah and his family and at least one pair of all the other creatures. He did promise, however, he would never destroy the world again in this same way, and He created the rainbow in the sky to be a sign, a reminder of this promise.

Humanity has been responsible for so much tragedy, so much pain, so much atrocity. It all has to break God's heart. There has to be a greater plan, some explanation for why God has allowed all that He has. Even so, what if once a century or so, *even God* questioned what He had allowed? Klaus wondered if his plan of going back to the past to assassinate Adolf Hitler before he ever rose to power might not be the first time such a thing had happened.

And then he wondered if *this* was his life's purpose, if maybe it always had been. Might God have predetermined that Klaus was born ... right when he was and in Germany?

Given him the mind he had for physics so that he would begin to grapple with the concept of time?

Encouraged him to create a time machine?

Saw to it he had Jewish ancestry?

Made sure his cousin would learn what he did, had them come together, and put it in their minds to go back in time to stop what might turn out to be one of the greatest atrocities to ever happen in the history of this world?

Klaus shared his idea with Armand, who knew nothing of Klaus's research. Only a handful of people did. Klaus did not want to sacrifice his life for any cause but began to believe this just might be worth it. Hopefully, he would be able to succeed and return to the present unharmed, but he knew this could never be assured. And he wasn't completely sure the time machine would work, but there was only one way to find out. And Klaus needed at least one man to stay behind in the laboratory. Armand agreed to be that man, knowing that he, too, was risking his life. The Reich had no mercy or compassion for traitors.

Late one night Klaus and Armand met at the laboratory. It was good the lab was in Munich, for Klaus often had to be in town for Reich business. They were both careful to make sure no one saw them leave their residences or followed them to the lab. Klaus had never married. His work was so consuming that he had never found the time. Which is just a bit ironic, is it not?

Klaus had secretly made all the preparations for the trip with no one the wiser. All he had to do was climb into the machine and strap himself in. There were several prototypes of suits that had been made; Klaus just needed to pick one that fit. He had already spoken with Armand at length and written all his instructions down. If everything went according to plan, they could be finished in six or seven hours, and Klaus back to February 18, 1940, around daybreak. It was a Saturday night, so no one would be working in the lab in the morning.

The date in the past that Klaus and Armand decided on was August 13, 1920. Hitler and the Reich were so egomaniacal that they kept very detailed records of every significant event, most importantly, all of Hitler's speeches. There might not be a better way to know just where Adolf would be at a particular time. Armand had access to these records and made good use of this.

It was this very habit of obsessive recordkeeping that came back to haunt the Reich after the war, as some of us know. The allies found many of these records, particularly those at concentration camps, and had indisputable proof of their war crimes. Maybe, just maybe, this could be a memory that could disappear from all of our consciousness and from existence altogether.

On this August 1920 evening in Munich, Hitler made one of his first popular speeches, attended by two thousand people. Ironically, his topic that night was, "Why are we Antisemites?" The speech lasted two hours. It was documented that he was interrupted fifty-eight times by the cheers of the crowd. Someone must have been keeping count.

Klaus and Armand agreed the best plan would be to arrive where the event took place, the Hofbrauhaus, a well-known beer hall. Klaus would be there several hours early and remain as inconspicuous as possible to listen to the speech and then follow Hitler afterward, making use of the best opportunity to assassinate him. Klaus realized he might have to murder more than just Hitler if he wanted to get away. He was not happy with this but felt the end justified the means.

To cut right to it, the machine not only worked, but when Klaus came to, he was sitting in an empty warehouse. This was just what he had hoped from the best information he had. Around the turn of the century, his current lab had been a factory but had sat vacant for many years after, including 1920. Klaus had several miles to walk to get to the event, and he arrived around six o'clock p.m., unsure when the speech would begin. He was dressed in clothes that were more working class and typical for twenty years earlier.

After arriving at the Hofbrauhaus, Klaus spent the next hour walking back and forth around the general area, trying not to be conspicuous while waiting for people to gather for Hitler's speech. Around seven, more people arrived, and it was time to go in. The crowd was already more than he anticipated.

The tavern was large, three stories tall, with many rooms. Klaus asked a man who was standing by himself if he knew when the "political meeting" was starting that night. The man looked at him briefly, sizing him up, and said it was to start at 7:30 upstairs. Right about that time, other men started up the staircase. The man nodded in their direction while looking at Klaus. Klaus thanked the man and started that way.

The staircase led to a large room upstairs. The tables had all been moved out to accommodate more people. Several men had gathered in the far corner of the room and were deep in conversation. They looked like Nazis to Klaus. That might sound strange to you, especially since they were in plain clothes. You might even be tempted to ask, "So what does a Nazi look like?" But if you had lived in Nazi Germany as Klaus had, you would know.

Even in 1920, these men believed they were on a mission to save the world. Their air of self-importance, their belief they were inherently better than the rest of humanity, placed them on a platform from which they looked down at the rest of the world. You could see the intensity in their eyes and in their body language. It was unmistakable.

Men filed in, and before long the room was almost full. Klaus recognized one man near the front—Rudolf Hess, one of Hitler's partners in crime early on who would eventually become deputy führer. Maybe Klaus would get a chance to get two birds on the same night. For the first time, Klaus did not feel the slightest sense of shame. He found a place to stand about halfway back in the room.

Just then Hitler made his entrance. A flood of anxiety coursed through Klaus's body. He tried to keep his eyes to himself just in case all the color had gone out of his face. The speech that night was extraordinary but disturbing.

We have all seen old black-and-white films of Hitler in his prime, speaking to the masses. For most animated speakers, the word emphatic would do. For Hitler, that would be grossly inadequate. His whole body would tense up, and he would not only use both hands but make them into fists as he jerked them up and down and thrust them out. If you had been within ten feet of him, his spit just might have reached you. And German is such a harsh language to those of us who speak another. It made Hitler's words even more abrasive. He was so self-righteous and so angry.

As the speech continued, Klaus nodded at the end of this point or that, as many of the other men did. And when the shouting started, he joined in, even shaking his fist in the air. But as the evening continued, he became more and more nauseous. He could see where all this was leading. The evil of it all affected him. He had never thought of spiritual beings, of angels and demons. But it occurred to him they might truly exist. There would be no better place on earth at that very moment for some demons to be listening and adding fuel to the fire. And angels would want to be there as well, as spies, but also to douse the flames of hatred.

It seemed like an eternity, but Hitler wound down and summarized his message. When he was finished, another gentleman spoke briefly, then the evening was over. Klaus had already made his way to the side of the room to allow a quicker exit. Hitler and several others left by a side door. Klaus tried to be as inconspicuous as possible as he found his way to that door and exited. It was a smaller stairwell that led downstairs. Hitler and several other men spoke in the main bar, but after five minutes left by way of the front door out onto the street. Klaus quickly followed.

It was so early in the Nazi movement that Hitler had not seriously considered there might already be individuals who would want to harm him. For the time being, the Nazis were more focused on creating credibility and recruiting new people to the movement, although they had known from the beginning where this was leading. No one else did. Everyone else in Germany would eventually learn who they were and what they believed, but by that point it would be too late to stop them.

Hitler did not leave in a car, as Klaus had feared. He and two other gentlemen left the Hofbrauhaus on foot, walking for quite a ways before they entered an apartment building. Klaus waited outside and did his best to stand in the dark. About two hours later, Hitler emerged from the apartment by himself. Klaus could hardly believe his luck. It was close to ten, and streetlights were scattered here and there, but much of the street was shrouded in darkness.

Klaus followed Hitler and struggled to decide just how far to stay behind, not wanting Hitler to notice or hear him but not wanting to lose him in the darkness either. As soon as they were far enough away from the apartment that a gunshot could not be heard, Klaus thought he would be okay to go ahead. Others would hear the shot inside their homes, but he should be able to disappear into the darkness and find his way back to the warehouse.

About five minutes or so into their walk, Klaus noticed that Hitler seemed to be slowing down. Then he realized it was not that, but he had stopped altogether. He was still facing the same way, away from Klaus but standing still. Klaus stopped at first but then realized if Hitler turned and saw him, he would have even more reason to be suspicious. And so Klaus continued to stride in that same direction, mostly looking down, trying to look like anyone else taking a walk in the evening. Hitler continued to stand there, and as Klaus moved closer, he turned around to face him. Klaus was not sure what to make of this—might Hitler suspect foul play? Might he have a gun himself? But then he realized if he played it right, fate just might be delivering him into his hand. It would have been more difficult to catch up to him if he had not stopped.

As Klaus approached Hitler, he raised his head to acknowledge him, as anyone would have done. Although it was dark and Klaus was not sure Hitler could see his face, he forced a little polite smile, then said, "Guten Abend," German for *good evening*. Hitler responded in kind and began to say something else, but Klaus was not listening. He had already pulled out his pistol from underneath his coat and within a second or two had pulled the trigger three times, the gun pointed right at Hitler's head. The pistol was eighteen inches away. Klaus did not want to miss.

The next thing Klaus knew was that he was not standing on that street with Hitler any longer. He was not sure where he was. In the first moment, he wasn't even self-aware. He did not know who he was, where he was, or where he had come from. I do not believe there are words for what I am trying to describe to you, but they are all I have, so I will have to use them. Moses may have had a similar difficulty in trying to describe what he thought and felt and experienced when he stood before the burning bush.

Just like Adam and Eve violated a standard when Eve bit that apple in the garden that caused an existential rupture that changed this world forever, it would seem that Klaus had done that very thing as soon as he pulled that trigger. Prior to that he'd been dangerously close to violating this standard already: traveling back in time, attending the meeting, talking to people in the past, etc. But he had not done anything yet that had truly changed the past from how it would have been.

Although it seems clear God reserves the right for Himself to change His mind and start over, He does not reserve that right for us. He will not allow us to be sovereign. We have always been subjects. We are only supposed to be subjects, not gods.

Klaus woke up sometime later and was in his lab with Armand. Both were utterly confused and speechless. They looked at each other for a few moments, struggling to become clearer in their minds, but just then they said good night to each other and went home. They never again mentioned anything about this night to each other, as if it had never happened. In their minds, it had not.

The rest of WWII came and went. I wish it had been that easy to say for the fifty to eighty million who died because of it. Klaus continued with his academic life in physics but not with time travel. For a reason he would never understand, after that evening on the streets of Munich in 1920, Klaus convincingly communicated to the Reich that although his research had seemed promising in the beginning, in the end it utterly failed. Equally mystifying, his superiors received his explanation without question or challenge. What had seemed to be time travel was not. No one ever spoke of it again.

Klaus became a more spiritual man as he grew older. That often happens. He even attended some seminary classes when he was in his sixties. As an older man, he began to write about theology, but one topic became almost an obsession for him: the sovereignty of God.

It occurred to Klaus, as clearly as he had ever realized anything, just how difficult the line between justice and mercy is, just how thin the line is between accountability and grace. He wondered what it must be like to be God. It must have been quite glorious when all was good before the fall. But after?

Klaus could sense how broken God's heart was because of His wayward sons and daughters. How hard it must be to have to let them learn from all their mistakes when He could change it all in a second. And the greatest of atrocities? How many tears must the Father have shed? Klaus knew deep down that all things somehow must be the way they are, that the Father could intervene if He wanted to, but this could very well be control and not love. Mankind would have to learn to *choose* the right way. They could not be forced into it.

Klaus's last theological paper before he died, strangely enough, was a little fictional piece about a German scientist who had invented a time machine during WWII. After realizing just how evil the Reich had become, the scientist hatches a plan to go back in time and assassinate Adolf Hitler before the Reich rises to prominence. Klaus was pleased with the main idea for the story—he did not believe anyone had ever thought of it. The scientist succeeds in going back into the past and is close to assassinating Hitler before he is interrupted by an angel of the Lord.

The angel and the man have a long conversation, just as the book of Job is a long book. But the net of it was this: Has the human race ever considered just how hard it is for God *not* to act? Sin has almost destroyed this world altogether. How do you pick and choose what to allow and what not? At what point does something become bad enough that you decide to disallow or change it? And at what point is something good enough to leave alone? Over time the pressure would only build in making these distinctions. God can manage this . . . but man?

Klaus felt a little odd as he penned the last words . . . the last words he would ever write. He had the strangest sense of déjà vu as he watched the words flow from his pen to the paper: "Man was never meant to be a god. If he ever could be one, he would greatly regret it. It might even turn out to be a living hell."

Author Bio

Sam Blumenthal is a retired clinical psychologist who grew up in a Reform Jewish home in Charlotte, North Carolina, where he still resides. He is the proud father of three grown sons and has two daughters-in-law and five grandchildren, whom he loves very much. He came to faith in Christ at the age of forty-five in the midst of life's struggles, which is another way of saying the God of the Bible opened his eyes to what had always been the truth of his life . . . he had just refused to see it. Sam looks for every opportunity to speak and write about the God who loves him so much He chose to run him down in another country and lovingly carry him back home. *Once Upon a Time* is Sam's first book, a collection of short stories about God's relentless pursuit of all His children.

ORDER INFORMATION

REDEMPTION
PRESS

To order additional copies of this book, please visit
www.redemption-press.com.
Also available at Christian bookstores and Barnes and Noble.